MADNESS
OF MARCH

ALSO BY BURT GOLDEN

Jericho's Walls

The Dead Listing

Dead Is Not Enough

Shadows

Jocks, A Memoir

These titles are easily available by googling
"Burt Golden Amazon"

MADNESS
OF MARCH

BURT GOLDEN

LITTLE JOHN PRESS

Madness of March is a work of fiction. References to real people, events, establishments, organizations, or locales are intended to provide a sense of authenticity and are used fictitiously. All other characters, and all incidents and dialogue are drawn from the author's imagination and are not to be construed as real.

Little John Press edition 2012, 2021

Printed in the United States of America

ISBN 978-0-9860044-0-7

Cover Design by Karen Phillips

To Maxine Golden, my wife and North Star

ACKNOWLEDGMENTS

Madness of March would not have been possible without the help of some very generous people, namely, my son Jay for his creative advice, Joanne Shelly for her guidance, Glenda Rynn, David Rosenfeld and Janet Ennis for there editorial work. I also appreciate the continued effort in my behalf of Maddie Margarita, Stace Dumoski, Melodye Shore, and the rest of the fine writers at PFL.

Special thanks to Valerie McGonigal, Director of Marketing at Boardwalk Hall in Atlantic City, and Orlando Ward of the Midnight Mission.

Lastly, my deepest gratitude to Larry Holcomb, retired principal of the Lyon School, who offered a perspective on young men who leave orphanages at a late age, and my friend Bill Taub for his basketball advice.

All men dream, but not equally.
Those that dream by night in the
dusty recesses of their minds, wake
in the day to find that it was vanity.
But the dreamers of the day are
dangerous men, for they may act their
dream with open eyes to make it possible.

— T.E. Lawrence
Seven Pillars of Wisdom

*T*he biggest game of my life, then I'll be dead.

Sweat glues the white shirt to my back as I pace the sideline of the empty, domed stadium and ask myself how I got here. Outside, seventy thousand fans wait in the snow for the gates to open. Only a few of them know what's going to happen.

My shoes click on the shiny hardwood as I pass two men connecting the clock on the scorer's table. Across the court are tall bleachers, maybe fifty rows with cameras at all corners. Three levels of seats are behind the baselines. Seats in the top level seem no larger than the head of a pin. The shots can come from anywhere.

I sit my butt on a white, cushioned chair—the chair I'm going to coach from. The chair I may die on.

If I call the cops, all I can report is my forthcoming death. And after I'm dead, the newspaper photo of my body will be much larger than my obituary.

I should never have walked into that HotShoe store.

CHAPTER 1

"Something tells me you had a tough day," I said to the tall, Black shoe salesman. "You can't find me a Gravity Breaker. Let me help you."

"What are you," he said, "a priest in shorts and shoes?"

"No. But if you want to talk, I'll listen."

At two-fifteen, I sat in the rear of HotShoe's Hollywood answer to Niketown, waiting for Jimmy Wheeler. When I called Wheeler's office that morning, I knew two things about him. One, in the basketball world he could make you or break you. And two, he catapulted HotShoe sales past Nike and Payday in basketball shoe profits. When I hung up, I knew he was going to visit a Hollywood Boulevard HotShoe store at mid-afternoon. I didn't know why and I didn't care. I was going to give him the chance of a lifetime.

The salesman was four inches taller and maybe ten years younger than I. Six-four if he was an inch; thirty-years-old if he was a day. He shook his head, knelt, and gathered up the boxes. My eyes drifted across the store to the sunny entrance. There, Wheeler strutted our way, passing large photos hanging from the ceiling of basketball players whom he had signed for millions to wear HotShoe apparel. The guy looked like he could strut sitting down.

The salesman followed my gaze and turned to Wheeler. With stress in his voice, he said, "Hey, Wheels, thanks for coming, man. The last three days have been hell."

They began to shake hands, then went to the half-hug. Wheels spoke Brooklynese with an edge, pronouncing *r's* as *a's, a's* as *r's*. He wore blue HotShoe sweats with the white flame logo over his heart.

"Mercury," he said, "what's goin down? I get your brother a basket-ball coaching job at Sheldrake College—then he disappears."

Mercury turned to me and said he'd be right back. As they walked away, I heard him say, "Wheels, I've talked to the cops. Nobody knows nothin?"

While I was sorry to learn about Mercury's situation, I was plugged in to take care of my business.

Two weeks ago, approaching Wheels wasn't a thought.

Two weeks ago, I was a defeated man with no focus. Then I read an ad: "Winning Dynamics Will Change Your Life. Take A Chance on You." Hell, I was Conrad Byrnes, the last person to take a chance on me. I was one of the living dead. Dead on the inside. When our eigh-teen-year-old son died in a tragic car accident, I lost my way. Nothing could replace my grief. Not my job as a high school basketball coach, not talking it out, not long walks. Soon, my marriage fell apart, ending in a divorce after twenty seasons. So like I said, I was the last person to take a chance on me when I walked into the crowded hotel ballroom for Winning Dynamics. But after four psychodrama days, I was sold on me, reenergized and retooled. And my subliminal dream of coaching the NCAA winner in March Madness had bubbled to the surface and was stronger than ever. Brainwashed and cleansed of any negative thinking, I believed that "Winning was the only thing." I was now plugged into positive Winning Dynamics rules but unable to edit their sayings that rolled off my tongue.

*　*　*

I found a pair of Gravity Breakers in a far corner of the store and brought them to the counter where I planned to get Wheels' attention. Behind the counter, Mercury bagged a shoebox and handed it to a tall, young man who quickly departed. Then, Wheels wagged a finger at Mercury and said, "I can find your brother. I know people . . . people in the shadows."

I applied Law 6 of Winning Dynamics: *Court Attention at all Costs.* "I'll take this pair," I said and pushed the box to the counter's edge. Hoping Wheels could equate shoe sizes with the heights of some NBA basketball players, I continued, "I also want a size twenty."

He glanced down at my size tens, then at my frame. "Whaddaya gonna' do with a twenty?"

Oblivious of passing customers, I looked him straight in the eye. "The best college basketball prospect I've ever seen came by my gym yesterday with holes in his shoes. I'm trying to find his size."

Wheels waved a dismissive hand. "There are no great prospects with bad shoes. They get 'em free from companies like mine. Who you talking about?"

"A guy you've never heard of. A six-nine kid who was six-six two years ago . . . and he's still growing. Doesn't even shave."

Wheels stared at me for a long moment, then asked, "What's the kid's name?"

"Pico Rimpau. Just turned eighteen, and he's amazing."

Wheels reached into the front pocket of his warm-up pants, pulled out a little black book, flipped through the pages, his eyebrows drawing closer and closer together. Then he held up the book as if it were his bible and he was about to preach the gospel. "Every blue-chip player is in this book. Your guy ain't here. Who you kiddin'?"

"That's his value," I said. "No one knows about him." Then I faced Mercury and applied Law 7, *The Feeling of Loss:* "Just give me a pair of twenties and I'll be out of here."

Mercury said, "We don't—"

Wheels waved a free hand to Mercury to shut him up and said to me, "What NBA player does this kid remind you of?"

"He reminds me of Bill Russell, the old Boston Celtic. Ever seen film on him? Trim, jumped like he was coming off a trampoline and dominated the game." I reached up and flicked my wrist. "Swatted shots for fun."

Wheels didn't take his eyes off me as he slipped the book into his pocket. "I've seen Russell. But any tall, Black, high school kid can dominate a game if they're playing with a bunch of white kids who can't jump."

"Pico Rimpau can rebound to the eleven and a half foot mark. Top of the square."

Wheels' face loosened and he raised his hand to his heart, skimming his HotShoe logo. "So you're a coach. Where at?"

"Polk High School, West Hollywood, a few miles from here."

Wheels snapped his head back. "Polk? Hey! . . . Conrad Byrnes . . . you coached Moody Moore! You can coach." He smiled and stuck out his hand. "Jimmy Wheeler, Vice President of HotShoe Marketing. They call me Wheels."

As we shook hands I inadvertently said, "Too bad you missed on Moody."

Wheels ignored my left-handed remark, said, "Shit, I thought we had him—he went to our HotShoe Basketball Camp. We treated him well. Then he signs with a Payday university, then Payday Shoes. Surprised the hell out of me." Wheels waved a hand again. "We screwed up, never included you in the process. We shoulda met a long time ago." He pointed to Mercury. "This is Mercury Mansfield."

Mercury, nodded, didn't smile or offer his hand.

I mirrored him, said, "Mercury Mansfield. You averaged four points in six games for the Pistons last season."

"Yeah," Mercury said without emotion. "I laced 'em up on a ten-day, look-see."

"I heard you say that something happened to your brother."

He glanced at the glass countertop, lowered his voice and said, "My brother's missing. He was working as an assistant basketball coach at Sheldrake. Now nobody knows nothin'."

Wheels shook his head. "He went recruiting in Philly last week—an hour from Sheldrake in Atlantic City. Never came back. Disappeared . . . vanished."

"But he knew his way around Philly," said Mercury. "That was his job, recruiting inner-city guys."

Wheels nodded to Mercury. "I'll get my feelers out. If I hear anything I'll let you know. And, Coach Byrnes, size twenty is a special order. But I've got a pair in my car. I'll give them to you, no charge."

Minutes later, he returned and handed me a dark blue box with a white HotShoe flame on the side. I thanked him and paid him, much to his surprise.

"Now why don't I know about Pico Rimpau?" Wheels asked, wrapping my bills around a thick wad of green, securing it with the snap of a rubber band. "It's May. Every eighteen-year-old who can drain it, shoot it, or handle it has signed with someone."

"You don't know him," I said, "because he's led a different life."

Wheels opened his hands as if he were about to catch a beach ball. "What is this, *Days of Our Lives?*"

"No big problem. Listen, if you think Moody Moore is great, you should see Pico Rimpau." I inhaled and went for it. "I'll tell you what. My car against yours, says if you come to my gym tomorrow to watch him play, you'll project him as an NBA guy destined for a shoe contract, and you can place him with a Division One team that HotShoe sponsors to wear their logo."

I didn't tell him that I got no callbacks from PayDay Shoes and all the college coaches I contacted about Pico.

Wheels smiled out of the corner of his mouth as if he were watching a bad comedy routine. "What kind of car you got?"

"Eighty Corvette, headers on a 305 V8 with a jet fuel tank. What are you driving?"

"BMW SUV."

"Good," I said, with a broad smile. "I've got a two-car garage."

"I'm bringing a tow truck for your Vette, Wheels said. "Bring your pink slip."

CHAPTER 2

Pico Rimpau, wearing tattered white shorts and new HotShoes, stood next to me behind my high school gym backboard, his shoulders slumped, his basketball tucked under his arm. In front of us, dressed in eclectic attire and warming up for Pico's audition, were five Black community college players who'd played for me.

I looked up at Pico's long face and immature goatee, then pointed at Wheels, sprawled out on the lowest bleacher seat as if he were taking a sunbath, and tried to explain his influence in the basketball world. When Pico gave me a blank look, I said, "'He da' man.'"

Pico said, "He doesn't look interested."

"But he does look interested."

Pico jogged onto the court and straightened as he cut across the baseline.

While jump shots swished through the net or caromed off the rim, I took a seat next to Wheels. In his blue HotShoe warm-ups, he checked out the old, gray double-decker gym that had black pipes for banisters and slab metal doors for exits. He turned to me. "Besides Moody Moore, what's Polk High School famous for?"

"Gang membership and teacher resignations."

"Sounds like you're not happy here."

"You got that right."

"So why don't you do something about it?"

"I'm trying . . . went to Winning Dynamics. Now I know that life is a rip-off when you expect to get what you want. And life works when you choose what you get. And, actually, what you get is what you chose. So to move on I have to choose it."

Wheels stared at me. "What the fuck are you talking about, man?"

"It's a life-changing experience."

Wheels' back straightened. "I don't have time for your story. I'm in a hurry. When the game starts, I'll tell you why your kid can't play."

His comment was no more than a towel snap. I countered with "I measured my garage for your SUV. It looks like I might rip off your side panel squeezing it in."

He chuckled. "You ARE funny."

Warm-ups were dull. After coaching and watching 108 games the previous season, I wasn't interested in practice shots, and my memory rewound:

Three seasons since I coached Moody Moore, since he went Division One, spotlight. Payday-sponsored colleges made me feel important, hosted dinners, left game tickets. College basketball recruiting looked good to me. Then death. Then divorce.

"Bill Russell dominated," Wheels said, "but that was a long time ago. He was playing against a bunch of white guys. We'll never see that again."

"Russell . . . yeah." I shouted to the players, "Half-court game to twenty, winners' outs. Pico, the two, five-ten guys will be on your side. Let's see what you can do against the six-six guys."

They played with Pico's ball. He wouldn't have it any other way.

For the next ten minutes we watched Pico perform like the second coming of Russell. He was a human elevator, blocking shots, rebounding above the rim. But he made no effort to score. Instead, he passed the ball out.

I kept my eyes on Wheels for some sign of approval. He didn't smile, nod, or hand me his car keys. But he didn't leave.

Then Pico riddled the net with several windmill dunks, and his opponents hung their heads in defeat. Wheels repositioned his bottom leading me to believe either he's interested or his ass hurts.

As if Pico sensed that he had to do something spectacular, he knocked a player to the floor on his way to a one-handed rebound, arm outstretched, high above the rim. Hovering like a helicopter, he slammed it through the twine. It was a circus act, an NBA highlight show.

"Holy shit!" Wheels said. "What's his name again?"

"Pico Rimpau. P . . . I . . . C—"

"I heard you."

Seconds later, Pico, playing defense a few feet in front of the rim, leaped high above the square, caught an attempted lay-up with one hand, and in one motion passed it out to a teammate at the top of the key who hit a jumper.

Wheels' head snapped toward me. "Coach Byrnes, that's impressive. How close are you to Pico?"

"You mean, can I influence him? We're friends."

"Good," Wheels said. "Now tell me why Pico Rimpau is an unknown."

I cleared my throat. "He's had a situation."

Wheels threw his hands up, raised his voice. "What kind of a situation? I hate situations."

"Pico's unfamiliar with the world as we know it," I said calmly. "But he's got a positive attitude."

"You mean he's been in the slammer?"

"No. He's been in and out of a facility for dependent and neglected kids . . . and he's been living on the street a lot."

Wheels shook his head vehemently. "I don't like street guys; they got baggage. They—"

I cut him off, raised my voice. "Pico's okay . . . I'm telling you, he's okay."

Unblinking, Wheels' eyes jogged to Pico and back to me.

I had to keep it simple. "Three years ago," I said, "Pico played for me as a tenth grader while he lived with foster parents. When they were arrested for selling drugs, social services placed Pico back in the facility, St. Andrews in downtown L.A. He'd been in and out of that place since he was a baby. He lived there for two more years until he turned eighteen. But during that time he escaped a lot, lived on the street, and played ball. You would too. They don't have a team at St. Andrews."

Wheels glanced around the gym as if he expected someone else to be listening. In a near-whisper, he said, "And nobody knows about this guy?"

"Nobody," I said softly.

"Don't go away," Wheels said as he bounced up. He pulled out his cell, punched in some numbers, and walked toward the exit mumbling. Then he made a 180 and returned to hear his cell go off. He glanced at the number on the screen, put the handset to his ear and spoke as if he were hard of hearing. "Babe, this is Wheels. Got a great post prospect for you. Guy named Pico Rimpau." Wheels listened for a moment, then got more excited. "No, not fuckin' Joey Pico. He's doing time. This guy's better. Future lottery pick. So, Babe, since you're a HotShoe team and I'm paying you seven hundred K, I'm going to deliver Pico Rimpau to you. But I want to sign him to a HotShoe contract when he's ready to go pro. He's going to be on my string, understood?" He paused. "No, I'm not joking. This is real. Yeah, take a look at him."

I understood that the coach was in bed with the HotShoe Company and was getting an offer he couldn't refuse.

Wheels continued. "Pico just got back in town. He's been on the move. That's why nobody knows about him. I'm telling you, he's a future shoe." Long pause. "Can he think? Does it matter?" Silence again. "Hold on."

Wheels turned to me with his thumb over the receiver. "Babe DeCarlo, the coach at Sheldrake College, would love to have Pico. He wants permission from Pico's foster parents to have him travel to Atlantic City tomorrow for a two-day visit."

I thought, *Sheldrake . . . Mansfield . . . the guy who's missing.* Then the power of Law 8 overcame me. *Negative Thoughts Are a Straight Line to Nowhere.*

"It's great that Sheldrake is interested," I said, "but Pico's former foster parents can't give permission. They're in jail. They lost custody."

"Where does Pico live?"

I shrugged. "I don't know. Somewhere."

Wheels repeated my message to DeCarlo and agreed to something. Then he hung up and said, "Okay, forget permission. Coach also wants you to visit and make Pico more comfortable."

"You mean make sure he gets there?"

Shut up.

Wheels' voice softened, like he had a winning hand at a poker table. "I'll make it worth your while." He motioned for me to follow him to the exit door where he pulled out his large roll of bills and peeled off ten hundreds. He held them out. "Here. This should cover your time."

"I'll cover my airfare."

Wheels was silent for a moment, then said, "Consider this as consultants' pay. Use it for your summer basketball camp."

He hit a responsive chord. I wrapped my fingers around the green and pocketed it.

"So what else do you want?" Wheels asked. "Everyone wants something else. Parents, coaches, uncles . . . everyone wants something."

"I'm looking for a college coaching job."

"Well. They're missing a guy at Sheldrake."

"Hey, Coach," Pico yelled. "We're finished. 21-0."

CHAPTER 3

I walked on to the court, thanked the players, and introduced Pico to Wheels. They bumped fists and Pico thanked Wheels for being there. Then they followed me to my office. We walked through a steamy locker room, where jocks dried off and dotted the floor with white towels, where the scent of underarm deodorant and smelly feet permeated the air.

Down the middle aisle, I spotted Aaron White, a troubled, rock-solid, six-foot member of my team. He was toweling down his backside.

"Wait a second," I said to Wheels and Pico before walking down the row. "Aaron. Heard your father's ill. I tried to call your house last night, but the line was busy. Tell him I hope he gets well soon."

We entered the P.E. office, a victim of cutbacks and neglect. Marred walls were covered with dusty, black and white team photos dating back to the Depression. Furniture that wouldn't be accepted at Goodwill was slotted in the corners.

Pico and Wheels slid into blonde wood chairs and sat around my cluttered desk. Pico gave me a questioning look, probably wondering what was next. His ball nestled on his quads. He leaned forward and perspiration leaked from his oblong face onto his ball like a drippy faucet, spilling over onto grease-stained, white trunks.

I extracted two water bottles from the corner refrigerator and grabbed a fresh gym towel from a neighboring chair, then handed out the water and draped the towel around Pico's neck.

Pico chugalugged whileWheels spoke with excitement. "Pico," he said, "you can jam and swat like no one else I've seen in years."

Pico's blank expression brightened as if he were being blessed by the Pope.

"I understand you just got out of St. Andrews," continued Wheels. "How are you managing?"

Pico looked away for a split second. "Maintaining. Just maintaining. Yep."

"Why'd you come back here?"

"When you're eighteen at St. Andrews, they let you out. That's the law . . . I played for Coach Byrnes three years ago . . . He said if I got good, he'd get me a scholarship. And I know what he did for Moody Moore."

Wheels slowly nodded. "And where'd you play in L.A.?"

"City playgrounds with men, old college guys, like that. Like Shattuck and Wilshire. They got lights and players . . . sometimes down by skid row. Anywhere I wouldn't get picked up by the cops. They'd return me to St. Andrews."

Wheels pinched his eyebrows. "Tell me about basketball on skid row."

Pico glanced at me as if he were looking for acceptance. "I got tired of being picked up by the cops in Hollywood, so I went down there. Lived on the homeless block. You got a choice down there . . . the homeless block, the recreation drug block, or the heroin block next to the police station. I disappeared on the homeless block for a while." He rubbed the ball's pebbled surface with his long fingers. "Got to be careful down there. They'd cut through your box in the middle of the night and slit your throat for a dollar." He took a breath. "If you're lucky, you wake up smelling shit, and being sprayed by the five a.m. street cleaner."

Wheels ran his fingers through his black curly locks. "How'd you sleep through that?"

"Light."

"And where are you sleeping now?

Pico glanced at me again. "In a cardboard condominium in back of the Pantages Theatre."

I swallowed hard, shook my head, looked at Wheels, and back at Pico. "You live in a box. I didn't know."

Wheels turned silent for a long moment. Then he asked Pico if he was ever in trouble on the street."

"I'm clean, Mr. Wheels. No nose candy, maybe a joint now and then. Never been collared."

"That's good," Wheels said, sliding his fingers over his HotShoe logo. "I have a home for you, Pico. I want you to fly back to Atlantic City and—"

Pico's dark eyes widened. "I got no money, man."

Wheels cracked a faint smile, said, "I'll take care of that. Just spoke to Babe DeCarlo, the Sheldrake coach, and he wants to talk with you about playing there."

Pico look at me. "Coach, you go with me?"

I can't handle being a father-figure again.

"Done," said Wheels, who stood and surveyed the office. "Coach Byrnes, you have a yardstick?"

You going to redecorate my office?

I fetched one from behind the three-drawer filing cabinet across the room and handed it to him.

Wheels stood and measured Pico's wingspan. Tip to tip. "Just what I thought," he said. "Seven-foot arms on a six-nine body. Great rebounders have a wing spread longer than their height."

I smiled. "Pico, you stay at my place tonight. And, Wheels, I need to talk to you about something."

He followed me into the locker room. When the door clicked shut, I said very simply, "I won the bet. You owe me your car."

Wheels's voice hardened. "You're a strange bird. That was a bullshit bet. Fahgetaboutit. Aren't you plugged in? Don't you know the difference between bullshit and applesauce?"

"Wheels, you don't get to vote on the way it is. You already did."

"You're out to lunch," Wheels said. "Nobody bets his car. You want to help this kid . . . make sure he doesn't get out of your sight. And don't answer your phone. It could be PayDay Shoes wanting to screw me again. I missed on Moody Moore. I'm not gonna miss on Pico Rimpau."

LUCAS STADIUM, INDIANAPOLIS, IN
NCAA FINAL GAME
APRIL 5
MINUTES TO TIP-OFF: 85

I sit next to the scorer's table, hunched over, staring at the floor.

All my assassin needs is a forged admittance pass and someone to have planted a weapon before the stadium locked down four days ago. Could be a guy posing as a cop on the floor, the official scorer, or a guy walking down the aisle selling ice cream, with a pistol under the cups.

I tilt my head back and study the catwalk above the far end of the court. *No moving shadows. No unusual angles.*

A woman's voice calls out, "Coach Byrnes."

At the far end of the court, a blonde gal no taller than five-feet-two in heels comes toward me. She wears a black wool overcoat. Trailing her is a short, hairy man in Levi's and a Mackinaw jacket, balancing a video camera on his shoulder. She's on the good side of thirty, wrinkle-free face, strong chin, shoulder-length hair and bright blue eyes. I step toward her. She offers her hand and announces, "Allison Crowe, MBC."

She shakes my hand that's wet with perspiration. I agree to do a quick interview.

The cameraman tilts his lens up at my face, and Crowe clips a small mike on my shirt before stepping back. Then the camera man counts down, "3-2-1."

Crowe says, "Coach Byrnes, you've come a long way very quickly—coach at Polk High School in Hollywood to head Sheldrake coach. Now the big dance—playing for the national title. How do you feel about being here?"

I stare at her.

Are you fuckin' kidding? I can't tell you the truth.

"Coach Byrnes?"

"I'm sorry. I've been . . . I have a lot on my mind. How do I feel? It's like an out-of-body experience. Nothing like it."

Crowe's eyebrows pull together. "Would you elaborate?"

"There's pressure from all directions. You'd have to be in my shoes to understand."

"Big game and all—I understand." Crowe pauses for a split second. "Do you think you've made a difference with this team?"

Have I made a difference anywhere? Have I made a difference on earth? What has my life amounted to?

"That's for someone else to answer," I say.

"What's the difference between coaching this game and coaching a high school game? You've been in both places."

"If you strip away the crowd, the TV cameras, and all the attention, it's the same. Some rule interpretations are different, some nuances in strategy. That's all."

Except now I'm a target.

Chapter 4

We're flying over the Rockies, an air pocket bouncing us around. Pico clamped his basketball between his knees, and squeezed his chair handles like he was going to be ejected. It was his first plane ride. Skid row he could take, but flying scared the hell out of him.

Pico's ball never left his person. Somewhere over Kansas, he returned from the bathroom with his Spaulding, settled into his bulkhead seat, and rubbed up the ball as though he were a pitcher on the mound. I slipped the *L.A. Times* sports section under my seat, turned to him, said, "How long have you had that NBA special?"

Pico glazed his long fingers over the ball's pebbled surface. "Before they let me out of St. Andrews, the staff gave me the ball and a Bible."

"Where's the Bible?"

"Traded it for a hot dog and fries at a hamburger stand."

My eyes narrowed. "You know what I believe in? Tough defense and high percentage shots."

"I believe in that, too," Pico said. He turned away and looked down at miles of agricultural fields. Within seconds, his head swiveled back. "That picture of the coach cutting down the net . . . the one that's over your couch. What's that about?"

"That's what I want to do . . . win the NCAA and cut down the net."

"I have a better chance of cutting down the net. You're a high

19

school coach."

I jetted out my chin. "Just the same, that's what I want to do."

An hour later, after reading a sports magazine, Pico, who only knew mean streets and incarceration, asked me about college workouts, strategy, and schedules. I told him what I knew about the college game, which wasn't much. I never played college basketball. I was a basketball coaching mutant.

On our final approach to Atlantic City Airport, he asked what the next forty-eight hours would bring. I said we would be making friends and signing a letter of intent. Then I thought about Moody Moore's recruitment and said, "Let's find out how many centers they have and what kind of guy Coach DeCarlo is."

"Is that all?" Pico asked.

"No. Act like you did at St. Andrews. Not on the street."

"I'm not stupid."

"I know."

*　　*　　*

While waiting for my luggage at the airport carousel, I called my brother Jordan. Jordan is four years older, married, and a sports columnist for the *Philadelphia Inquirer*. After our father died, our mother remarried and Jordan took our stepfather's last name, Taylor.

"Jordan, this is—"

He cut in, "I know who this is."

I stepped away from background noise and strolled toward the tall, sun-drenched windows that looked out onto a large parking lot across the street while I explained to Jordan why I was going to Sheldrake College.

"You're as excited," he said, "as the day you set sail for Hawaii on a 28-footer, with no fuckin' idea how to get there."

I raised my voice. "Jordan, I had books on basic sailing and celestial navigation."

"You were getting bored sailing your 16-footer into the ocean with small craft warnings. You needed a bigger fix."

I stated Law 9 of Winning Dynamics. *"A Man Has to Reach Beyond His Grasp."*

"Conrad, one of these days that vine you're swinging on is going to snap, and you're going to break your ass."

"Hey, coach," Pico yelled.

My head jerked back. The baggage carousel began to rotate and a swarm of ex-passengers closed in, as if they thought they were going to get their luggage back.

I put my finger over the mouthpiece and shouted, "Pico, I'll be right there." Then Jordan asked what I knew about Sheldrake College.

"I know they can help Pico Rimpau, that they return every starter on a team that went to March Madness, and that one of their assistants is—"

"Missing, Conrad. The guy's a missing person! What kind of operation is that?"

"Jordan, you see the dark side of everything."

"And you've always been in the dark."

I glanced back where Pico stood. "Well, I now know that I have to ride the horse in the direction that it's going."

Momentary silence, then, "Conrad. I beg you. Get some therapy."

"You just don't get it because you're not an ultimate achiever."

"So you paid to have your brain washed?"

As Jordan rambled about why I should get some help, lead a normal life, and remarry, I spotted my luggage, walked back, and snagged it. Then I cut into his lecture with, "Jordan, meet me in Atlantic City. It's an hour away. That's why I called. I thought we could get together."

"I'm in Chi-town covering the Cub series. But tell me how your visit goes. And don't tell anyone at Sheldrake that you know me. I just ripped Sheldrake Basketball in my column."

I ended the conversation with, "Jordan, we have different last names, and I'm only going to be here for two days. Talk to yah."

I surveyed the arrival area for anyone looking like an assistant coach, a "ball face" in HotShoes that was supposed to pick us up. A few overweight men reading the racing form queued up at the rental car counter. None of them came towards us or looked our way.

Pico followed me to an empty bench next to the windows where I picked up a strewn *Philadelphia Inquirer*. I opened it to Jordan's column, sat down and read it.

THE WHOLE TRUTH
By Jordan Taylor

It has been five days since Sheldrake Assistant Basketball Coach Michael Mansfield disappeared. While I hesitate to say goodbye to Mansfield, I am concerned that he may never reappear. Missing persons are almost a daily occurrence in Atlantic City. The stats are worse in Philadelphia. Twenty-six people disappeared in Atlantic City last year and 34 in Philadelphia. It's getting so that when you are about to go shopping and say goodbye to your parents or your spouse, it might be for the last time.

I know Michael Mansfield. He worked his way up from high school coaching and recruited Nitro Nixon to Sheldrake. Mansfield has no blemishes on his resume. But Mansfield labored for a basketball program that was formed by gamblers for gamblers. It wasn't that long ago that Atlantic City Casinos suffering from lack of attendance at the gambling tables during the winter, encouraged the formation of Sheldrake's basketball program to get more traffic. Now look what happened. I'm not saying that there is a connection, but that program smells all the way to Philly.

Glad I'm not working at Sheldrake while Jordan batters the program. A forty-eight- hour visit with Pico and I'm outta here.

Chapter 5

"Hey! You Pico Rimpau?"

My eyes shot over to the rental car counter again. There, a young man with bright eyes and a Bluetooth in his ear came towards us with the urgency of someone who had loaned us money. I judged him to be in his mid-twenties. Wearing green and gold HotShoe sweats, he had a prominent nose under slicked back, black hair. He had the body of a six-four guy and the legs of a guy five-three. In basketball parlance he was a "low post." Pico pushed off the bench and stood, his shoulders slouched, his ball tucked under his left arm. "I'm Pico."

The young man gaped at Pico for a moment, reached up, bumped fists with him.

"Buddy Giranda, assistant at Sheldrake, pleased to meet you." Giranda spoke rapidly, as if he were trying to sell a hot item before the cops caught him. "How was your flight? Ever been east? Babe DeCarlo's looking forward to meeting you."

Without waiting for a response, he introduced himself to me. Then he looked down at my black bag, then at Pico.

"Where's your bag, Pico? Is it lost? I can fix that."

"I don't have any," Pico said, standing in his complete wardrobe: windbreaker, a T-shirt, the pant legs of his Levi's above his ankles, and new HotShoes.

Giranda's eyes widened like he didn't understand why Pico's wardrobe was limited. Then he reached for Pico's ball. "I'll carry that."

Pico's face etched with rage as he jerked the ball away from Giranda's outstretched hand. "No one carries my ball but me."

"Okay, okay," Giranda said, throwing up his hands. "We're here to please." He glanced at Pico's pants. "You need some game shorts: we've got some."

"I've got shorts under my Levi's."

* * *

Giranda, at the wheel of a white SUV, sped us down a tree-lined highway. I sat behind him, envisioning smiling faces and good times in Atlantic City. Pico sat in front, staring at the road, his seat pulled all the way back, his knees above seat level.

Giranda's cell went off. He pressed it, listened for a second, and said, "We just took off. Get everyone ready. We'll be there in fifteen minutes."

Must be a reception committee.

"Did Wheels get you guys on the plane okay?" Giranda asked.

"Everything went okay." I cleared my throat. "Sorry to hear about Coach Mansfield."

I focused on Giranda's rearview mirror and waited.

Giranda held the wheel steady but stared in the mirror. "He went recruiting in Philly and disappeared. Tough neighborhoods there, but wow, I never thought this would happen . . . Could've been me, huh?"

"Was Mansfield the number one assistant?"

"Yeah. What about it?"

"So now you're the number one assistant?"

Giranda gave me a look that was somewhere between "I killed him" and "Don't fuck with me." Then he said, "Bobby Charles is our other assistant. You won't meet him. He recruits Africa and Europe. He's always on the road."

"So you're down one assistant . . . What did Mansfield do besides recruit?"

24

Giranda hesitated for a moment. "That was his main job. He did some other things, but mostly recruited."

Before I could ask Giranda, "What other things?" he looked fleetingly at Pico, then said, "I heard you're a hell of a player."

I cut in. "Pico may turn out to be the best player you ever had in this car."

"Oh, yeah? Where'd you play, Pico?"

"Anywhere there was a game in L.A, like playgrounds."

Giranda said condescendingly, "You played on playgrounds and you're a blue chipper?"

I leaned as far forward as the seat belt would permit. "Pico's not on any recruiting list. He developed his own game. There ARE players out there you don't know about."

"Not in this day and age," Giranda said, speeding by cars in the slow lane. "Pico, you ever match up against a real good player?"

Pico looked at Giranda. "Dude named Springs."

"Springs? Never heard of him."

"Six-nine, two-forty . . . played at Quentin."

"Quentin? Never heard of it."

"San Quentin. Armed robbery! Played there ten years."

I smiled.

Pico does need some polish.

Silence lingered in the car before Giranda said, "That's one place I've never recruited." He paused, then asked, "Does this guy Springs have any eligibility left?"

"He was eligible for parole last year and got out."

Giranda gave Pico a double take, then shot into the outside lane to pass another car. "How good is Springs?"

"You couldn't move him out of the low post with a bulldozer."

More silence before we crossed a thin strip of marshland and saw the outline of tall buildings against a clear blue sky, about five miles away.

"Atlantic City. There it is," Giranda said. "See the casinos? We're on the small Island of Absecon."

Pico scratched his cheek with his bony fingers. "They promised me the ocean."

"We're coming to it."

We passed two blocks of factory outlet stores on the edge of town, stopped at a light on a run-down main street where Blacks were curled up in doorways of dirty, red brick buildings. On the next block, we saw nothing but "For Lease" signs.

In seconds, we came to a newer, more appealing, vibrant area: dense street traffic, the back end of a high-rise casino, and a bus loading up stooped, senior citizens, who moved slowly out a side entrance.

Giranda made another turn, rolled down all the windows, and I got my first whiff of the Atlantic Ocean—cool salt air, cotton candy and hot dogs. "Smells like an amusement park bathed in salt water."

"That's boardwalk business on the next block. But take a look at the domed building on our left, our home court, Boardwalk Hall. The first domed arena, built in 1929. We're next to the beach, Pico. Imagine going to school twenty yards from the sand. We were 13-0 in the dome last year—got the edge."

"What edge?" I asked, getting no response. Then I gazed at the dome that could hold a football game: one block long, four stories high. I wondered what it looked like inside.

Giranda said, "We're going to workout now."

"Hey," I blurted, "tryouts are illegal."

"Not here."

Pico glanced at me over his shoulder as if he were taken by surprise. I reached forward and patted his back.

What happened to making friends and signing an agreement?

I took a breath. Applied Law 21 of Winning Dynamics. *Happiness is a function of accepting what is.*

CHAPTER 6

Giranda drove down a steep ramp into a dank, Boardwalk Hall parking garage. He led Pico and me upstairs to a glassed-in first floor, level with the boardwalk. Then, up a tall escalator to a streamlined foyer, walled by art deco painting with geometric shapes—a step back in history. As we got off the escalator, I said, "How'd your program get started?"

Giranda kept walking and barked over his shoulder. "I saw the *Inquirer* in your hand at the airport. You must have read that asshole Jordan Taylor's column. What Taylor can't figure out is that we don't control how many gamblers pay admission. But you win and there's always someone who wants to take you down."

"Isn't that the way it always is?"

Giranda said nothing, kept walking.

After a short tunnel, we found ourselves on a light-showered horse-shoe walkway above 10,000 green and gold seats. Below, there was a basketball court. And at the end of the building was a large stage. I envisioned myself coaching at Boardwalk Hall: hollering player instructions, hearing the roar of a packed house.

Seconds later, we walked across a portable court where five tall, black players warmed-up at the far end. A stout man, who I believed to be Babe DeCarlo, stood on the baseline.

In green-and-gold sweats, DeCarlo had black hair slicked back just like Giranda—or was it the other way around? I gauged him to be six-two, two-forty. His red-webbed eyes and substantial girth said "bar time." The look on his fleshy face said he would just as soon eat me as talk to me.

DeCarlo craned his neck and growled. "Pico Rimpau . . . Babe DeCarlo. Good to meet you." He didn't offer his hand. "You know what you're here for, Pico. Put your ball down and go to work."

Bad reception after 3000 miles.

Giranda stood on the other side of DeCarlo and shook his head as if he expected Pico to reject DeCarlo's instruction.

Pico held out his ball to DeCarlo. "That's the ball I play with."

DeCarlo exploded. "We play with whatever fuckin' ball I want to play with, and yours ain't it."

Blunt force trauma kind of guy.

Pico straightened as I headed off a lava flow. "I'll hold your ball," I said.

While DeCarlo's face softened, Pico calmly handed me his most valuable possession. Then he headed for a cushioned, foldout chair on the sideline where he stripped down to his HotShoes and white shorts. He jogged to the key, straightened his shoulders, and bumped fists with a couple of frontline body-types who were hanging around the basket rebounding shots.

"Y'all want a piece 'o me?" Pico said loudly. He positioned himself under the basket and extended his arms, encouraging a pass from a player at the top of the key. The other players watched with curiosity as Pico received the ball chest high, ripped it down to his waist, sprang, snapped the ball back over his head, and swished it through the net like a rocket going down a shaft.

"You be on my side," said the player who had passed him the ball, bringing laughter from the others.

DeCarlo spoke to me out of the side of his mouth. "If he can't do more than stuff backwards, you guys will be on a seven a.m. flight tomorrow."

I looked through DeCarlo. "I thought we're here to sign a letter of intent."

"In the first place, Byrnes, I don't like eighteen-year-olds running around with my wallet. In the second place, Wheels has been wrong before. Mistakes are costly here."

I considered Winning Dynamics rule number 43: *Make Your Enemy Envision the Future You Choose*, and said "Pico Rimpau will be your best athlete. He's trainable and he's a year away."

"Now is not tomorrow," DeCarlo shot back."

"What if you like him?"

DeCarlo crossed his arms. "Then he'll be green and gold."

I scanned the green and gold seats and assumed that they were school colors and symbolized the money that changed hands in Atlantic City.

The half-court game took twenty minutes. Pico asserted himself near the basket and sucked up every rebound like a human vacuum cleaner. He never left the basket while playing defense and swatted away short shots. At the tail end of the game, Pico had the audacity to toy with jump shooters within eight feet of the rim, faking to block their shots, distorting their release, and causing them to miss the basket.

But Pico was raw. He lost his man on defense and had no rudimentary offensive moves other than a dunk that would break someone's hand if they tried to block it. But Pico's team won.

DeCarlo glanced at a slim white-haired man who had slipped into the bleachers during the game. The man stood, nodded his head, then walked up and out.

Pico, more winded than the other players, placed his hands on his knees for a few seconds, straightened, bumped fists with the players, and came toward us, his body a sweat machine.

"How'd I do, Coach Byrnes?"

"I think you did good, but that's for Coach DeCarlo to decide."

"You're out of shape, kid," DeCarlo said. "But you've got promise. Let's talk at dinner after you shower and Coach Giranda checks you into the Mardi Gras Casino next door."

DeCarlo isn't the caring person I read about. Could be difficult for Pico.

CHAPTER 7

The Mardi Gras registration area was designed like Bourbon Street in New Orleans. On an open mezzanine to the right of the registration desk, a huge throng of partygoers hung over an ornate, wrought-iron balcony, talking, laughing, drinking, tossing strings of beads downstairs. The party spilled out onto stairs that led from the first floor to the mezzanine. At the head of the stairs, a Wynton Marsalis look-alike trumpeted "As the Saints Go Marching In." On the far end of the registration floor, colored lights flashed from slot machines and soft calliope music sounded the gambler's call.

"Welcome," said a young woman in a low-cut black dress, standing behind the registration desk. She waved us over. She had the face of an angel, set atop a devilish body. I glanced to my left at Giranda checking us in with another woman not as attractive. Then my eyes moved helplessly back to the woman who would definitely make my All-Casino team.

"Does the partying go on all night?" I asked.

"Fun never sleeps, Honey."

"Can we go upstairs?" Pico asked.

"Our trip is all business," I said.

"Coach, if I haven't seen it, it never happened."

The woman gave Pico a somber look. "You'll be drinking Budwater here," she said. "You have to be twenty-one to drink or gamble."

* * *

An hour later, Pico, DeCarlo and I entered the packed 26th floor Mardi Gras Restaurant with a three-sixty view. Pico's uncommon height and the basketball at his side drew many eyes. However, after we slipped into padded chairs, Pico sat only slightly taller than me. In basketball jargon he was really split down the middle with unusually long legs.

From our corner table, I saw miles of high-rise casinos adjacent to the boardwalk, then noticed customers in casual attire, heard mellow conversations, clinking glasses and soft, piped-in jazz.

DeCarlo, dressed in a beige suit and a green and gold Sheldrake tie, sat with his back to the window and looked over my shoulder. Turning to see what caught his attention, I spotted a white-haired man standing near the entrance—the same man who had watched our workout. He pointed at DeCarlo, who nodded back.

Pico, his ball under his chair, examined the shiny silverware and crystal goblet before him as if they were puzzle pieces. I studied the menu. Cajun I didn't know. An accommodating DeCarlo chose our entrée, then regaled us with basketball stories of himself as we waited for dinner.

When we were served a tray of hot dinner rolls, Pico's large hand operated like a steam shovel, removing all four. When we were served lobster bisque, he slurped it down before DeCarlo and I lifted a utensil. After the plates were cleared, the waiter placed a silver tray of steaming folded cloth napkins in the center of the table. Pico reached out, took one, bit into it, and twisted his face. He looked at me sheepishly, and said, "Thought it was a burrito."

DeCarlo curled his lips in a failed attempt at a smile. "The burrito napkins fool a lot of people," he said, removing a fresh napkin from the tray and wiped his hands and his mouth. Pico followed his lead.

Before I knew it, it was dusk and the overhead lights brightened.

DeCarlo leaned back and asked Pico about his course work at St. Andrews. I knew something about NCAA admission requirements, nothing about Sheldrake's standards, and listened closely.

Pico shot me a furtive glance.

"Go ahead," DeCarlo said. "No secrets here. Say it like you gotta say it."

Pico nodded, said softly, "I didn't go to a regular fuckin' school. St. Andrews wasn't that kind of place. 'Charm School,' that's what I used to called it. Different kids every day . . . dumped by social services . . . waiting for their parents to square with the law, going to a foster home, or climbing the fence to hit the streets."

I interjected, "Pico got a grade every day."

"Last two years was like—I escaped every other week."

I interrupted. "He went to school when the cops brought him back."

"Or when it got too cold," Pico added.

DeCarlo slouched in his chair, clasped his hands on top of his head, and asked, "Did you ever have any science classes?"

"Science" Pico said, "was a bad fuckin' dream." He glanced at me as if to say, *Sorry, I cussed.*

"Go on, Pico," DeCarlo said.

"Science was like . . . I remember one class. Dazed kids with a Prozac hit, a burned girl on a stretcher, a guy walking around with his eyes on the ceiling, and another guy sitting next to me drawing a horse with a separated head. Nobody watching the teacher." Pico gazed out at the neon lights on the strip and rolled the ball around under his chair with his heel.

Pico can't meet the standards. Can't get around the eligibility thing.

"I'm glad that's behind you, Pico," I said.

DeCarlo changed the conversation as if he had a handle on prerequisites. He said, "I once recruited an L.A. kid who lived on Rimpau Avenue."

Pico looked at DeCarlo for a long moment. Then he said, "That's where they found me when I was a baby . . . in a box at the corner of Pico and Rimpau. That's how I got my name."

My breathing stopped, my mouth dropped, and there was silence at our table. Finally, DeCarlo said, "I'm going to make you Pico Rimpau of Sheldrake."

How the hell you gonna do that?

"There's great opportunity for you here," DeCarlo continued as if grades were no problem. "You can have the American Dream."

"I've heard of that," Pico said with a frown.

"So what's your dream, Pico?"

Without hesitation, he said, "NBA star."

"Why?"

"Because I'll be somebody. That's why."

DeCarlo nodded. "That's what Sheldrake's all about. We develop future NBA stars. We went to the first round of the tournament last season, and we have everyone back, including Nitro Dixon and Americus Hart, two guys that are going NBA. And Babe DeCarlo will win because Babe DeCarlo can coach. Then everyone on our team will get the American Dream." He twisted his water glass clockwise. "We need you to complement Americus, our post guy. You'd be a star in a year, Pico."

"How many centers would be in front of Pico?" I asked.

"Just one," DeCarlo said, twisting his glass counterclockwise."

"That's all good," Pico said, "but I'm not comin' here without Coach Byrnes."

DeCarlo froze for a long moment, then erupted. "What the hell you talking about?"

Pico's not comfortable with DeCarlo.

"Coach Byrnes could make things easier for me here."

DeCarlo turned to me. "You can coach, but I don't know if you fit in." Shooting a look over my shoulder, he said. "I'll be right back." I watched him in the window's reflection as he zigzagged across the room, then spoke briefly to the white-haired man now seated at a table near the entrance.

The waiter cleared our table while Pico and I waited and said nothing.

DeCarlo returned and eased into his chair with his eyes on me. "Had to talk to a booster." He leaned forward slightly and spoke slowly. "So, Coach Byrnes, what would you think about being an assistant at Sheldrake?"

My heart went tachycardia.

A door is opening for me just like Winning Dynamics said it would . . . without a resume, an interview or references.

"Coach Byrnes," DeCarlo continued, "we're looking for someone with a positive attitude. Negative attitudes are a killer. Are you positive?"

I took in more oxygen. "I don't think you're going to find anyone more positive."

Our table was quiet when a white-coated waiter returned with cups of orange sorbet. When the waiter left, DeCarlo said, "Are you security-oriented, Coach Byrnes? We don't hire security-oriented coaches. To get the American Dream, you have to be free of your umbilical cord."

I looked into DeCarlo's eyes and saw myself standing in the center of the Grand Ballroom of the Biltmore Hotel in downtown Los Angeles, listening intently to the Grand Meister at Winning Dynamics. Three hundred attendees sitting in long rows listening to him say:

> *"Go for it, Mr. Byrnes.*
> *Step into the deep water.*
> *Leave your secure job.*
> *Burn the ships in the harbor.*
> *There is no turning back, Mr. Byrnes. Go for it."*

I said, "Let's talk about that tomorrow morning. Just you and me."

"Good," DeCarlo said. "After breakfast in my office. Nine sharp."

"I look forward to that."

DeCarlo turned back to Pico. "And Pico, you've led a tough life, but now we'll take care of you."

The waiter returned and handed DeCarlo a folded note. He read it, crumpled it, and looked at the white-haired man, who nodded in his direction, got up and left.

*   *   *

The elevator door to our hotel floor opened. DeCarlo told us to leave our shoes in the hallway. "Someone will shine them."

Pico said, "Someone is going to really shine my basketball shoes?"

I gave him a shrug and we stepped out.

The elevator door slid shut and I was about to say, "Good night," when Pico displaying a full set of teeth, mimicked DeCarlo.

"'What's your dream, keed? American Dream? I'll get you one of those.' That's jive, mother-fuckin' street talk. DeCarlo feeds you enough to get high . . . just enough to come back for more. I get it, Coach. That's why I want y'all to come with me. I don't trust him."

My mind gyrated with the day's events. "Pico, I'm with you, no matter what you decide, although I'd like to be hired by Sheldrake. It is too late for you to be recruited by another school the caliber of Sheldrake. Just understand this—college basketball is a business. It's all about winning. You win—you get what you want. DeCarlo gets what he wants."

"Yeah. Just like the street."

Then silence you couldn't cut through with a knife.

I broke it, asking, "Are you going to walk away from Sheldrake?"

"No. I didn't eat garbage to turn this down. I can deal with his ass if you're with me."

"Well, I'm not employed by Sheldrake at the moment, and you haven't even been admitted yet. Do you know that you need certain classes and grades to get in here and be okayed by the NCAA?"

"Really."

*   *   *

Inside my basic hotel room, I opened my suitcase to unpack. Two hours earlier my shirts were on top of my pants. Now my pants are on top of my shirts. I rifled through the case, checked for missing apparel. Nothing missing. No windows open. The door was locked when I entered.

You're tired. You don't remember.

After I put my shoes in the hallway, I sank into soft cushions on the couch, clicked on ESPN, put my feet up. My mind drifted.

Who's Whitey? Admit Pico without grades or classes? Job offer . . . what kind?

CHAPTER 8

The next morning, I retrieved my loafers from the carpeted hallway. They weren't shined and I didn't care. I sat down on the couch, slid my right foot into the shoe, and felt loose lining. I took off the shoe, reached inside, and, to my surprise, pulled out five crisp, hundred-dollar bills.

Does this seal the deal? What did Pico get?

My inclination was to keep my mouth shut and wait for someone to say something at breakfast. But neither DeCarlo nor Giranda said anything about the shoe money. I assumed it was the Sheldrake culture. But I was edgy about this culture that crossed into dark areas of recruiting. Accepting money would make me guilty of influence peddling. Then I rationalized that it was a done deal and that I wasn't breaking any laws. But it wasn't going to be my last rationalization.

* * *

At mid-morning, Giranda showed Pico and me around campus, a block-long, twelve-story, former turn-of-the twentieth century hotel between Belleview and Texas on Boardwalk. It was next door to the dome. No ivy covered walls, meandering walkways or park-like settings. Only a full-on view of the beach. Built in 1910, the hotel had been donated to

Sheldrake College in 1950 by the Sheldrake Family Trust.

Giranda also took Pico to meet with the players. I headed next door to Boardwalk Hall to meet with DeCarlo in his office, breathing in salt air and avoiding dive-bombing seagulls all the way.

On one side of DeCarlo office was a green-and-gold cement block wall adorned with action shots of him dribbling a ball for the Knicks and jump-shooting for Penn. No Sheldrake team photos. It was all Babe DeCarlo.

The opposite wall was plastered with a large HotShoe advertisement, serving as a reminder that Wheels was a conduit for Sheldrake play-ers. Edging the doorframe that led to the assistant coach's office were framed photos of men I did not know.

"Those pictures around the door frame," I said. "Who are those guys?"

DeCarlo's jaw jutted out. "They're the coaches we'll beat this year. They all want to deprive me of what is rightfully mine . . . the national title."

Just then, I recalled a Winning Dynamics session. The speaker could have been DeCarlo.

> *Winning glorifies, intensifies and ratifies your life. Winning, you see, is happiness. Therefore, winning is your only reason for being.*

"Let's talk about your job," DeCarlo said, bringing me back. "I've made package deals before. Sometimes they don't work out." He pointed an index finger at me with the thumb up as if his hand were a pistol. "The only reason you'd work here is because of Pico Rimpau. You'd be our number-two assistant. Bobby Charles is number three. But he's overseas recruiting and won't come back until he signs those recruits."

"So what's my job?"

"You'd have special assignments. Mostly helping kids succeed."

I nodded. "All my life I've helped kids succeed."

DeCarlo stared at me for a long moment. "Now it's nut-cracking time. Tell me, Byrnes, what <u>wouldn't</u> you do to win?"

What <u>wouldn't</u> I do to win? His question kept rolling around my brain.

Finally, I said, "I wouldn't break the law."

DeCarlo chuckled. "We wouldn't ask you to break the law." He grabbed the NCAA manual that was lying flat on his desk and held it up. "There are some rules in here everyone breaks. But they aren't laws. You see, we help kids succeed. It's like cheating on your income tax. Everyone does it." He slapped the book down on the desk. "I think you're our kind of guy. My people will be happy that you're with us."

I said, "You're alluding to other people in the program beside yourself and Giranda. If you don't mind, I'd like to know who else I'm working with. Who are 'my people'?"

DeCarlo looked surprised, said, "My people are those who want to see Sheldrake basketball win. They pay any price for success. They're friends of mine."

Apply Law 16. *"Enter Action with Boldness."* "Friends of yours are friends of mine."

"No. These are *my* friends." DeCarlo reached into his top drawer and pulled out a contract. With an edge, he said, "When you become a head coach, you get your own damn friends."

Hierarchy of friends is no big deal.

DeCarlo placed a twelve-month contract before me. It was ten thousand more than I was making at Polk. I smiled at the number, scribbled my name, gave it back. Tight-faced, he leaned forward and shook my hand. Then he closed the door to his secretary's office, returned to his chair, and quietly said, "When you return to L.A. this afternoon . . . "

I cut in. "This afternoon?"

"At Sheldrake you work when you have to work. You leave this afternoon. Pico stays here. We're going to train him and get him ready for December. It's only June, but the season will be here in a hurry. Don't worry. We'll take care of him."

"I've got a connection with Pico. I don't think he'll go for this."

"You can talk to him on the phone," DeCarlo said, punching his computer keys. "This is your schedule. The SAT is coming up and Pico's records have to be accepted by both the NCAA and Sheldrake. Get on it. When you get to L.A., you'll meet with Wheels and work out something at St. Andrews. You guys will make Pico eligible. Then I want you to talk to our SAT test-taker. Let's not fool ourselves. Pico can't be admitted anywhere." He slipped the contract into his top drawer. "If you don't help him he'll be back on the street. Coach Byrnes, all your life you've been helping kids. Now you need to help one more."

"I'll tell Pico what I'm doing."

"No," DeCarlo erupted. "He'll figure it out."

My mind spun.

Don't take the job . . . it's not you. What about Pico? Take it. Winning Is The Only Thing.

"What are you thinking?"

"Nothing."

"Good. Thinking hurts you. Now you need to resign from Polk High School. No leave of absence."

Burn the ships in the harbor. The only way.

Winning Dynamics in control of my destiny, I nodded. I felt like jumping out of my chair. I was in the big time.

DeCarlo reached into his bottom drawer, pulled out a cell phone, and handed it over. "Use this disposable phone. Throw it away when you finish the L.A. business. I'll get you another."

I put the phone in my pocket. "What if Pico can pass the SAT on his own? Shouldn't we let him try?"

"You kidding? . . . Where you been, man?"

DeCarlo spent a few minutes briefing me on my L.A. assignment. He gave me written instructions, reached into the top drawer again, this time for a thick envelope, and handed it over. "This is for the guy taking the SAT. Three grand. It's a good deal."

I took it like a drunk taking one more drink. The drinks were beginning to taste like water.

DeCarlo got up and waved me into the next office. He said I would be using Mansfield's desk and told me to look it over. Giranda would take me to the airport.

I pulled out the chair and sat down as DeCarlo left the office. All the drawers were empty, as if Mansfield went up in smoke.

*   *   *

I spoke to Pico by cell as I packed, told him that I signed a contract and that we were still connected at the hip. Pico gave me his social security number. I didn't tell him what it was for. He said he liked the players. Then he opened my eyes with, "I'd like to come back to L.A. with you."

Still fighting off the darkness of my son's death, I said, "We'll talk. In the meantime do what Coach DeCarlo tells you. This is going to be a good life for you."

In the hallway outside our locker room, I lean against the cement block wall, trying to get my mind on the game. Across from me, my assistant Giranda dials his cell. I give him a long look, wondering if he's the guy that's going to kill me.

He's got motive—my job.

But Giranda wouldn't shoot me in front of millions of viewers. What then?

I checked under the team chairs. *No dynamite there. None under the scorer's table a foot away from my chair. Anyone could wrap plastics around themselves and dial a cell number setting off an explosion. I'm dealing with the insane.*

Giranda knows every recruiting angle. Now it's Facetime calls just before the title game to tell these high school All-American that we want them. He's recruiting three power forwards to get one six-eight, two-hundred-forty-pound animal to beat up players on the weak side board. But they don't know that. Not one of them has made a verbal commitment to any school. But a verbal and thirty dollars can get you into a Philly game. A letter of intent is everything, and the signing window is coming up. But I won't be around.

Giranda smiles. "Patrick, our players are excited, huh! Millions of eyes will be on us tonight, and you can be a part of this . . . we'll be back here . . . I'm telling you, we're comin back."

In a short minute his conversation ends. He punches another series of numbers. A few seconds later his face brightens. "J.C. You know who's calling from the locker room of the team playing for the title?" Pause. "Yeah . . . this is your man from Sheldrake." He gives me a thumbs-up, meaning J.C. is interested in signing with us. He points at me, then at the phone. He wants me to hustle J.C.

I shake my head no.

My dying words aren't going to be, "Please come to Sheldrake."

Giranda places his finger over the mic and says to me, "He can't remember my name and I've been recruiting him for two years." He looks away. "J.C., you're our number one power-forward. We want you very badly. You can lead us back to the Promised Land, the Final Four . . . you the man, J.C. Sheldrake, HotShoe contract. You'll be somebody."

When he hangs up, I say, "Giranda, you'd be a very good head coach. You're going to get a lot of attention after this game. Are you looking?"

He gives me a wide-eyed smile.

I caught him off guard. He's thinking about it.

"No, Coach. I'm with you."

Liar.

CHAPTER 9

From Los Angeles International, I edged north on the 405 Freeway in bumper-to-bumper five o'clock traffic. When I crossed the Santa Monica Freeway, my cell went off. It was Jordan.

"I couldn't wait for you to call me," he said. "What happened?"

"You wouldn't believe it, Jordan. They hired me to be an assistant coach. A dream job—I'm on my way."

Drooling with skepticism, Jordan said, "That's a fantasy. How did that happen?"

I briefed Jordan on things that wouldn't make his column—the mundane, the boring. Told him how much DeCarlo liked Pico and that Sheldrake needed one more assistant. "Now I'm back in L.A. to sell my condo and take care of some business. Probably take me two months to get back there."

"Is Pico Rimpau eligible?"

My voice spiked. "Do you think Sheldrake would be interested if he didn't have grades?"

"Thanks for the non-denial denial. How about this? Were there any clues to Mansfield's disappearance in his desk?"

"Jordan, you'd rip the cover off a baseball with your fingernails if there was a story inside." I hit the brakes as an idiot cut me off, took a breath, and said, "For your information, there was nothing in his desk that you'd be interested in." I waited for him to respond. Dead silence. "Hello?"

Jordan spoke as if he had just discovered penicillin. "Conrad, I'm in my hotel room watching CNN on the net. A black hand was found on the beach in front of Boardwalk Hall. Could be Mansfield's hand."

"That's sick, Jordan."

"There's more. A source close to the investigation says they're checking to see if the DNA matches the arm that was found last week on the beach. This could be it. Mansfield could be coming up in pieces."

"Mansfield went into a rough neighborhood and didn't come out. That's good enough for me. You've been looking under rocks so long you only see dirt." I turned east on Wilshire, passing the shadows of the Federal Building.

"Listen, Conrad. Resign. Give back the job. I'm telling you there's something very wrong at Sheldrake. Go back to Polk. Are you going with any one? You should get married."

"I'm glad your marriage works. Mine was a nightmare. And for the hundredth time, stop being my father. I've got the chance of a lifetime." I stopped for a light on Veteran next to the cemetery. "Do you know how many high school coaches in L.A. have taken a big-time job? Me. I'm the only one."

"That's because the other coaches are smart."

"If I'm going to make something of myself, it's now."

* * *

Two days later, under a warm Southern California sun, I drove Wheels down a winding alleyway on the backside of Chinatown to St. Andrews. The orphanage was located a short distance from Civic Center. I wouldn't have known it existed if I didn't have directions. Thick trees and brush masked the small campus from North Broadway. Pagodas and two-story restaurants hid St. Andrews from Chinatown tourists.

Wheels sat back and gazed through the windshield, his briefcase under his legs. "I'll do most of the talking," he said, as if he had done

44

this before. "I'm selling the sizzle. You take care of Pico's classes."

My heart in my mouth, I turned into an alley, then passed several gray restaurant dumpsters that smelled of yesterday's fried rice. Putrid, nauseating. The alley dead-ended into a tall cyclone fence on a cracked sidewalk laced with weeds. St. Andrews. At the gate I pressed a buzzer. A tall thin man with a ponytail shuffled towards us. Mid-thirties, no smile, all business. He directed us past low-rise classroom buildings to the principal's office in the center of the campus.

I had called ahead and told Principal Ford that I wanted to meet with him about Pico Rimpau, the basketball player, and that it was important. I didn't tell him that Wheels would attend. Ford didn't ask any questions, only said that Pico had spoken highly of me.

Ford stood behind a messy desk under a whirring ceiling fan. He looked like an unmade bed: messy gray hair, shirttail out, three-day beard. I introduced him to Wheels as the HotShoe VP. We took hard seats on the other side of the desk. Wheels set his briefcase between our chairs. I glanced at the secretary on the phone in the next room, concerned that she would hear our conversation. Wheels, sitting comfortably in his chair, did not display an aversion to being overheard.

I told Ford that I had just taken the job at Sheldrake. He gazed at me through large framed glasses and said in monotone, "So now you're here about Pico Rimpau, the basketball player. I thought someone would ask about him sooner or later. Pico came here as an infant. Someone left him on a street corner; then we got him. He wasn't a cuddly baby, didn't smile much. I always thought he was going to be adopted. Never happened. Some kids aren't lucky. Maybe it's the smile, you never know." Ford leaned back. "Pico's had some angry moments. You'd be angry too if no one wanted you."

Wheels cut him off like a hangnail. "Thank you for the information. We're here because we want Pico to play at Sheldrake College in Atlantic City."

"Finally, someone wants him," Ford said. "He can really play. Wants to be a pro. But we never had a team. I let him practice after school out there." He pointed to a window behind him that looked out onto a blacktopped court in the middle of a small playground. Rusted metal backboards, bent rims, chain baskets. Then Ford turned back to us. "So you guys want Pico Rimpau to play at Sheldrake. Coach Byrnes, I understand why you're interested in Pico, you coach there . . . But you, Mr. Wheeler, why is HotShoe interested?"

Wheels nodded once and said, "We like to help young people."

Ford held up both hands as if he were stopping traffic. "Hold it right there. HotShoe isn't a charity. It's a shoe business."

Not breaking stride, Wheels said coolly, "Basketball relations is my side of the business. Helping kids succeed. That's my job." Then Wheels shot me a look. It was my turn. Ask for the transcript.

I hoped the place handed out grades like candy.

"May I see Pico's transcript?" I asked.

Ford gave me a narrow-eyed look, as if he wasn't buying our presentation. Then he got up and crossed the room. His back to us, he said, "Pico's a nice kid, but he's unpredictable."

He pulled out a large file from a three-drawer cabinet next to the glass front door. Then he returned to his chair, placed the file on his desk, and walked his fingers through the pages. He latched onto a document and handed it to me.

As I reviewed Pico's record, Ford stood over me and said, "Pico was here almost eighteen years. He escaped a lot. It's tough living here that long. He had a foster home, but that didn't take."

Pico had A's in science, math, and English, but plenty of academic deficiencies. I looked at Wheels and shook my head. "Not enough semesters of anything."

"He never graduated," Ford said. "No one ever graduates from here. This a way station." I visualized myself cutting down the net at the championship game, snipping the last strand of twine to the roar of thousands of fans. I said, "Pico could use your help. He's a good kid. He deserves it."

Ford returned to his chair and said, "We can't give them any help after they're eighteen. The gate opens and they're out. That's it."

Wheels placed his forearms on the desk, feigned sincerity, and quietly said, "Mr. Ford, we can help each other."

Ford stared at Wheels and kept staring. The only sound in the room became the squeaky ceiling fan. Finally, he asked, "What are you getting at?"

"We're both in the business of helping young people," Wheels said. "And Pico needs your help now more than ever. He can play at Sheldrake, graduate, and have a pro career if he has the right grades and classes from St. Andrews. He needs four years of English, three years of advanced math, two years of natural or physical science, and more." Wheels continued to outline the entrance requirements, then said, "Pico could be the first one to graduate from St. Andrews. He'd be a hero to every kid coming through here."

He got up, walked to the cabinet, and pointed to a blank wall. "Pico's NBA photo could be right here."

The more Wheels spoke, the more uncomfortable Ford looked.

When Wheels returned to his chair, Ford got up, and closed the door. Walking back, he said in a clandestine tone, "You want me to create a new transcript, is that it?"

Wheels poked my leg. I hesitated. My brain was spinning with ethics questions. Then I remembered the grand Meister at Winning Dynamics. *"Indecision," he said, "is the seedling of fear. You can't be afraid of winning. Every step forward leads to winning, your only goal in life."*

I took a deep breath. "Mr. Ford, in his whole life, Pico never got a break. We'd like to give him one right now. This is his only chance. He'll never get another one."

Ford eased into his chair and listened.

Wheels reached over, picked up his briefcase, and placed it flat on Ford's desk. "And in turn," he said, clicking open the locks, "the HotShoe Company will pay you a consulting fee of fifty grand." He opened the lid where fifty big ones screamed for ownership.

Holy shit. So Ford gets 50K, Sheldrake gets Pico, and HotShoe makes 2 billion selling Pico Rimpau shoes.

"Jesus," said a startled Ford. Reaching out with a shaky hand, he slammed the case shut, stared at it for a second, and looked at Wheels.

"What if something goes wrong? Someone finds out?"

Wheels waved a dismissive hand. He was good at that. "The HotShoe Company," he said, "doesn't take big risks. I'm not saying I've been down this road before, but I can assure you, you won't have any problems. Here's your story: Pico had these classes with you. You tested him. He earned top grades. You know teachers give kids breaks all the time who are inches away from being admitted to college."

Inches? Shit. Try a mile.

Ford slammed the case shut and placed the case under his desk. Then he glanced out at the basketball court and mumbled, "We've had a lot of teacher turnover. No witnesses." Then he looked at me. "What grade point average does he need?"

"A 3.3."

Ford took the transcript back, scanned it with his finger as he spoke. "I'll have to change his attendance record." He shook his head. "That's a big job . . . When do you need the transcript?"

I said, "In a couple of weeks. End of May. The transcript needs to document that he graduated. I'll come by and get the sealed record. Write this down: Sheldrake College, Office of Admissions and Records, 166 Boardwalk, Atlantic City, New Jersey 08401."

It's all about winning . . . winning is the only thing.

Ford nodded. The deal was done.

CHAPTER 10

That evening, I called Ronald Washington, a senior at the University of Southern Califoria, to set a meeting time and place. Washington was going to be Pico Rimpau when he took the SAT. At ten a.m. the next morning, we met on the second deck of a USC parking structure off Figueroa. I parked in a shady corner. Fifteen minutes early, I had called my Realtor to say that I had signed the listing agreement and she could pick it up that afternoon. Then I reread DeCarlo's plan with very damp fingers:

1. *W gets P's social security number, your address, your home phone.*
2. *W fills out P's app and signs P's name.*
3. *W gets P's driver's license downtown. Pay expedite fee.*
4. *App fee paid by money order with P's name.*
5. *Tell W date, time, place of event. You receive by mail.*
6. *Get results 30 days later.*

I placed a cell call to Washington and told him where my Vette was located. Five unnerving minutes later, he knocked on the passenger side window. He was handsome, black, looked seventeen, stood six feet and carried a brown backpack.

I opened the door. "Ronald Washington?"

"Right."

Washington sank into the passenger seat. I took a deep breath, let it out, and looked through a number of car windows on both sides of me. Only a young guy reading something three cars away. Something said to keep going, so I did.

"You got the cash?" he said coolly, unblinking.

My chest was heavy, my mouth dry. I handed him a number-ten envelope with almost as much money as I made in a month, and all the numbers he needed to know. "Where do these meetings usually take place?"

"Airports, parks, coaches offices, libraries . . . no special place, man."

Washington had the prerequisites for taking someone's test. Fearless, intelligent, in need of money. He placed the envelope deep in the pocket of his khakis. When I began to go over procedures, he said, "Don't worry, I've got this down."

My mind went blank. I said the first thing that popped. "Well, until that moment."

"Until then." He opened the door and disappeared down the shady ramp.

*   *   *

Two weeks later, after I had resigned my job at Polk to every security-oriented teacher's amazement, I returned to St. Andrews. Ford met me at the gate, rushed me into his office, and handed me a stamped envelope with the school's seal across the flap. Getting my hands on the document was insurance against Ford's second thoughts. Now all I had to do was mail it.

I drove to a mailbox in front of a Chinese restaurant on North Broadway and parked. The sidewalks were empty. At the mailbox, fear of getting caught overwhelmed me. I looked up and down the street. Except for a man reading a newspaper in a white panel truck, the street was as empty as the morning after New Year's Eve. Taking a deep breath,

I slipped the envelope down the mouth of the box. Heard a ping at the bottom. Now Pico was half way home.

CHAPTER 11

PRESS OF ATLANTIC CITY.COM

> *The body of a black man that washed up on the beach in front of the Trump Taj Mahal yesterday was identified as Donald Fleming, a forty-six-year-old homeless man. Fleming had been shot in the back of the head and had his right hand amputated at the wrist. The Atlantic City medical examiner matched his DNA with the hand that had been found on the beach two weeks ago.*

Sitting in my birthday suit in my Hollywood Hills condo, I glared at the computer screen on my bedroom desk. "Of course, it wasn't Mansfield."

My front door clicked open. "Hello . . . Realtor."

"Shit."

Sunday, 9 a.m. No sense of decency.

I peeled my butt off the leather chair, scrambled into my khakis that were strewn on the floor.

Voices—two women.

Barefoot, bare-chested, I stormed down the hall to the living room but stopped under the archway. Hands on hips, I was seemingly invisible to my intruders: a gray-haired lady in a yellow suit, fiftyish, who stood between the sofa and the soft chair and a tall blonde in a T-shirt and Levi's with a nice backside.

The older lady, presumably the Realtor, said in a gravelly voice, "This two-bedroom, two-bath has been listed a short time." She stepped to the windows that overlooked the city and reached for the blind pulley.

"A real steal. The owner went through divorce." As she pulled up the blinds, light shot across the living room. "Look at the oasis of skyscrapers downtown and Catalina Island in the distance. Great view property."

Appraising the view, the blonde said apprehensively, "And the Hollywood sign on the cliff is right below us."

"Good morning," I said, "and welcome to the top of the world."

Heads swiveled my way.

"I didn't know anyone was home," the Realtor said. "I rang the bell, waited, then used the lockbox key."

"I'll wait outside," I said.

When I approached the front door, the buyer said me, "The basketball hoop that's at the end of the driveway on top of the cliff. I used to play hoops, but I wouldn't shoot at that basket. You miss and the ball winds up miles away on Hollywood Boulevard."

"Missing isn't part of my philosophy."

The Realtor pointed to the kitchen. "Here we have a new refrigerator."

"She got most of the furniture," I said. "I got two burritos and the refrigerator."

My guests glanced at each other but said nothing.

I answered my ringing cell. "What's new, Coach?"

Giranda's voice was harried. "Pico wants to go back to L.A."

I squeezed the hell out of the phone.

"You mean he quit basketball? I talked with him yesterday. Everything was okay."

I stepped out of the house and onto the blacktop driveway, felt the chill of morning air, glanced past the hoop at the city that was just waking up. "What happened?"

Giranda raised his voice. "I don't know! Pico disappeared for a day. He's a problem. We're making some decisions. Call you tomorrow." Click.

Pico screwed up, damn it.

Someone with high-octane perfume tapped me on the shoulder. My head spun. The Realtor's face looked older in full sun.

She handed me her card. "Thank you for the showing." Then she lowered her voice to a conspiratorial level. "I'll give you a tip. Box those bedroom trophies and clean up your house. And get those Post-It notes off all the mirrors. That 'Head Coach, National Title' sign detracts from the value of your home."

"The trophies were my son's. He's gone now."

"Get this place organized. I'll get you a buyer."

* * *

The next morning after a sleepless night, I was crunching Corn Flakes at the lone kitchen counter stool when Giranda called back. "Listen," he said, "Coach DeCarlo wants Pico to come back to L.A. and live with you while your train him, get him up to speed. I know the NCAA frowns on this, but who's watching you in L.A., huh?"

I heard something scrape across the mouthpiece, then muffled voices in the background. DeCarlo got on the phone and yelled like he needed a distemper shot. "If Pico's gone," he said, "you're gone! I'm not running a fuckin' nursery. Pico lives with you until you move back here. You train him like you did Moody Moore. Work on his jumper and free throws. He arrives LAX tomorrow at four." Click.

I pushed away from the counter and went to the window shaking my head.

If I don't have that job, I don't have any job. Get on it.

* * *

A day later, Wheels conveniently came knocking at my door. He said he was in town calling upon a southern California university, but I knew he was lying. He had a national job and was sitting on a potential shoe in Pico Rimpau. We spoke briefly in the entry. There, he doubled down on his investment by handing me a HotShoe box packed with twenties. "This will cover Pico's expenses in L.A."

I said, "He's already got enough money."

Wheels gave me a hard look, then lectured me with, "Talent is the lifeblood of basketball and cash is its nutrient."

I stood on the front step and watched Wheels get into a silver 500 Mercedes and drive down the hill. *I know kids. Pico just needs stability, not money.*

CHAPTER 12

During the drive from LAX, I didn't ask Pico why he wanted to return to L.A. and he didn't offer anything. We talked ball. Driving past the high rises on Wilshire Boulevard, I thought, *Training and organized ball are going to be a shock to this Greystoke in shorts and shoes. He hasn't been coached in two years.*

When we entered my condo, Pico threw his duffel bag on the couch, plowed into my only soft chair, and slammed his ball down on the hardwood floor. Then he unlaced his gunboat-size shoes and flung them across the room.

I gave him a look.

Having distaste for his taking over my space, anger welled up inside me. I watched him stretch his legs, pick up his ball with one hand, and wrist it at the ceiling.

I raised my voice. "Hey . . . we got some household rules around here." I threw his bag on the floor and plowed my butt into the couch. "My condo's up for sale. It's got to be neat all the time. No crap on the floor, no basketball playing. Buyers like it neat."

Pico shot another ball at the ceiling. It rebounded off the plaster, smudging the finish. "Yeah, whatever."

He could give a flying fuck.

"I don't know what the hell happened to you back East. But let's

56

get this straight—around here we play basketball outside. This place is going to be neat at all times: we pick up our own crap, we make our beds, I'll wash our clothes, I'll make our meals, you put the dishes in the machine and put them away when they're dry."

Pico looked at the ceiling, then shot the ball straight up. The ball ascended only few feet. He caught it with one hand, said, "Eighteen fuckin years I've been told when to get up, when to go to sleep. Been marched to class, marched to the cafeteria. No more."

I stared at him.

I can take Pico out of the darkness, but I can't take the darkness out of Pico.

"Pico, I understand that you've been through a lot. And you're trying to figure things out. But we still have rules here." I took a breath. "And Coach DeCarlo thinks you're a problem. You got money, a free room, and free food. Then you disappear on him. How's he going to trust you on the court? Playing time is about trust. This is a real problem. That's why you need boundaries and some self-discipline."

Pico stared back.

I wanted to scream, *"You're really fucked up."* But I took a deep breath and said calmly, "So you had no control of your life at St. Andrews and any home you were in. Is that it? Now you want control?"

Pico's eye's narrowed. "You don't know what it's like."

"You're right. I don't know what it's like." I pushed off the couch and stepped over his ball. Upon opening the refrigerator I surveyed the last remains. "Looks like spaghetti sandwiches for dinner."

"Huh?"

I closed the door, faced him, and the drill-sergeant in me surfaced. "Everything I eat is a sandwich. I make simple meals. I'm single. But I'm independent and I have control."

"Is that why you live alone?"

"Look—I'm divorced and my son's gone. Now basketball is number one and everything else is number five." I placed my hands on my hips. "So can you agree to those household rules?"

"Man, one day at a time."

I didn't know whether to hug him or kill him, and I didn't think I could handle two months of one day at a time.

I walked back to him. "Let's start all over." I stuck out my hand. "Welcome to my house. I think we'll get along just fine." We shook hands. "Now let's shoot some free throws."

Gathering himself like a man with erector-set legs, he collected his shoes and his ball. As he laced up, I said, "Defenses are going foul you and send you to the line. That's the only way they can stop you from scoring and dominating the defensive end. If you don't hit free throws, DeCarlo will take you out. But hit those free throws and you'll earn a living playing this game."

"I'm not real good at that," Pico said.

I opened the door, stepped outside, and leaned into a strong wind that blew my hair to one side. All five connecting condos on the western rim now blocked the setting sun, creating a broad shadow over the long driveway in front of us. Straight ahead was a short white line, fifteen feet from the basket, and the Hollywood sign about a hundred feet below the cliff.

Pico took both stairs with a single step. Stopping at the driveway, he eyed the hoop. His ball pinned solidly against his hip, he said, "I'm going to lose my ball. This is crazy, man."

A crosswind cooling my left cheek, I said, "Well, I don't miss. Gimme your ball."

Pico stiffened. "No way."

"Come on, pass me the ball. I haven't missed this shot in five years."

Pico made a face but flipped me the ball. Then he took a few giant steps toward the edge of the cliff and stood under the backboard prepared to catch a missed shot.

"Get away from there. You're bothering my shot."

Pico shook his head, wouldn't move. I dribbled once and was ready. Looking at the hoop, I said, "I can do this blindfolded."

"Damn," he muttered.

I set my feet behind the line and eyed the basket. Aiming above the left side of the rim to compensate for the wind, I snapped off a one-handed set shot with a lot of backspin. The ball arched, drifted right, angled through the rim rippling the nylon sideways, then bounced back to me. I caught it belt high, looked Pico in the eye. "The trick is to make the shot with enough backspin to make it come back to you. Try it. If you can make this shot, you can hit free throws anywhere."

"My ball's not ready for that."

"Okay. We'll go to a park and I'll teach you how to make a living at this game. You know all the parks. Where do you want to go?"

"Give me back my ball."

I snapped it over.

"Shattuck," Pico said. "By MacArthur Park n' Alvarado. They make free throws *and* driver's licenses down there.

"I know it."

A car started up behind us. My eyes spun back. A white Crown Vic, four condos away, made a sharp U-turn and disappeared down the hill. I hadn't seen that car around here.

Chapter 13

At 7:30 a.m., I was cleaning up the living room for another real estate agent when something shattered on the kitchen's tile floor. My eyes jerked to Pico emptying the dishwasher. Standing over the dish fragments he stared at me with sad eyes. "You gonna to kick me out now?"

"Is that what happened to you . . . one mistake and they kicked you out?"

He said nothing.

I crossed the living room, calmly approached him and noticed he was teary-eyed. "You'd have to do something worse than that—like burn the place down."

I pulled out a dustpan and broom from the closet next to the dishwasher, handed him the broom, and I held the pan's edge against the floor. "I know you've got better hands than that. You dropped it on purpose. You're testing me. Look, I'm with you . . . I'll hold, you sweep."

Pico clamped his lips and swept.

Minutes later, while Pico watched ESPN in the living room, I slipped into the bathroom, locked the door, and dialed Bob Edwards, playground director of Plummer Park in Hollywood. A longtime friend, he would help me get some breathing room. When I asked him to give Pico a morning job, he gave me a flat-out "No." But then he agreed to put Pico to work when I said I would cover his wages. Pico would check out equipment at the park each morning.

At nine, I dropped Pico off at Plummer and told him I would pick him up at noon. After lunch we would workout. A simple plan.

When I returned a few hours later, Pico had disappeared.

I called his cell. No answer. Thinking that he couldn't have gone far, I drove down Sunset Boulevard, checking out the doorways and sidewalks in front of cheap motels and fast food restaurants. No Pico. I turned west on Hollywood, eyeing the homeless sprawled on the Walk of Fame. Then I doubled back on apartment-lined cross streets. Still no sign of him.

Frustrated and out of ideas, I floored my yellow Vette up the winding streets of the Hollywood hills and waited for Pico to call me at home.

It was pushing four-thirty when I received a call from Mr. Ford at St. Andrews. My heart in my mouth, I thought the NCAA had found out about Pico's grades. I held my breath and pressed the phone to my ear.

"Coach Byrnes," Mr. Ford said in his usual monotone, "I suspect you're concerned with Pico's whereabouts. He told me you thought he was at work. But he was here most of the day. We had a nice talk. He's excited about playing college ball."

"Where is he now?"

"I took him to the Union Station Subway. He'll be home soon."

"I appreciate your call. I was going to call you. He's unpredictable and the abandonment thing hangs over his head like a black cloud."

"Yeah," Ford said, "and he's got a record of flipping out when anyone calls him a bastard."

Momentary silence before Mr. Ford went on. "At St. Andrews I was like a father to him. Now it's your turn. He looks for fathers everywhere. I hope you don't disappoint him."

"This is complicated, Mr. Ford. More complicated than you can imagine."

"I tried to tell you."

"Let me ask you this—you counseled him a long time. How would you work with him if you were me?"

"It's all about trust, Coach Byrnes. Something you're familiar with."

*   *   *

An hour later, I opened the front door for Pico. "Welcome back," I said with relief in my voice.

He entered with a smile, said, "How's it going, coach?" Then he stepped toward the shadows of my living room as if nothing had happened.

"Where you been?" I asked.

He stopped, turned back. "Been home to St. Andrews."

"What happened at Plummer Park? You were supposed to be working."

"You gave me a job without asking me if I wanted one," he said with an edge and stepped into the living room.

Say something, Dad.

I followed him. "Well, it's good that you're upfront with me . . . telling me what's on your mind."

Pico sank into the soft living room chair where thin lines of bright sunlight streamed across the room striping his body.

Sitting on the couch now, I leaned forward, and said, "Tell me about your visit."

He nodded once. "Had a good talk with Mr. Ford. I also went to see my bro. He wasn't there. Probably climbed the fence. Could be anywhere."

"Learn anything else?"

Pico pursed his lips. "Mr. Ford said this is period of adjustment for me. But if I hang in there I'll be okay."

"He got that right. New life, preparing for college basketball with the freedom to chose who you are."

"Mr. Ford called it identity."

"That's the most important part. We'll start working on that tomorrow."

CHAPTER 14

Long morning shadows from the old Sheraton Hotel fell across Wilshire Boulevard and covered Shattuck Park. A small grassed-in, triangular block, Shattuck had a fenced-in basketball court as its centerpiece. A homeless man and his rollaway luggage were parked under a leafy tree just outside the court. The only sounds came from Pico's bouncing ball, chirping birds in the trees, and the whir of Wilshire Boulevard traffic.

I was breaking the rule that forbade working out a recruit, but the NCAA would never find us at a mid-city park.

Our workout session began with free-throw shooting fundamentals. I rebounded under the hoop. Pico, in HotShoe black shorts and shoes, clinked a few shots off the rusty metal backboard. Then he held the ball out in front of him, staring at it as if it had let him down. "Fuckin' free throw," he yelled as he kicked the ball past me, rattling the fence. "How am I going to play if I can't make a free throw?"

"Relax. You've been a half-court player. No free throws there." I bent down, picked up the ball. "I'll show you how." As I walked him back to the free throw line, I said, "Shooting a free throw is like placing an egg into the basket without cracking it . . . very gently, with one delicate motion." I propped the ball over his head. "Hold your ball so high above your head that it will take all your strength to shoot it into the hoop.

Then snap your wrist and have your middle and indes fingers guide the ball to the basket. Try it."

Pico extended his long arms and shot. Although the ball bounced away, his form was good.

"You've got a nice-looking motion. Now let's add something. Before you shoot, visualize making the shot, then look at the hole during your entire motion."

He did and the ball curled around the rim and fell out.

He raised his voice again. "Damn! . . . I can't do this."

"Pico. Do you know what the most important shooting muscle is?"

"The arm?"

"No. The heart. Now take your time and shoot another one."

He did and the ball went down.

He smiled at me. "Hey. All right."

A gravely voice outside the court yelled, "Shut the fuck up!"

I looked through the cyclone fence at the homeless man sitting against the tree. Overgrown brown beard, shoulder-length hair, worn clothes. Maybe forty.

"Sorry, mister," I calmly said. "We're going to workout every morning at nine."

"Fuck!"

His message was clear.

Pico tucked the ball under his arm and walked to the fence. "Hey, man. How's it going?"

The man mumbled, "Out of work, out of luck, out of time."

"Sorry, man."

Pico and the man shared street experiences before he came back. Then Pico spent a half-hour shooting free throws. Thinking motion, visualizing, and putting his heart into it.

During that time I said, "Nice going," more times than I could count.

* * *

Next on my morning agenda was to have him receive the ball in the low post, six feet from the hoop. As I demonstrated the stance, Pico stood on the sideline with his arms crossed and his face twisted, as if he weren't into it.

"Look at me!" I barked. "Feet wider than your shoulders, knees bent, weight evenly distributed, vertical back, elbows out. Now you do it."

"You showed me how to do that when I was a tenth grader."

"We're starting all over. From the beginning. Now get in the stance."

As Pico and I exchanged spots on the court, he gave me a serious look. "You're treating me like a kid, teaching me beginning basketball and all."

"Trust me. You're a great athlete and you need to be fundamentally sound—these are building blocks for playing major college basketball. Stay with me."

The next morning at Shattuck, I spent an hour teaching Pico how to shoot the jumper. I reviewed how to pivot with the ball from his low-post stance and shoot a turn-around jumper with his arms extended high overhead. Thirty minutes later, he was ready to try out his shot against competition. There wasn't any. But I had an idea.

I walked a short distance to my Vette at the curb, took out a long handled broom that I had brought from home. Clutching the broom in one hand, I walked through the court. Pico followed me to the homeless man, the same guy he had talked to the previous day. Leaning up against the tree within reach of a battered piece of luggage, the man eyed us.

A couple of paces away, I said, "Excuse me, mister, want to make ten bucks?"

He stared at me. I couldn't help staring at the bulge in his mouth.

"Ten bucks." I repeated and held out the broom. "Just wave this thing in the air. Try to block some shots. You'll be like a seven-foot player, just what we need. You interested? Ten bucks."

He growled, "Been there, done that."

"You played?"

"Basketball. Once a Jackrabbit, always a Jackrabbit. That's what the coach said when he recruited me."

"What happened?"

"There are those who watch it happen, those who make it happen, and those who don't know what happened."

He could have gone to Winning Dynamics.

"Twenty," Pico said.

"Okay, twenty bucks," I said.

The man puckered, turned his head to the left, and spurted brown juice, darkening a small patch of grass, an arm's distance away. "When?"

"Now."

The man stood, grabbed the handle of his luggage.

He probably had a seven-feet-six-inch reach. With the broom his reach would be somewhere between eleven to twelve feet. A monster.

"What's your name?" I asked.

"You can call me Proverb."

"Okay, Proverb, follow me."

Proverb trailed us to the fence, and bounced his luggage up and over the lip of the cement court.

"Leave your luggage by the fence," I said.

He froze, gave me a "Don't fuck with me" look.

"Your stuff will be safe. Don't worry."

He wheeled his luggage against the fence a few feet behind the goal, took a step forward and to my surprise, spat on the end line.

"Proverb, we don't want anyone slipping on the court. Spit out your chaw and let's get to work."

Proverb looked at me again as if I had gone too far.

I took my wallet out of the front pocket of my sweats, flashed a Jackson. "Twenty bucks."

He turned and spat a soggy wad that resembled thick brown hair. It arced a few feet, hit the bottom strand of chain link, wrapped around it, then dripped ugly.

I could be taking roll at the high school with normal people.

I inhaled, let it all out, handed Proverb the broom. "Now stand behind Pico and block his shot with the head of the broom."

Pico took his position down low on the left side of the key with his back to Proverb, who stood behind him holding the broom high.

"Remember, Proverb. He shoots, you swat."

He growled back, "I'm not stupid."

Out of the corner of my eye, I saw a white Crown Vic pull up behind my car. It looked like the same car in front of my house two days earlier. I could barely see a shadowy figure behind the wheel. The ball under my arm, I walked quickly out the gate, crossed the grass, and yelled to the driver, "Hey! Hey you!"

The car pulled out, peeled rubber, and sped down the street.

Somebody wants to see me without me seeing them.

Wondering what that was all about, I quickly returned to the free throw line extended, (near the sideline) and asked Proverb, "Ever see that car before?"

"I only notice cops."

I looked down the empty street, then back to Pico and Proverb. "Okay," I said, holding the ball above my head. "Back to basketball."

Pico assumed his stance. I lobbed him the ball. Upon reception he spun right, went up in one motion, tried to shoot over the head of the broom. When his shot was ten feet up, Proverb whacked it back into his face. Then Proverb gave a wide-eyed Rasputin look, like he had a vision.

Pico picked up the bouncing ball, snapped it back to me, his face angry, combative, just what I wanted.

"Pico," I said, "think about this on your next shot. Imagine facing a seven-footer who wants to send you back to the streets." I waited a couple of counts to let my message sink in. "This time, get up as high as you can, extend your arms, and bank it over that asshole."

I lobbed the ball into Pico again. He pivoted and sprang. Went higher. Snapped off the shot. The ball looped over the bristles, pinged off the metal board, and angled into the net.

"Yes!" I shouted, pumping my fist. "I knew you could do it!"

Proverb brought down the broom, and cracked, "The angle of fuckin' incidence equals the angle of fuckin' reflection."

Pico turned to Proverb. "One coach is enough."

I lean against the cold tunnel wall outside our locker room. My assistant, Giranda, stands across from me, finishing up his last recruiting call. My mind drifts to last spring.

Morning sun warms Sheldrake Park. Pico's shooting actions become fluid. Proverb's actions bring a smile to my face. Good times. Pico and I are in sync. Proverb gets a laptop with Wheels's money. Pico teaches him how to use it.

I should have stayed in L.A. Never expected what was waiting for us when we returned to Atlantic City. Never expected a free apartment and what came with it.

My contract doesn't state what I do. Nothing is written down. No paper trail. No connecting dots.

Giranda slips his cell into his pocket, saying, "It's the waiting that gets you."

I stare at him, feel like throwing up. "Yeah, it's the waiting."

CHAPTER 15

DeCarlo, dressed in slacks and a HotShoe polo shirt, waved me out of his office. I followed him out of the arena, across the boardwalk, and down a wooden ramp that hugged the sand. The seashore was hot and clammy. Oppressive for a southern Californian dude like me. DeCarlo stopped at the edge of the walkway where small green waves slapped the shore and the edge of the ramp. Several yards away, two gray-haired women with rolled-up pant legs tested the water, and a couple of bikini-clad girls kicking sand and behind them made a mad dash for the Atlantic.

DeCarlo said, "Now that Pico's been admitted to Sheldrake and you're settled, you're going to meet Peter Townsend III." He looked over his shoulder and waited for two teenage girls to walk by us along the shoreline. "Peter Townsend is the owner of the Mardi Gras. Big booster. Big name in Atlantic City. Give him a call."

Sounds like a guy with a position but no job, wears a blue blazer, white duck pants, lives on a large estate with a winding driveway.

"Classy name, Peter Townsend III." But I thought *this could be my chance to get more responsibility. Work my way up the coaching ranks.*

DeCarlo said, "I don't want to know anything about your dealings with him."

I said nothing. I had no idea what to expect, and I couldn't ask

69

DeCarlo.

DeCarlo gave me Townsend's cell number and asked me to repeat it, which I did. He also slipped me a new throwaway phone. I gave him the old one. There were never any written records of our business.

I phoned Townsend III fifteen minutes later. He answered in a soft voice, speaking clearly as if he had practiced with marbles in his mouth. He instructed me to be at the Cockatoo Bar across the street from the rear of the Mardi Gras at three. Then he told me what to say to the bartender. I had thirty minutes.

CHAPTER 16

The Cockatoo Bar was a dirty brick, single-story building in need of an acid bath. Inside, light came from a neon sign behind the bar and a large window to its right. Two men leaned over the bar sipping doubles, and through the window I saw a man loading a Topas Beer truck in the alley. The beer keg the man was lifting slipped out of his hands and hit the pavement without a bounce. He picked it up, loaded it, closed the sidewalk cellar door, and hopped into the cab.

"Hey, what do you want?" the bartender said like I was trespassing. Middle-aged, fleshy faced, he wore his pants below his gut like he had decided long ago that a size 36 belt was the last one he was going to buy.

Taking a whiff of stale air, I used the code: "I'll have a keg."

"Pick it up now?"

"Yes."

The bartender glanced though the window at the truck motoring away. Then coming around the bar, he motioned me to follow him. We passed a bricked-in doorway, several worn leather booths, and stopped at a marred door in the rear of the room. After he unlocked the door, I followed him down worn wooden stairs to a dingy storage area. He hit a light switch on a wood post, brightening a room half-filled with Topas Beer kegs and cartons of hard liquor. After another door he unlocked, we entered a long, dark tunnel, illuminated by two hanging light bulbs, one at each end of the underpass. I inhaled. The scent was unmistakably salt water. We were below sea level.

"Wait a second," the bartender said. He dialed his cell and snapped, "He's comin." Then he faced me. "You need to go down this old escape route."

"Why?"

"The Cockatoo used to be a speakeasy way back when. Had some raids. This was the escape route."

"What am I escaping from?"

"You're going to the Mardi Gras."

I raised my voice. "I just came from the Mardi Gras."

The bartender gestured for me to get moving. "You're going back."

I shook my head and made my way past the first bare light bulb; the only sounds coming from suction cups in my HotShoes gripping the wet cement floor.

All this for a fuckin' booster meeting?

In a short minute, I stood at the end of the tunnel next to the "greeter," a big man in a dark suit with a bad job. The overhead light bulb brought a light sheen to his bald spot, an airport security wand in his hand, and the elevator door behind him.

"Stand still," Big-Man said as he scanned me.

"Hey, I'm a basketball coach. What are you looking for? My offense?"

"A wire," he said. Then he stood. "Never keep the boss waitin." He thumbed a lone elevator button. The door slid up open.

I entered thinking, *what didn't DeCarlo tell me about Townsend? Is this some kind of joke?*

I took a long ride up on the express, my brain trying to come up with a Winning Dynamics reason for doing this. There weren't any. Seconds later, I entered a large sun-filled room. Sixteen-foot ceiling. Maple paneled wall behind me, sunlit windowed wall about twenty feet away. A large maple desk to my right. Above the desk hung a large black-and-white photo of a toddler holding the hand of a man in black-and-white wingtip shoes. The man wore a dark, pinstriped suit, and a white tie on a white shirt. They stood in front of a hotel surrounded by miles of desert sand. I guessed the little boy to be Peter Townsend III, the place to be 1940s Vegas.

In front of the desk sat a coffee table on a red Middle Eastern rug bordered by two facing, white leather couches.

I called out, "Mr. Townsend?"

"Over here, Coach Byrnes."

My HotShoes squeaked on the hardwood floor as I stepped towards the windows.

There, a tall, trim, gray-haired man about my height with steel-blue eyes that could melt granite stood to meet me. He was the same man who had observed our workout and dinner during Pico's forty-eight-hour visit. He wore a dark pinstriped suit, black-and-white wingtips, and a white tie on a white shirt. A carbon copy of the photo. He flashed a smile that wasn't worth two cents, didn't offer his hand, nor did he introduce himself.

The warmth of an ice sculpture.

Unemotional, unanimated, he said, "You've represented yourself well, Coach Byrnes."

"Thank you."

Taking a seat, he gestured for me to sit on the white leather chair across from him. I didn't take my eyes off him as I lowered myself onto the chair's edge.

Townsend leaned back, crossed his chicken legs, and said, "You have brought us a good prospect, a little raw, but good."

"He'll make his mark, Mr. Townsend."

"Will you, Coach Byrnes? Will you make your mark?"

I repositioned my sweaty bottom. "I intend to."

The landline on the table rang. He picked it up. "Townsend." He listened for a short minute before saying, "The Mardi Gras will be glad to donate twenty grand to the American Cancer Society."

He replaced the phone and looked at me. "Coach Byrnes, I brought you up here to give you more responsibility. Responsibilities that Mansfield had before his unfortunate disappearance. Handling Pico Rimpau is just part of your job. The other part is distribution. We deal in cash . . . nothing on paper, no records, no deposits, no wire transfers, no mistakes."

My eyes widened. *You talking drug money?* "Distribution of what?"

"Player payoffs. How do you think the players got here? Natural selection?"

Feeling real stupid, I said, "Of course."

Townsend gave an imperceptible nod and continued. "You'll find a zipper on the side of your mattress."

My mattress?

"Unzip the side of your mattress and take out the two envelopes."

Son-of-a-bitch. Your people went through my luggage at the Mardi Gras back in May.

"The envelopes are for the grandmothers of Nitro Dixon and Americus Hart. We're helping them survive the inner city while their grandsons win for Sheldrake. A fair exchange. Don't blow it, Coach Byrnes. Coaches that can't handle it don't last long here."

Not going to blow it. It's all about winning, my only goal in life.

"Coach Byrnes, you're to meet Mrs. Dixon and Mrs. Hart in Philly and New York. We're buying their American dream. Isn't that what you want . . . the American dream? A head job some day? The NCAA title?"

Townsend went on to tell me where and when the payoff would take place. If he blinked during that time, I missed it.

"Any questions?" he asked.

"Yeah. Do all your guests come through the tunnel?"

Townsend raised his voice slightly. "Would you like anyone to know you were here? I don't."

I nodded. Understood the importance of leaving no tracks for NCAA investigators.

He got up indicating the meeting was over. I stood. He walked me to the elevator and pressed the button, and said, "What's your understanding of our meeting?"

I thought, *You're crazier than I am,* but said, "This meeting never happened."

Townsend gave me his best icy stare. "We're going to get along just fine, Coach Byrnes, just fine." The elevator door opened, and I stepped in.

"Oh," said Townsend, holding the door open. "I got a car for you waiting at my dealership, Townsend BMW/Audi on Pacific."

As the door began to close, I said to him, "Winning is the only thing."

CHAPTER 17

A white two-door BMW sped down the long car dealership ramp. It screeched to a stop a few feet from me. The driver's side door opened and a barrel-chested man got out.

"This a loaner?" I asked.

"Yah, it used to be Mansfield's."

"How did you get the car back?"

"Cops brought it back after they went through it. We cleaned it up."

"See anything unusual?"

"No. Only 3,000 miles on it. Still in good shape."

I got in. The leather seats smelled of money. The car was quiet and powerful—my kind of machine. I opened the glove box. Nothing. Lifted the consol. No hints of Mansfield's demise.

The man stuck his head in the window. "Where you off to?"

"No special place."

Where I'm going isn't your business.

*   *   *

I drove west on Highway 42 to a big steam room they called Philadelphia. My destination—Independence Hall. After making a drop to Mrs. Dixon, I'd meet my brother Jordan for a drink. The closer I came to

Philadelphia, the more I needed to raise the AC.

I found a parking garage in Philadelphia's historic district, then stepped out into wet heat. Two blocks later, drenched in sweat, I stood shoulder to shoulder with a large group of tourists who had assembled inside Independence Hall for a history lesson. We stood behind a low, Eighteenth Century wood railing.

A female park ranger addressed the crowd. Behind her was a large room of antique desks and chairs used by the signers of the Declaration of Independence.

I positioned myself next to a far wall where Mrs. Dixon could easily recognize me. I had emailed her to look for a clean-shaven white guy, wearing a beige HotShoe cap. She had Emailed me back, "You won't miss me."

A man about forty moved next to me. He wore dark blue shorts, and damn if he didn't wear a beige HotShoe cap. But he held a young boy on his shoulders. I looked around for a Black lady. There were two in the crowd, one of them tall, middle-aged with a baby in her arms. The other, sixtyish, average weight, five-feet eight, long gray hair, dark glasses, and a Sheldrake cap.

Shit. A Sheldrake cap. I hope there's no photo of our exchange on the eleven o'clock news.

She worked her way towards me. It had to be her. I was nervous. Not a good feeling for a bagman.

The park ranger surveyed the crowd, spoke, "During the blistering summer of 1776, fifty-six courageous men gathered here to sign the Declaration of Independence. They were going to risk everything— their lives, their fortune, and their sacred honor."

The lady tapped me on my right shoulder, whispered the code word, "Franklin."

Eyeing the park ranger, I reached down, pulled out one of two envelopes from my red HotShoe sack, and handed it over. I hoped the lady wasn't looking for the Ben Franklin Museum.

She said nothing. Smooth as silk, she stuffed the envelope in her handbag and quietly made her way to the exit as the park ranger continued to lecture. I looked around. No eyes on me. I felt like I just shot through a red light. Guilty but exhilarated.

CHAPTER 18

I exited with the crowd. Outside, it was so hot that if you dropped an egg, it would have been hardboiled before it hit the pavement.

I walked to the corner of 5th and Chestnut, a pitch shot from Independence Hall. From there it was a short walk to the Washington Building, a two-story, Nineteenth Century restaurant. I was eager to see Jordan. It had been a long time.

On the first floor I pulled open a heavy, steel elevator door, pushed an accordion iron gate to one side, and stepped into an antique contraption, which I assumed was Otis' first creation. A man in a lightweight blue suit followed me in. A few inches shorter than I, clean-shaven, short haired. He nodded. I nodded back, jerked the gate closed, and pressed UP. The elevator rocked and rose slowly. Then the man hit STOP, jiggling the car to a halt between the floors.

"The hell you doin'?" I blurted.

The man gave me a pissed-off look, the kind that precedes a technical foul. He pulled out a business card from his side pocket, handed it to me, saying, "Special Agent Streeter, FBI."

Now I had an FBI card in my right hand and a thousand dollar payoff in my left.

I froze.

"We've been watching you."

"What's there to watch?"

"Byrnes, we're not interested in the NCAA rules you're breaking. We have our eyes on you because you're working with a person of interest."

A buzzer went off. Someone else wanted the elevator.

I looked at the stop button. I was tempted to press it, but didn't.

As our contraption struggled to ascend, Streeter pulled out a five-by-seven, black-and-white photo from his inside coat pocket. "You're working with this man." He held up a head shot of Peter Townsend III.

My mouth dryer than the L.A. River, I said, "I don't know what you're talking about."

Streeter's voice hardened. "You have a choice, Byrnes. Talk to us or go down as a co-conspirator when we nail him. What do you say?"

Breaking NCAA rules is not a felony. What's Townsend doing? I've got to talk to DeCarlo.

I looked through him. "Fuck you! Stop harassing me. "

Streeter didn't flinch, said, "Don't get in so deep that you can't find your way out." He slid the photo back. "Think about our offer . . . think real hard. We'll be in touch." He pulled out the Stop button. The elevator jiggled and rose to the second floor. Streeter jerked the gate open and headed towards a far staircase.

CHAPTER 19

I stepped out of the elevator feeling as though I was underwater, holding my breath, hearing mumbled voices of the packed restaurant. Customers, elbow-to-elbow on wood benches, ate off white ceramic plates on picnic tables covered with white paper tablecloths.

I spotted Jordan to my right at a corner table and crossed the room.

He got up, gave me a hug. Just what I needed.

I heard him say, "Been a long time, kiddo." Then he pulled back to look at me as I appraised him.

A five-eight candidate for Jenny Craig. Turns controversy into a conviction. I love him in an odd sort of way.

"What's wrong, Conrad? You don't look so good."

"Caught something coming up the elevator. Felt fine on the street."

Jordan looked down at my right hand. "That your new business card?"

Jesus! FBI card in one hand, payola sack in the other.

"No," I said sharply and slid the card deep into my pants pocket.

We sat down. I casually placed the sack on the chair to my left, next to the wood-framed window. Then I gazed out the window and watched the FBI agent cross the street. I wondered if I would see him again.

"How's your job going?" Jordan asked.

I looked over my shoulder at patrons apparently minding their own business. "It's exciting." *Pay-off city.* "Meet interesting people." *FBI.* "And it's all basketball."

"Assistant coach," he said. "Perfect job for a basketball addict."

I reached out, wrapped my sweaty hand around a cold glass of water, and drained it.

Silence for a long moment as Jordan read the menu and questions rolled around inside my head.

How did Agent Streeter know where I was? How did he make the Townsend connection? Is he going to stay after me?

Jordan put the menu down and said to my surprise, "Mom would be proud of you. On paper you look good."

I took a breath. "Mom told me I'd never make it and I'm still trying to prove she's wrong."

Jordan's pale brown eyes narrowed. "She had that effect on both of us," he said softly.

As a waiter placed a dish of rolls in the center of the table, I assessed my brother. "Jordan, you were the one who was supposed to make it. And look at you—big-time sports columnist for a major daily. Cracking heads everyday. You're at the top of your game. That's got to be satisfying in a odd sort of way."

He gave me a Cheshire cat smile. "I haven't made it yet. But I'm close."

Close to what?

I took a stab. "They don't give the Pulitzer Prize for gossip."

"They do for good investigative reporting."

The waiter suddenly appeared and we ordered. Our glasses were refilled and I drained mine again.

Jordan glanced around and leaned forward, his striped tie brushing the edge of the table. He spoke in a conspiratorial tone. "Ever heard of Peter Townsend III? He's a big Sheldrake booster. I thought you might know him."

You're not going to step on <u>my</u> back to get the award. Send Jordan off in a different direction.

I said with an edge, "I coach Pico Rimpau. Don't know any boosters."

Heads turned our way.

"Calm down," Jordan said. "All I did was ask you about a guy named Townsend III."

I took a breath. "I don't know Townsend whatever number he is."

Jordan leaned closer still, this time his gut pinning his red tie against the table. "He's a Sheldrake booster. Surely you must know him."

I studied his eyes and guessed what was stirring behind them. *The closer he gets to Townsend, the closer he gets to me. He's always been a twisted Boy Scout—he'd turn on me.*

"Well, Conrad, <u>here's</u> a story. Townsend's father was Tiny Cielo . . . Las Vegas 1947. Tiny Cielo was a silent partner in one of the first casinos but he wanted more. He wanted the Vegas narcotics concession. But so did the mob. They turned on him during the Kefauver Committee hearings. Got him deported. But before Cielo waved goodbye in New York Harbor, his wife took custody of young Peter and changed his name to Peter Townsend III. There was no first or second, only a third. And Cielo left an incredibly large trust fund for Peter that kicked in only when the kid entered Harvard. And the kid is smart—"clear admit" as they say in your business. Then the kid returned to Vegas and built the Monaco. But the gaming commission forced him out for Mafia connections and brawls on the casino floor that Townsend started.

"Present day picture, Townsend owns the Mardi Gras Casino, a car dealership, and is marinated in the Atlantic City community. Board of directors of the hospital, cancer drive leader, donates to both political parties."

Jordan glanced over his shoulder. "But he's dirty. I know it."

"What makes you think so?"

"He's too clean."

Good thing he's not on to Wheels and HotShoe.

I threw up my hands. "Jordan, there is no Pulitzer for creative journalism."

The waiter appeared holding a tray of burgers and a mound of fries and placed them before us. Jordan smiled and gave me a hearty thumbs up. "Best burger in Philly."

I bit into mine. Tasteless.

After washing down a mouthful of burger with a swig of dark ale, Jordan wiped the catsup off his fingers with his tongue. Then he tried and failed to hold back another smile. "Did you read this morning's paper?"

"No. Why are you smiling?"

"Because a homeless guy admitted murdering Mansfield." He chuckled. "But he also said that he killed JFK." He waited for me to laugh. It didn't happen. Then he looked at my plate. "Hey, aren't you hungry?"

"I've had all I can digest today."

My brother extracted a few fries, wolfed 'em down, then came at me again with, "How do you like working with DeCarlo, the most unethical coach in the business? One more NCAA violation and he's banned from coaching."

Trying to cut him off, I said sharply, "DeCarlo is a winner. And 'Those Who Condemn Winners Are Those Who Never Won and See No chance of Winning.' Winning Dynamics, Law 8."

Jordan rolled his eyes. "More Winning Dynamics' bullshit. Conrad, you've lost touch with reality. Come to your senses and take a high school job before the NCAA suspends you for breaking rules."

"Just don't tee me up, Jordan. You know I wouldn't do anything wrong. I just coach Pico Rimpau and evaluate players." I glanced at my watch. "How about a lift to the train? I've got to see a recruit in New York." I reached over and grabbed the red sack.

Jordan took out his pad, placed it on the table. "Who you looking at?"

"None of your business. I don't want to see it in your column tomorrow."

CHAPTER 20

Icaught the two-thirty to New York, arrived at Penn Station on 33rd Street and 8th Avenue at four-ten. Twenty minutes before the exchange—Townsend's money for Mrs. Hart's goodwill. I darted in and around heavy sidewalk traffic for three blocks, yellow cabs shooting by me like it was the end of world. Covered with sweat, I entered Grand Central Station, glanced at a tall, four-faced clock. Four- twenty. Ten minutes to my meeting.

On the main concourse, travelers scurried in every direction like they were members of an ant colony that someone just stepped on. I ducked to one side of the central information booth, picked up a *New York Times* out of a garbage can for a prop. Coming around the backside looking for a tail, I narrowly missed a couple saying a tearful goodbye and a man wheeling his luggage at my shoes. Feeling that there were no eyes on me, I took the Vanderbilt Archway stairs two at a time, then stepped out onto Vanderbilt Avenue. There, I spotted a small store-front with a red awning sign, "Campbell Apartment, Cocktails from another era."

I sidestepped a drunk who looked like he was walking up hill and entered. It wasn't my kind of place. No tap beer. No peanut shells on the floor. I inhaled perfume and after-shave. Saw art deco, dark wood, red leather chairs, stained glass, and standing room only. A large room with maybe seventy people dressed to the nines. Laughing, drinking, talking. No free stools at the long bar where men with over-tanned faces and bottled hair flirted with attractive younger women with expensive breasts.

A waitress in a hot black dress came my way. I smiled and winked. She smiled back and gave me a head-to-toe. Behind her, in a far corner, two men got up from overstuffed chairs. I stabbed my index finger towards the chairs. Glancing back, she dropped her smile and gestured to a gray-haired man in penguin attire behind a podium, a few yards away. There, three men waited in line.

Time's running out. Go for it.

I approached the maitre d', shook his hand with twenty bucks neatly folded in my palm. He slipped it into his coat pocket and guided me to the leather chairs.

I sat down, checked the front door and nearby customers as I carefully slid the envelope out of the red sack and between the folded pages of the *Times*. Then I held it in my sweaty hand and waited. A few minutes later, a stout, gray-haired lady shuffled in. Probably Mrs. Hart. Black, prune-faced and sloped shouldered, at least twice my age.

I got up and waved. She edged towards me and I cleared the last few yards. She carefully sat down and rested her large white bag on her lap.

"Franklin," she said, providing the code word in a crusty old voice that mixed with the crowd noise.

"I know it's you, Mrs. Hart. Good to meet you in person."

"Let's have it."

I tried and failed to generate a Winning Dynamics Law that would calm her down. Nothing came out. It was like I lost air in my Winning Dynamics sail and was mentally adrift in a dead sea. I looked down and considered not giving her anything.

Mrs. Hart raised her voice. "Don't tell me you don't have it."

I hoisted my eyes and said reluctantly, "It's in the paper." At the same time, two middle-aged men moved into an open space next to us. They exchanged cards. I put up a hand to Mrs. Hart and nodded, meaning, "Stop salivating. You're going to get it."

A moment later the men looked towards the bar and I placed the *Times* on the cocktail table, my sweat prints all over it. "It's in here."

A waitress trying to do her job reached down, clamped the paper, and said, "Let me get this out of your way."

"No!" Mrs. Hart barked, snatching it back like she caught a fly.

My heart went into a freefall. All eyes would be on me if the money fell out of the newspaper.

The waitress straightened. "Okay, fine." Her eyes darted from Mrs. Hart to me. "So what'll youse have?"

She's wondering what a seventy-year-old Black lady is doing with a forty-year-old white guy . . . So do I.

Mrs. Hart waved her off.

"I'll have a Ja . . . Jack and water."

The waitress left.

As Mrs. Hart stuffed the newspaper inside her purse, she said, "How well do you know my grandson, Americus?"

"I haven't met him yet. I just took the job."

Her eyes twinkled. "Americus is something special. Going to be a lottery pick. Going to buy me a house in the country where they only do over-the-counter drugs. His photo is in the living room, right next to Jesus. Know mean?"

"Yes, Ma'am."

She rocked forward, struggled to her feet. "Too bad about Coach Mansfield."

I stood. "Yes. Terrible."

"He never liked our meetings. Always looked guilty, just like you." She looked across the room to the entrance before turning back. "One more thing. I told DeCarlo to make sure Americus gets twenty shots a game . . . no points, no lottery pick, no house."

In seconds she disappeared into the crowd.

A cold chill ran through me, like I just got away with murder. I had to get the hell out. I sprang from my chair and wormed my way out of the bar. Outside, I sprinted to the station, ran down the steps and through the concourse, darting to open space like a tailback running to daylight.

Cloaked in guilt and sweat, panting, and in desperate need of a shower, I finally stopped blocks later inside Penn Station. There I looked behind for anyone chasing me. There was no one.

After sitting down on a bench seat near the entrance, I tried to get a grip. I hadn't felt guilt since the day before I entered Winning Dynamics three months ago. But now I do. Winning Dynamics was wearing off. And I couldn't go back for a tune up. I knew I was in quick sand that rules did not apply, that I would be targeted by the mob if I talked. My thoughts turned to DeCarlo. *Tell him about your elevator meeting and find out what Townsend is up to.*

CHAPTER 21

DeCarlo, holding a large stuffed envelope, lurched from his chair and waved me outside.

Thinking "FBI," I followed him as he scampered down the arena steps and spoke about the Junior Olympic team he was taking to Barcelona for a tournament. They were going to begin workouts at Boardwalk Arena the next day.

We breezed across the shiny court and around the bleachers, where we entered Sheldrake's dressing room. There, DeCarlo locked the door behind us. We sat down and straddled a long plastic bench with enough room between us to play cards.

DeCarlo emptied the contents of the envelope on the bench. "This will get our starters eligible," he said.

"Coach, there's something . . . "

DeCarlo cut in. "They don't know that they're taking these classes in summer school.

We want them working out, not wasting time in class."

I perused the papers: Atlantic City Community College summer school registration forms, printed names of our starters, social security numbers, birthdates, game tickets, and a short stack of hundred-dollar bills.

I blurted, "Look . . . "

DeCarlo interjected, "Deadline for registration is today. Chucky Primera, the basketball coach at the college, is a good guy. He's going to take care of it . . . he knows you're coming . . . the gifts are for him."

"The forms haven't been signed."

"Sign 'em."

I took out a pen. Felt a moment of guilt that was quickly overrun by ambition, and penned in the player's names.

DeCarlo stood and gave me directions to the college. "When you come back, I want you and Giranda to get on a plane for HotShoe Basketball Camp near Pittsfield, New Hampshire. Every blue-chip high school player in the world will be there. And every big-time coach will show up to be seen by the players they've been recruiting."

I looked up. "I've read about it. And there's something . . . "

"Marquee Smith, a point guard from Philly will be there. We want him very badly. So does Wheels. All you have to do, Conrad, is wear a Sheldrake Shirt and pump up his ego with positive gestures. Pound your heart with your fist, then point at him."

Finally, I blurted, "Coach . . . FBI."

DeCarlo froze with an expression that said we could get five to ten— scaring the hell out of me.

I said, "I was approached by an FBI agent yesterday. The agent said he wasn't interested in the NCAA rules Sheldrake was breaking, but he wanted me to rat on Townsend. I told him to get fucked." I took a deep, quick breath. "Now tell me what Townsend's up to."

DeCarlo sat down, his face drawn. "Townsend bankrolls our program." He held up both hands. "That's all I know and I'm not supposed to know that." Then he let out an incongruent laugh. "You know that's great news. We're under their FBI radar. The fewer eyes on you the better."

Fuck. My prints are on everything. I'm a pawn, the first one to be thrown off the raft.

The air sucked out of the room, I stuffed the summer school documents back into the envelope.

"There's something else," DeCarlo said.

"More?"

"I'm going to have Pico workout with the Junior Olympic team. That won't cost us anything and it's legal. I'm in charge."

"Pico's not ready for that," I said. "He's never played full court, never been in an organized offense, and I'm supposed to be with him at all times. But I'm out for two days."

"He won't miss you."

"That's a mistake, Coach. I'm telling you. I gave him my word that I would be with him all the time. I've gotten to know this guy. Don't do it."

"I'll handle him."

"Handling isn't what he needs. He needs understanding."

"Bullshit. He's a teenager running around with my wallet. Now deliver the papers."

* * *

Wanting to drive to southern California, I drove from Atlantic to Albany Avenue, thinking about Pico all the way. Then I crossed a bay and found AC Community College on a small island surrounded by marshland and diving seagulls that couldn't give a damn about the FBI or the NCAA. I passed tennis courts and a baseball field, then pulled into a parking lot in front of a gym building that would be mistaken for a factory in Los Angeles.

Brick-faced, no plants or trees.

I called Pico's cell from my car.

"Pico, I'm taking a trip tomorrow and I'll be back in two days. You're working out with the Junior Olympic Team at Boardwalk. DeCarlo will call you. It'll be fun."

Silence. Then he gave me an earache. "You're supposed to be with me. That's our deal."

Jesus. I held the phone out a fraction. "I'm sorry, Pico. I do what DeCarlo tells me to do. Take your ball. Everything will be okay. Coach DeCarlo will work with you."

"I hate DeCarlo."

Oh, shit.

"You can make it without me."

"I hate you too."

"Just hang in there. I'll be back."

*   *   *

I found Chucky Primera in his small office, leaning back, looking at nothing. He was a square man with dark circles around deep-set eyes. Looked like he hadn't slept, ever.

Pico still on my brain, I stood just inside the doorway, introduced myself and said, "It's about the thing."

Primera didn't move a muscle. "So you're the new guy. Too bad about the last guy. He was a good recruiter and did some other things." Getting up, he said, "Follow me." We walked out into a cool breeze coming off the marsh. As we passed a number of students in assorted attire, Primera said, "Too bad about Mansfield. I saw him the day before he disappeared. He had a worried look on his face—the kind of look one of my players gave me after he stole a government check off my desk."

Minutes later, we entered Admissions and Records, a one-story building surrounded by low-rise classrooms. I followed Primera as he shot around a half door that said "Keep Out." Behind the counter, he waved to a couple of clerks like he owned the place. Then he spoke softly to a middle-aged woman who feverishly stamped papers at her desk.

I'm amazed we got this far.

The woman pointed to a large windowed conference room across the way. Inside that room, Primera closed the Venetian blinds and locked the door. I checked the handle just to be sure, then emptied the envelope on the large conference table. Primera checked out the materials.

"What kind of grades do you want?" he said, stuffing a roll of hundreds into his pocket.

"A's," I said with guilt dripping all over myself. "All A's."

As Primera was repackaging the envelope, there was a knock on the door followed by a woman's voice. "Coach, we have a meeting in this conference room."

Primera barked at the door, "Be out as soon as I pick up my winnings."

His remark gave me the same security that came moments before my last bungee jump. Nothing but fear..

Then it struck me. He was in the right kind of work. He had no conscience.

Primera tried to close our transaction with, "Tell DeCarlo that the forward he sent me looks great in summer league. I had to cash in my life insurance policy to get him. But I didn't need the policy ... that's for sick people. I need insurance against losing. If I get fired I can't draw unemployment, and my family would be in the street." Then he picked up the envelope and gave me an understanding look. "Don't you love the high you get from winning?

I appraised Primera. He was no different from me, from DeCarlo, from everyone else I had come in contact with in Atlantic City, a city of addictions.

"Are you questioning this business, kid? Don't worry. There's light at the end of the tunnel."

"What if the light is a burning fuse leading to a stack of dynamite?"

"You better not talk that way in front of DeCarlo."

"Just kidding," I lied.

On the drive back to the city, my cell rang. It was Townsend. His voice sounded like I had done something wrong. He told me to head for his office. Said it would take me fifteen minutes.

When I hung up, I thought, *how the hell does he know it would take me fifteen? I didn't tell him where I was.*

* * *

Once again, the greeter in the dark tunnel leading to the Mardi Gras Casino welcomed me. I wondered who else he was greeting. I also wondered why the Topas beer keg that was loaded onto the truck a month earlier didn't bounce when it hit the pavement. It was supposed to be empty.

I stepped warily into Townsend's penthouse. Sunlight streamed in through the tall windows across the way brightened the room. Townsend sat on the couch that faced away from the elevator. His back to me, he said, "Come in, Byrnes."

Wondering what was next, I sat gingerly on a couch across from him and shut up. Townsend said, "It's time for your performance review."

I leaned forward, once again overwhelmed by blind ambition and spewed my guts out. "I've got something to tell you, Mr. Townsend. An FBI agent came to me yesterday and said he wanted to know all about you."

Smile creases formed at the corners of Townsend's mouth, as if he was an untouchable. "What did you tell him?"

A door swung open to my left and a voice said, "He told me to get fucked."

Agent Streeter stepped out.

My eyes shot back to Townsend. "The hell is this?"

Streeter came forward, laughing all the way, and stopped behind Townsend. "He's good to go, Mr. Townsend."

My eyes darted back and forth between them.

"Relax, Byrnes," Townsend said. "Meet Special Agent Streeter, alias Bob Tully, my general counsel. Sorry to put you through this, but there are some people who want to run me out of the casino business. They spread rumors about me to the FBI. They'll say anything to get me out. I wanted to make sure they didn't get to you."

Lucky that Tully didn't see me with Jordan. I'd be out of a job if they knew my brother was trying to bury Sheldrake basketball.

"Nothing like being in a steel cage with a shark," I said. *Wheels isn't here because he's a different entity. DeCarlo has two sources that don't get in each other's way. What an operation!*

Townsend continued with, "If there's one thing I learned from my father, it's quality control . . . no slippage. That's why we don't do wire transfers. Hand-to-hand worked in the old days. It works now." Then he leaned back and placed his arms over the backrest.. "Glad to have you aboard, Byrnes. Now that you're with us, just remember what Ben Franklin said after he signed the Declaration of Independence. He said, 'Gentleman, we must all hang together, or we will hang separately.'"

CHAPTER 22

Giranda and I landed in Concord, New Hampshire, at noon. Dark clouds threatened our drive to Wild Goose Pond in the White Mountains. But arriving at our destination for one o'clock games seemed feasible until I asked directions. The diminutive woman behind the chest-high, rental-car counter gave me a blank look and said, "Hard tellin', not knowin'."

I didn't know if she was putting me on or putting me off.

The woman abruptly dialed her cell and told me to take notes, which I did on a small pad. Between a number of *eh-huh's* she said, "You can get theah from heah. Take Highway 393 a short distance. Right on U.S. 202 for miles. When you get to Jeff's Restaurant on the hill, turn left for a while. Pass fah stacked mailboxes and a 'Live Free or Die' sign on the roof of the blue barn. You'll be close to the yellow house. Turn right at the yellow house, then take the dirt road at the fahk after the big tree."

"Where'd you say the dirt road goes?" I asked.

"Road don't go nowhere. Stays there year around."

Thirty minutes later, raindrops the size of thumbtacks pelted our windows from a passing storm as we rolled by what appeared to be the blue barn. Then the sky cleared as suddenly as it had closed in, and Giranda said, "When we get to camp, I'll point out Ace Hunt from NYU, a real nut case. He's after your number one recruit, Marquee Smith."

I raised my voice in astonishment. "My number one recruit?"

"Marquee's your guy. DeCarlo told me. He liked the way you did the Pico deal."

"News to me, but okay."

The more responsibility the better.

"At camp," Giranda said, "we can't talk to the players. So when you see Marquee on the court, tug at your Sheldrake shirt to get his attention. He won't know who you are, but that doesn't matter. What matters is that Sheldrake was there and loves him." Then Giranda smiled broadly. "It da love, baby."

Miles of green countryside and one yellow house later, Giranda said, "The camp will be an eye-opener for you."

I took my eye off the road, glanced at him. "I haven't blinked since I took this job."

"The coaches who spoke to these players on Zoom will try and refresh their memories. After a while, the players don't know one recruiter from another."

Turning after the yellow house, I said, "Tell me where the players come from."

"Thirty-five international players were flown in by HotShoe to show their wares. Many don't speak English well, but they communicate with long range jumpers or by swatting a shot."

A big tree and a muddy road later, we entered a narrow, unpaved forest road. After bumping and lurching for a long minute, we saw a tennis court on our left and A-frame bungalows to our right, then a clearing that the storm had avoided, and a large wood-sided building fifty yards away with a 'HotShoe Basketball Camp' sign on a pitched roof. It was five minutes before game time.

I parked on the dirt road, just above a set of bleachers. When I slid out of the car, the sun peeked out and instantly warmed my face. We stepped down onto the top row of hillside bleachers and took seats above three rows of coaches, half of them white. Below them were seven rows of high school players, most of them black. In shorts and shoes, Wheels was lecturing below the bleachers on an asphalt court. Behind

Wheels were four basketball courts and a large pond with a glass surface. Clean air, tall trees, lots of sun and water—a welcome change from the scent of varnished hardwood and putrid sweat.

My head pivoted to the middle of the players' section where there was laughter at something Wheels just said. Then he changed his face from friendly to threatening.

Wheels, who knew how to buy grades and courses, pointed at the players and yelled, "This is no bullshit. You've got to take the right classes and get the right grades in order to play college basketball."

A few minutes later, the players hopped down the wood planks and headed for court games. Wheels stayed to shake hands with smiling recruiters who swarmed around him, hoping to be anointed with a blue-chip player or two that would extend their careers, maybe promote them to a better job.

I needed to be brought up to speed on Marquee Smith and waited for the right moment.

We crossed the first court, joined coaches on the periphery of Court 2, which was surrounded by tall pines only a few feet away. There, Marquee Smith's team of Northeastern players was matched against a select group of Europeans. I had never been in the woods, so I listened for the birds and looked around for bears. But the only sounds were bouncing balls, and the only moving objects were players streaming back and forth. As Giranda predicted, coaches to both sides of me smiled at certain players, then gestured their recruiting interest by pointing, saluting, or winking at them.

It's a meat market—coaches salivating over prime and choice beef.

Giranda said, "Marquee is the sullen-faced, six-footer, waiting in the mid-court lay-up line. Number 8. Do your thing."

I faced Marquee and, like an idiot, tugged at my Sheldrake shirt, gave a self-assured, kick-ass smile, then pounded my chest and pointed at him. Thank God, he pointed back.

"He just told you that we're in the running," Giranda said out of the side of his mouth.

I nodded and watched our target.

After Marquee layed one up, a very tall coach on the opposite side-line pointed at him. Marquee, jogging back to mid-court, returned the gesture.

Giranda said, "Marquee just told Ace Hunt that NYU is also in the running."

Marquee was a show. His first three times on offense he flushed a 360 dunk, hit a 25 foot rainbow jumper, then drove the lane and drilled a pass to the corner for a three-point assist. He was an NBA prospect.

After another possession, Ace Hunt came around the backboard and walked towards us. Up close he looked like he had been around a while. Deep facial wrinkles, slumped shoulders, beer belly. He wore a dark blue NYU T-shirt and HotShoe sweat pants.

"Giranda," he barked.

The game going north-south, Giranda turned, gave him a cordial smile. "Ace Hunt, NYU."

Ace's face twisted in anger and the veins popped out of his neck as he raised his voice. "I came over to tell you to stop fucking around with Marquee. He's committed to NYU."

Giranda met his voice level and raised him a notch. "You should be committed. Nothing counts until he signs a Letter of Intent."

Nearby coaches watched them go at each other, some of them shaking their heads.

Giranda eying the action on the next court, said, "Got to see someone." He walked away, leaving me to be the target of Ace's verbal assault.

But to my surprise, Ace switched gears faster than a racecar driver taking a turn at high speed. Suddenly, he looked at me like I was his new best friend and waved an arm at the glossy, fluttering leaves above us. "Great job, isn't it? Getting paid to stand out here in the sun and watch basketball. So you're the new Sheldrake assistant. How do you like the camp?"

"I've got Marquee in the bag. And this is the first human zoo I've ever seen."

"Well, we got Marquee, and there are other players in the zoo for you."

I said sharply, "Marquee is going to Sheldrake."

Ace backed off. "Where you from that you know so much?"

"Polk High School in Hollywood."

"Hollywood, Florida? Been in that gym."

"No. Hollywood, California."

"Oh." He paused. "So you're a surfer type Hollywood guy. Think every chick on the beach is yours?"

I smiled. "Yeah, and I'm looking forward to kicking your ass when we play in December."

Ace stared at me as if he wanted to twist the verbal blade he had shoved into my back. "Well, you'll be tough with those kids Mansfield got out of Pago Pago. They're a year older now."

My face dropped. "Pago Pago? What the hell you talking about?"

Ace laughed. "That's where your starting five came from—Pago Pago Community College in American Samoa. They flunked out of every community college in the states, wound up taking classes at Pago Pago."

Nothing surprises me any more.

A tall, thin, Black coach approached Ace, tapped him on the shoulder, smiled, and said in deep baritone, "Hey, Ace. George Whitely from Cal. Where you at now?" He glanced at Ace's shirt. "Oh, NYU . . . great opportunity, great city."

Whitely handed Ace his card. "I heard you're on the bubble to get a head job. You'll need an assistant who delivers. Give me a shout-out."

As Whitely walked to another court, Ace said, "He recruited the 'Long Shadow.' Mansfield couldn't do that." He paused. "But, hey, too bad about Mansfield. I shouldn't say this, but he was almost too nice for this game."

After Marquee's game I joined Giranda on the corner of Court 4, nearest the pond, where another pack of coaches encircled the game site to watch two, six-nine power-forwards go at each other.

Giranda, who seemed to enjoy dripping information about Ace, said, "Ace applied for your job. An opportunity to get a good head job if we have a good March. Now he's desperate. Fifty years old. No retirement. Too old to recruit teenagers."

Giranda paused, then said, "Ace was one of the last people to see Mansfield alive. They attended a basketball clinic in Philadelphia the day he disappeared."

"You suggesting Ace knocked off Mansfield to apply for his job?"

"Ace is capable of anything. And he did apply for Mansfield's job."

I smiled. "What is he, an axe killer?"

"Listen, before he got into college coaching, he was an AAU coach, selling his players to Payday-sponsored colleges. When the father of one of his AAU players didn't want his kid going that route, somebody broke his arm. End of story."

I filed the ridiculous story. Saying nothing, I let my eyes drift across the facility to where Wheels was holding court with a few coaches under a shade tree next to the bleachers. I had to keep my connection with him alive.

"Watch these two big kids," Giranda said. "10 blue, 20 white. We're recruiting both of them. They've committed to NYU, but they don't have grades."

I understand. We'll fix their grades.

"I'll be right back," I said, and worked my way through the coaching crowd to the bleachers. Wheels was talking to a few recruiters. I stopped, got a long drink of water, and waited for his admirers to disperse. After several seconds, he walked down the sideline towards me.

When he got within handshake distance, I said, "How you . . . "

He walked right by me like I was invisible.

"Son of a bitch," I said to myself.

CHAPTER 23

It was time for another payoff.

Two weeks had passed since HotShoe Camp, and I welcomed the break from my day-to- day work with Pico. It was difficult being both his surrogate father and his coach. I needed some breathing room.

I entered a hot and damp Independence Hall. I was going to meet Jordan for a drink after my delivery. I would need one. Winning Dynamics had washed away, and my conscience had washed in.

When the park ranger said, "Welcome," Mrs. Dixon came around the small crowd wearing a white silk dress that clung to her body like wet paper. I slipped her the envelope. It was as easy as an unguarded lay-up. But I felt guilty.

Two sweltering blocks later, I greeted Jordan at Ben's Tavern, a tenth-floor bar at the Franklin Park Hotel. The room was in oak. The glossy bar, the ceiling planks, and the paneled walls emitted the faint smell of varnish. Customers packed the square bar in the center of the room. I sat down next to Jordan across from the entrance. Then I turned my thirsty eyes to the bartender and ordered.

Within seconds, the bartender slid a tall *Jack* and water my way, and Jordan opened his big mouth.

After three more drinks and a lengthy argument about my employment at Sheldrake, Jordan turned to me and said, "There's a filly eyeing you."

"A horse or a baseball player?"

"Across the bar. The blonde with long hair on the corner stool."

I gave her a look-see. *A face somewhere between beauty queen and the evening weather girl.*

Feeling a sudden thirst for more than the companionship of *Jack* and my brother, I said, "I'll see what's on her mind."

I slipped off the stool, came around the bar, put my hand on an empty stool for balance, heard two guys arguing about baseball and a lady arguing with herself. From her corner spot the blonde gave me an encouraging smile, watching me all the way. I took the seat next to her.

My eyes took a quick reconnaissance trip.

Tall and shapely, mocking eyes, wide mouth, broad shoulders. Mid-thirties.

I smiled. "I'm Conrad Byrnes. How am I doing so far?"

She made a quarter-turn, said in a deep, soothing voice, "Kaycee Brewer. And you couldn't be doing any better."

Great approach shot. I'm on the green, close to the flag.

"The guy you're sitting next to . . . is he your date?"

"My brother."

"These days you need to know up front."

Kaycee inhaled through her nose as if she were getting my scent, then said, "And what do you do Conrad?"

"I'm a psychiatrist."

Boy, am I ever.

"Interesting people make my day." She puckered, glancing at the glass of clear liquid before her. "I'll bet you can't guess what I do."

"How many questions do I get?"

"Everyone gets ten."

She pointed at the bartender, then at me. "*Jack* and water for my friend, please."

"How'd you know what I was drinking?"

"Asked the bartender. And you have nine more questions."

The bartender placed my drink before me. I thanked Kaycee and took a gulp.

"So you're a take-charge woman. Are you salaried?"

"Yes."

Ask any damn question. It doesn't matter.

"Are you in the private sector?"

"No."

"Government worker, huh. Do you work with the public?"

"Yes, and you've got six questions left."

I gave her another look. *Beige pants suit, buttoned jacket, white-collared shirt, no briefcase, no computer, no wedding ring. Small bag on the counter.*

She read her watch. "I've got to go, but you can walk me to my car and continue your questioning."

I slid off the stool. "Let's go." I gave my brother a thumbs-up behind my back and walked out of the bar with Kaycee to the elevator, a pitch shot away.

Tall as I am. Played ball? Called the plays?

As we stepped inside the elevator I said, "You work for the federal government."

"Oh, that's good."

I pressed the garage button.

In seconds the elevator door opened to warm, damp air in a parking garage jammed with cars. We walked leisurely to her dusty Crown Vic, a couple of aisles away.

"Are you an attorney?"

"Yes." She stopped and turned to me in front of her driver's door.

I said, "I won." Reaching out, I placed my hands on her hips, about to yank her towards me when she pushed my hands away hard.

"I've got to go," she said. "But you don't know what I really do."

As she began to reach inside her right, coat pocket, I went to plan B. "How about a road game or a home-and-home series?"

She fished out a thin wallet and flashed a silver badge. Her face and voice suddenly hardened. "I'm Special Agent Kaycee Brewer, FBI. And you're not Conrad Byrnes, the psychiatrist. You're Conrad Byrnes, the basketball coach, and your life is in danger."

Another trick.

"Don't joke. I've been through this before."

"I'm not joking." She pulled a card out of her bag and handed it to me.

Embossed FBI. Not like Tully's.

She opened the left side of her coat, revealing a gun resting in a shoulder holster. Then she slipped a document out from her inside right, coat pocket and handed it to me.

I unfolded the paper. Arrest warrant with my name on it. After the *herein's* and *wherefore's*, the words "mail fraud" hit me in the face. I took a short, quick breath.

"Mail fraud?"

"You committed mail fraud when you mailed Pico Rimpau's forged transcript to Sheldrake Admissions. That's federal penitentiary, ten to fifteen. And you're good-looking, Byrnes. Those would be long years if you know what I mean."

My ambition splashed in a cesspool of reality.

Truths are lies. Heaven is hell. Fuckin' Winning Dynamics. Dumb, Dumb, Dumb.

My mind spun like a roulette wheel, stopped on leniency. "I'm just a basketball coach."

"That's no defense, Byrnes." She clicked open her door. "If you stay on the same path, there's going to a murder . . . yours. I may be able to help you. We'll talk tomorrow morning. Nine o'clock. My office. Federal Building. Chestnut and Second, near your last drop. Room 1200. Make sure you're not followed. Park in the garage you always park in and leave your cell in the glove compartment."

She slid into her seat, slammed the door, rolled down the window. And in her soft, bar voice, said, "Now have you ever had a better offer?"

I froze, wondering what she had in mind as she pulled away.

Minutes later, my brain still swimming, I rejoined Jordan at the bar. He gave me an approving smile, putting down his drink. "Well, you going to get lucky?"

"Yeah, real lucky."

I pointed at the bartender. "I'll have another."

Jordan said, "Wow, she had some effect on you. Tell me about her."

"She's like no other lady I ever met."

"That's positive. Going to see her again?"

"Yeah. She's real interested in me."

CHAPTER 24

After a sleepless night at Jordan's condo, I wheeled around town with my eyes on the
rearview mirror, cut through several alleys, sped through a red light, and skidded into a parking spot in the garage nearest Independence Hall. Ten paranoid minutes later, my mouth parched, I had been searched by guards in the lobby of the Federal Building before I rode up to the twelfth floor. I had left my cell phone in my car, per request.

"Conrad Byrnes for Special Agent Brewer," I said to the man behind the thick glass window in the waiting room. After I studied the flag and the FBI wall-plaque for several minutes, a man in a cheap black suit escorted me down a hall to the second door on the left.

The room was stark and clean. My eyes were drawn to a manila folder, flat on Agent Brewer's desk, labeled, "Conrad Byrnes."

Not the way my Winning Dynamics life is supposed to turn out.

Her blonde hair pulled back now, Special Agent Brewer wore the black version of last night's suit and sat tall behind an institutional desk. I gave her a tight smile. She gave me a cold look, pointed to a chair on the other side her desk. "Sit down, Byrnes."

I took it. *I've got to find a way out.*

"Byrnes," she said, "I'll start from the beginning. Peter Townsend III has been the subject of an investigation by this office. A few months ago,

Michael Mansfield, your predecessor, made an appointment to come up here to talk to me. He mentioned Townsend. The next thing we know Mansfield's missing. Then you take his job, drive his car, and do his dirty work. We figure you now know or will soon know what Mansfield wanted to tell us about Peter Townsend III."

Fuckin' death trap.

"I don't have anything to add."

"You seem to be confused, Byrnes. We aren't negotiating." She dug out an eight-by-ten black and white from the folder, placed it before me. "United States of America vs. Conrad Byrnes. Exhibit A."

A photo of me depositing an envelope in a mailbox on North Broadway in Los Angeles. A date and time at the base of the picture.

Damn! Think of an out.

"Pretty good photo, isn't it?" she said, taking back the picture and slipping it into the folder."

"I was mailing a gas company bill."

"You mailed this." She fished out a document from the folder and slid it across the desk.

Pico's transcript. All A's. Graduation with honors.

"You don't have the authority to break into a mailbox."

"My authority is in your face! And this is your reality, Byrnes. We go down downstairs, put you in the tank, and start the paper work on mail fraud. Then your protégé Pico Rimpau gets blackballed by the NCAA and it's a one bedroom for you in Attica. Or you help me nail Townsend and we forget about the charge."

The full impact of her message sloshed over me like a bucket of ice-cold Gatorade.

Pico on skid Row! Me in ten years—toothless, in rags, begging for change in front of an arena.

"What do you want?" I asked.

"I want to get Townsend and the other characters you hang around with, if, in fact they're linked to Townsend. I know Wheeler is about power, DeCarlo is about winning, and Giranda is a pawn. I need to find out what Townsend is up to. We know he has a violent streak—that he was kicked out of Vegas for violence and Mafia connections. And that he was suspended from Harvard for smashing in his roommate's face. But what did Mansfield know about Townsend and why did Mansfield disappear? That's why I need you."

I repositioned myself in the chair. "So if anyone finds out I'm working with the FBI, I'm dead, just like Mansfield, because you don't know what the hell's going on."

Kaycee held up a hand as if she were stopping traffic, said, "Don't worry, Byrnes, I'll have your back." She leaned forward, placing her arms on the desk. "This is my plan. I move to Atlantic City, pose as a life insurance agent and your girlfriend. You continue to coach at Sheldrake and feed me information."

The cheap black suit who led me down the hall appeared with what looked like my cell phone. He handed it to Kaycee, tech-spoke to her for a few minutes, then left. Holding the cell in her hand, she gave me an ominous look. "This cell that you left for us in your car has a T Chip. Answer it and someone taps your line and maps your location. Someone's been tracking you, Byrnes. I suspect someone tracked Mansfield and listened to him talking to me." She clasped her hands and said in her bar voice, "Now who would want to do a thing like that?"

I was about to say, "Townsend" when Kaycee pulled a silver-tone, cell phone from her bag on the floor, held it out, and said, "You have two phones now. We placed this model in your glove compartment. Your new cell number and my number are taped to the phone. Remember which one is which. Only call me from the silver one. And don't call me from your apartment until we sweep it. It may be wired."

"Wired?"

I unraveled, spent several minutes telling her about DeCarlo's giving me the phone, Tully's FBI impersonation, and Townsend's knowing how many minutes driving time I was from his office without my telling him where I was. Tightlipped, she listened and made meaningful nods. Then she outlined our relationship with, "As far as the boyfriend thing is concerned, you play grab ass with me and I'll kick your balls through the goal posts. I am not the gal in the bar."

I listened to her tell me who she was now, providing me with shallow background information—the essentials every boyfriend knows after two great dates: family, education, job, favorite team, favorite drink, and pubic hair color, just in case the wrong people don't believe she's my girlfriend and hold a gun to my head.

When she finished, I said, "I hope you're as convincing in Atlantic City as you were in the bar. It takes great talent and skill to conceal great talent and skill."

"I've been trained to be deceitful," she said, "and you seem to come by it naturally."

"You picked me up. I didn't pick you up."

When she said nothing I asked, "Did you have me followed in L.A.?"

"From the moment you took the job we've been all over you. The tails, the Realtor, all FBI."

I took the long walk back to my car, got inside, slammed the door, and stared through the windshield at the concrete wall.

I'm attracted to a new girlfriend who's packing, but she's not really my girlfriend. And I have someone who wants to kill me, but they don't know that yet.

"Fuckin' Winning Dynamics!"

CHAPTER 25

I rolled down Highway 42 to Atlantic City, a bright sun on a gray day. I was riding the Tiger. It wasn't that I wanted to ride the Tiger, but I didn't want to get off it either.

Then I thought, *Call a friend.*

DeCarlo, no. Townsend, no. Giranda, no. Kaycee, no. Jordan, no. My ex, no.

No friends. Can't trust anyone. I'm all alone.

Before I could feel sorry for myself, my Sheldrake cell rang.

"Coach Byrnes, this is Peter Townsend."

The son-of-a-bitch IS my shadow. I sucked in a deep breath.

"How did things go?" he asked.

"No problems," I said, wanting to sound friendly.

"Philly is such a great town. What did you do last night?"

"Went to a Philly game," I said, wanting to get off that subject.

"I missed the score," Townsend said. "What happened?"

Get an answer. "I'm entering a toll booth. Be back to you in a second." I pulled off the highway onto the shoulder, got my FBI cell, researched the game, then hit the accelerator. "Sorry. About the Philly game, it was ten-zip. Johnson all the way. Nice crowd. Thirty-eight thousand."

"Good," Townsend said." He paused. "Next Saturday evening I'm having a fund- raiser for the American Cancer Society at my home in

Margate. Everyone who's anyone will be there. I'm inviting the Sheldrake staff. It won't cost you guys anything. I'll email DeCarlo directions. He should be back from Europe in a couple of days."

"Can I bring a date?"

"Sure."

*   *   *

It was late afternoon when I arrived in Atlantic City. Driving past the rear of the Mardi Gras, I remembered I still had a job to do and headed for the dorm. I pulled up in front of the twelve-story building, placed my Sheldrake parking pass on the windshield, and took an archaic elevator to Pico's upper floor. His door was open. Inside, the rancid odor of dried sweat attacked me. The drapes were closed and light glared from ESPN across the room. In shorts and shoes, Pico's roommate, the six-five Nitro Dixon, slouched in bed glaring back at the TV. I noticed a hole in the plasterboard between the two beds.

"Hey, Nitro, where's Pico?"

Nitro looked over. "He gone."

My voice harried, I said, "When? Where?"

"Just took off."

Panicked, I said, "Come on. Where is he?" I scanned the room for any leads. Pico's bed didn't have a wrinkle, just like they taught him at St. Andrews. On his pillow was a large stuffed bear, the kind you win when you do the impossible at the Steel Pier Amusement Park. On the floor next to the clothes closet was Pico's suitcase, wide open, neatly packed.

"I'm not his mama," Nitro said.

I shot back, "Don't fuck with me, Nitro. Where is he?"

"Sorry, Coach. Try Steel Pier."

I tried to get a heads-up, dialed Pico's cell, listened to his message. "This is Pico. Please leave a message and an NBA contract."

I frowned, said, "Pico, this is Coach. Call me right away." Clicking off, I turned to Nitro. "If he comes back before I return, tell him to call me."

Several minutes later, fearing that every hour could be my last,

I walked quickly down Boardwalk to Steel Pier where stars like Bob Hope and Annie Oakley once entertained huge crowds. Foot traffic had thinned out, and the offshore breeze cooled the perspiration on my forehead. Booth operators on the pier told me they hadn't seen any six-nine Black guys all day.

Picking up my walk to Olympic pace, I had no luck checking with Boardwalk's trinket and fast food stores on my way to the arena.

Unnerved by the dark corners of my life and Pico's disappearance, I sprinted for several minutes to the long shadows of Boardwalk Arena. There, drenched in sweat, I stepped onto the walkway that ran the width of a nearly empty beach and spotted Pico fifty yards away. He sat upright near the edge of the ocean, his basketball serving as an armrest.

I trudged across the warm sand in damp dress shoes, the sand spilling into my heels. Finally reaching him, I knelt down on the sand and stretched my legs out next to his ball using my hands to prop up my body. Pico in a blue HotShoe T-shirt and knee length shorts gave me a double take, but said nothing as if he were upset.

I said, "The kids at St. Andrews would love the peace and freedom of this beach."

"Where you been?" Pico asked.

"Philly."

"I like Philly."

I looked into his eyes. "What's goin' on, man?"

"Maybe this isn't the place for me. I don't like being rushed to be a player, and y'all are rushing me. I can't learn that fast and I know I'm disappointing y'all."

Forgetting my dilemma, I shot back, "That's not true! You just worked out with a great bunch of college guys that are all going to be drafted. You did some things well... blocked some shots, made some free throws. Sure, you were a little lost, but that was expected. I'm pleased with your progress."

"I got lost on offense," Pico said stone-faced. "Then DeCarlo flipped out like a fuckin' skid-row druggy... I can't handle that shit."

"I was worried that might happen."

A small wave slapped the shoreline, and Pico said, "I didn't know you worry about me."

"I worry about you because you're worth worrying about."

A thin smile crossed his face. "I'm glad you're with me."

I said softly with meaning, "I've always been with you."

Momentary silence before Pico said, "I gotta' tell you. I punched a hole in the dorm wall."

"I saw it. What happened?"

"Frustrated."

"You ever act out like that before?"

Pico looked at me for a long moment. "Yeah, at a group home . . . they finally sent me to a level fourteen place. Level one is for normal people. Level fourteen—you're fuckin' out of your mind. They used to drug me when I'd break a window or a wall. Then they sent me back to St. Andrews. I learned to keep my bags packed."

"Well, you can unpack. Everything's going to work out for you," I said, not knowing but hoping. "And Pico," I reached over his ball, putting my hand on his shoulder. "You're okay. You've always been okay. Now about the hole . . . what would you think about paying to repair it? Would that be the right thing to do?"

Pico focused on the sea for several seconds, then looked over. "You're right. Take responsibility." He paused. "Do you take responsibility for what you do?"

I repositioned my sweaty bottom on a piece of hot, uneven beach, leaned forward, made a couple of deep circles in the sand with my index finger. "I've made mine. And I take responsibility." Thinking of something else, I grabbed a handful of sand. Squeezed it. Felt the grains pour out of my palm. "Pico, if you ever . . . I mean you might hear something . . . aw forget it."

S tanding on the stadium floor, death on my mind, I look up at the enormous erector set of catwalks. Something moves between diagonal steel beams high above the field seats.

Shadows of my mind? Or a sharpshooter with a scope waiting for the final buzzer?

Across the long catwalk on the far side of the stadium, the structure dives into what appears to be an enclosed stairwell.

I can get that far. I've got a pass.

I gaze up at the clock. Fifty minutes, twenty-nine seconds, fifty minutes, twenty-eight seconds.

I cross the court, working my way up to the third level using stairs and ramps, the big erector set coming closer.

No one around.

The base of the catwalk has a four-foot-high enclosure. A gate and a lock. I swing it open and enter. There's a ladder inside the steel structure. Another gate needing a key. I pull the door. It squeals open. The latch has been taped. Someone is up there.

"Hey, get out of there!" yells someone.

A man in a blue sport coat and beige slacks, holding a walkie-talkie trots towards me. "Only stadium personnel are permitted in there," he says. "And you aren't one of those."

I point up at the catwalk. "Someone's up there. Up on the catwalk."

"We've been under lockdown for four days. No one's up there." Moving closer to me he spots the pass hanging from my neck. Then he points down to the stadium floor. "Participants are down there. Not up here."

"But there's tape on the latch."

The man removes the tape. "Move out, mister."

CHAPTER 26

I opened my apartment door to Kaycee Brewer. A slinky black dress revealed all her curves. She was lightning waiting to happen. She held a finger to her lips. I got the message and shut up. Inside, she reached into her bag and pulled out a thin metal card with short antennae. She proceeded to wave the scanner in front of every item in my apartment—including the print of a coach cutting down the net that hung over my couch. The instrument beeped rapidly when she scanned the table lamps in the front room and in the bedroom. She waved me outside. Behind a closed door, she said, "Byrnes, if I remove the bugs, they'll know that you know—and you're dead. Do you understand?"

My mind spinning like a wheel with no end, I said, "I understand that Townsend doesn't like slippage. That's why he gave me a free apartment—so he can bug me. But I'm only talking basketball. What the hell is he listening for?"

"You may find out tonight."

I raised my voice. "At Townsend's party—when we celebrate with the guy who's bugging me? I don't get it."

Downstairs in a ten-car garage, Kaycee swept the interior of my car, then pulled out a fingernail-sized, listening device behind the speedometer. She displayed it in her open palm, then wrapped her fingers around it. "If you ever wondered why you got Mansfield's car—here it is. Three hundred bucks, direct from India."

I stared at the bug. "Son-of-a-bitch."

As she replaced the bug, she said, "Don't forget that our goal this evening is to make Townsend comfortable with me."

We said nothing as we motored in the darkness, south on Atlantic. When we connected to Ventnor Avenue, several miles short of our Margate destination, I rehearsed, "I want you to meet Townsend. He's a great guy." I made a face.

Kaycee said, "He must be." She made a face back.

Ten minutes later, we entered Margate, an upscale, beachside community bordered by power lines. Passing large, expensive houses, we chatted about Sheldrake's upcoming season, her insurance business, and the weather. Then we turned left on Jackson toward the beach. A block later, I braked in front of a massive iron gate flanked by high walls, manicured trees, and mature hedges. There, two well-built men in dark suits eyed me suspiciously. I gave my name. A clipboard was checked.

Beyond the gate was a long circular driveway. Seventy-five yards ahead, a limo had pulled up to a vintage, U-shaped mansion with ornate architecture; its walls were lit up like an arena on game night. It was the kind of property the park service would manage.

The gates parted and my wheels crunched gravel toward the entrance where valets waited in front of a wide, marble walkway dotted with potted junipers.

Gazing at the structure, Kaycee said, "Impressive. Something the Great Gatsby would have owned."

"The Great who?"

"I guess the Great Gatsby didn't make *the ESPN Magazine* this month."

A valet welcomed the two men getting out of the limo in front of us. They unbuttoned their suit jackets and scattered in different directions. Then a short, silver-haired man in a black dinner jacket emerged from the back seat and walked up the steps. He looked like someone's grandfather. Kaycee pointed at him and gave me a thumbs up.

The limo driver waved the valet off and drove on.

I edged my car forward, stopped for the valets who clicked our doors open. I took a deep "here I go" breath and got out. As we walked up the steps, Kaycee asked softly, "How are you under pressure?"

I took another deep breath. "Watch me."

Near the front door, Townsend greeted the silver-haired man between two tall columns. As we passed, Townsend glanced at me, then locked in on Kaycee.

"I want it now," the silver-haired man said to Townsend as if he expected people to jump when he talked.

Not looking back, we entered a great hall filled with black-tie party-goers, laughing, drinking, talking. A string quartet played something I had never heard at a ball game.

"Did you see Townsend check me out?" Kaycee said, her voice mixing with the crowd noise.

"Everyone is checking you out," I said as we filtered through the crowd. "Who's the silver-haired man?"

"Scurto from Cleveland."

"And?"

"Mafia."

"Jesus." My heart did a drum-roll.

A couple of men stared at me. My senses heightened, I stared back. Then my eyes wandered about the massive hall. White marble walls and floors brightened by two crystal chandeliers suspended from a tall ceiling. Everything glittered. Across the room, warm ocean air puffed through several large open windows and the long gold drapes fluttered.

Everywhere I look, I see money.

A lady wearing a red-jeweled necklace and black suit walked by and gave me an odd look.

Kaycee asked, "Byrnes, why did you have to wear a blazer and khakis?"

"Goes with everything."

She looked away, mumbling, "Why did I have to hook up with a jock?"

Across the room I found DeCarlo speaking with two men.

"C'mon." I grabbed Kaycee's hand and guided her between clusters of guests across the large room. "I want you to meet DeCarlo."

I introduced Kaycee to DeCarlo, who gave her an up-and-down, mostly up. He introduced us to Mike Canadeo, the mayor, and Bob Hanson, the Chief of Police. Canadeo was six-foot, mid-forties, and paunchy, but with friendly eyes on a round red-webbed face. Hanson was around fifty, a couple of inches shorter than I, with black hair and a military stance.

"Coach Byrnes," DeCarlo said, "why don't you get me and Kaycee a drink?"

I grabbed a glass of white wine from a passing wine steward and handed it to DeCarlo. "Kaycee wants to see the rest of the house."

With that we squeezed through the crowd toward an adjoining hall.

I said softly, "I feel like I'm on ice skates."

"I didn't know you skate."

"I don't."

In the next hall, the room's centerpiece was a long buffet table. It was surrounded by guests who piled food on their plates, as if it were their last meal.

I motioned to an open door in the far corner that led to the balcony. Near the door I spotted a copy of Winning Dynamics on a large bookcase that wrapped around a marble fireplace. "Wait a second," I said, reaching up to pull out the copy. I opened the book to a dog-eared page of Winning Dynamics and read Law 31. "Control the Options. Get Others to Play Your Game."

"Kaycee said, "What's the game?"

"That's why we're here," I said, replacing the book. Then I grabbed two glasses of red wine from a waiter's tray and handed one to Kaycee. We stepped out onto a long dimly lit, cement deck, and kept moving to the middle, away from earshot. My lungs filled with salt air and my ears with the whisper of the rolling surf, I gazed down at floodlights that brightened a short beach, and my mind spun the questions:

Who are the players in Townsend's game? Townsend's a coach. DeCarlo's got to be the point man. But, Scurto . . . Scurto I don't know.

What's my position? And what's the game?

Kaycee brought me back with, "I'm going to let Townsend come to me."

I straightened. "You are wicked."

"You have to play the cards you have."

"I'd say you were handed a stacked deck."

Kaycee gave me a weak smile. "Wonder what Scurto wants?"

The corner of my eye caught a glimpse of someone coming our way. I turned. *Shit! Townsend.*

I forced a smile and hoped he didn't hear Kaycee.

Upon joining us, Townsend said, "Glad you could make it, Conrad. Who is your gorgeous companion?"

I took an imperceptible breath. "Kaycee Brewer, meet Peter Townsend III."

Kaycee delivered a sinful smile. "I've heard good things about Peter Townsend." She held out the back of her hand. Townsend bent forward and kissed it like she was the princess of Atlantic City.

Kaycee gave Townsend her card. "Kaycee for life insurance," she said. "Everyone needs life insurance."

Townsend read the card and said, "Life insurance?" as if it were an incredible concept.

Slipping the card into his coat pocket, he smiled at Kaycee. "How do you like my beach house?"

"Fabulous," she said.

Then, like he was old Atlantic City money or delusional, Townsend said, "My father, Peter Townsend II, bought this place from Theodore Sheldrake in 1945 . . . the man who built Sheldrake Hotel and Sheldrake College. My father came from England, invested in real estate. When people sold, he bought." He paused. "I love this old house. It reminds me of my youth." Then he glanced back at the party. "My guests will wonder what happened to me." He made a slight shoulder turn as if he were heading back to the party, then rotated back. "Where did you two meet, Kaycee?"

I interjected, "We happened to sit next to each other at a Phillies' game."

Townsend stared at her for a long moment, finally said, "Your voice sounds familiar."

Townsend was getting warm. So was I. A bead of sweat rolled down my forehead and hung on my eyebrow. I held back from brushing it off.

"I can't explain the unexplainable," Kaycee said.

Townsend nodded. "I hope to see you again." In seconds he disappeared inside.

I turned to Kaycee. "Townsend's onto you. He's probably got a recording of you talking to Mansfield and he's listened to it more than once."

"He doesn't know. He's fishing. Hang in there."

"Hang is a word I don't like."

Back in the great hall for the next hour, I was introduced to people whose names I quickly forgot, and chatted with guests about nothing in particular. Then someone tapped me on the shoulder and called my name. My head fishtailed to a smiling Mayor Canadeo, standing next to Scurto. Then I glanced at Scurto longer than I wanted to. His dark face made me think about death. Mine.

"Coach Byrnes," Canadeo said, "I wanted to be a college coach when I was playing high school basketball. I thought it would be a trip. Is it that kind of job?"

I glanced at Kaycee, before saying, "There's nothing like it."

"I thought so," Canadeo said, who then introduced us to "Mr. Scurto from Cleveland."

I shook Mr. Scurto's meaty hand and swallowed hard. "You're a long way from Cleveland, Mr. Scurto."

"I'm here to gamble," He replied, as if he were on the witness stand.

"And what do you do in Cleveland?" Kaycee asked.

"I'm in the temp-agency business."

"There's always a need for temporary help," I said.

Scurto stared at me, like I was a dumb ass.

A half-hour later, waiting for our car on the far side of the driveway, I said to Kaycee, "What kind of temp work does Scurto do?"

"Assassination, drug smuggling, prostitution, extortion, money laundering. It's all temp work."

"Why do you think he's here?"

"I'm on it."

Chapter 27

ATLANTIC CITY TIMES

*POLICE SEARCH FOR BODY IN
MARSHLAND*

*A tip from a Johnson Marina boat owner prompted
police to dredge the marshland for the body of Michael
Mansfield, assistant coach at Sheldrake College, who
has been missing since May 10. The marina liveaboard
stated that he saw a white man and a Black man motor
out to the marshland early in the morning on the date
Mansfield disappeared. Approximately one half-hour
later, only the Caucasian man returned. Crews spent
yesterday dredging the marshland and the marina area.*

It was a page-three story. Page one with me.

At the kitchen table, I sipped steaming coffee and questioned the story's plausibility.

What would prompt Mansfield to motor out in the middle of the night? A gun in his ribs? Dumping something? Or picking up something?

My FBI cell vibrated on the table. I read a text message: "L 12 O."

Code for "Lunch. Kaycee. Noon. Her office, Michigan and Atlantic.

It was morning. Seven-thirty. Cloudy. And I had time to coach Pico.

*   *   *

A half-hour later, in shorts and shoes, I rummaged through the remnants of a torn-down building next door and found two mortar-free bricks. I edged them into my backpack and pedaled my mountain bike through muggy air to Pico's dorm a few blocks away.

Pico, in no more than his boxers, opened the door. Greeted by the unmistakable scent of dried sweat, leather, and yesterday's pizza, I made a face as I surveyed the terrain. HotShoe apparel and pizza boxes strewn everywhere.

"Funny thing," I said, "the hurricane hit your room but missed the rest of the town."

Nitro, still under the covers, rolled towards us. "The man is on your ass already and it's not even the first day of practice."

I stepped over a shoe barrier, dug the bricks out of my backpack, and placed them on the chest of drawers to my right.

Pico said, "What now?"

Enthused, I said, "This is for our workout. Did you ever notice that NBA players on defense have their knees bent and carry their hands above their waist so they can move when the ball moves and cover-down and defend the ball?" I grabbed the bricks, faced him, and pumped weighted arms. "By running with these bricks, you'll build stronger hands and biceps and be in a state of readiness on the court."

Nitro rolled away, growling, "Too early in the morning for this."

Ignoring him, I looked at Pico. "Get dressed, big guy. We're going to make a player out of you."

"This better be good," he said, picking up his workout clothes and a towel off a pile of socks in the far corner. Seconds later he was out of the room headed for the bathroom down the hall.

"Nitro," I said, "You get the news about Mansfield being in the bay?"

He rolled toward me again. "Saw it on the Internet last night. I hope it's not him. Around here people disappear in parts."

I considered the Atlantic City reality. "Mansfield recruited you. What do you remember about him? Was he a night owl?"

"My role model, Mansfield?" Nitro said. "He went to bed at 10:00. Didn't drink, smoke, or run ... what else? ... . He liked gadgets. Took pictures with his phone. Used to email me photos. I haven't looked at them since he disappeared."

"Let's see what he sent."

Nitro pushed up, reached under his pillow, and pulled out his cell.

"Always keep your phone under your pillow?"

"Never know when the NBA is going to call." He sat up, pressed his index finger against the device a few times, said, "Here," and handed me the phone.

Holding up the cell, I flipped through the collection. About twenty historic scenes of New York and Philadelphia. Then one photo that I examined carefully. The top portion of the picture was a rearview mirror. It reflected the front end of a trailing yellow Audi with backwards license numbers and letters. Two head rests and a cell phone were just below the mirror. The lower portion of the photo revealed a front view—the white hood of Mansfield's car and the rear license plate of a car in front of him.

This photo was taken intentionally.

I walked to the window overlooking the beach and emailed that photo to my FBI cell, then deleted the shot on Nitro's cell. Trying to create a diversion, I said, "Hey, Nitro, tell me about Pago Pago Community College. Didn't you go to school there?"

"Pago Pago? Oh, yeah. Coconuts, palm trees, nude women."

"What did you take there?"

"I didn't take nothin', man!"

"I mean classes."

"Oh. A lot of things."

At that moment, Pico returned in shoes and shorts and said again, "This better be good."

Ten minutes later, I straddled my bike, inhaled salt air, and glanced at Pico retying his shoes on Boardwalk and Mississippi. In front of us, an army of seagulls bobbed for breakfast, and a couple of pigeons emerged from the Mardi Gras casino. To my right, a bald man with a long nose, wearing khakis and a short-sleeved shirt sat on a park bench and snapped pictures of everything, including us. I emailed the Mansfield photo to Kaycee with a note, deleted any record of it, slid the cell in my pocket, dug out the bricks from my backpack, and handed them to Pico. "Pico, you run, I'll pedal. Keep your arms in an L. There's no one in our way."

Pico, with his fingers completely wrapped around the bricks, and his arms curled, looked down the boardwalk, and said, "How far do you want me to run?"

"To the end."

"I can't see the end, and if I can't see the end, I'm not running."

"Okay, only to about a 440 . . . let's go," I commanded. "Hard as you can."

Down the boardwalk we streaked, passing casinos, a pier, and a few shopkeepers unlocking a world of chotchkies, as well as comfort-food shops.

A quarter mile later in front of a hamburger joint, Pico, out of breath, pulled up, handed back the bricks, placed his hands on his knees, and sucked wind.

"Great work," I said. "Now carry the bricks back."

A few minutes later and about seventy-five yards from where we began, I spotted the long-nosed man kneeling in the middle of Boardwalk, his camera pointed in our direction. Suspicious, I told Pico to swing up the next block.

*　*　*

I opened the door to agent Kaycee Brewer's life insurance office. Located on the second floor of an old brick building in a crap neighborhood of Atlantic City, her office was as inviting as a cheap motel room.

Kaycee sat back in a swivel behind a clean desk.

Closing the door, I asked her if she received my email with the license plate photo.

She responded as if she were being questioned about her dissertation. "The photo was taken at 3:13 p.m. on the day Mansfield disappeared—just before Mansfield was going to meet me at my office. There were a couple of unclear photos. One very clear. It's the plate in the rear-view mirror that's the important one. He was probably being followed, panicked, took the photo, then pressed any name in his directory, and happened to send it to Nitro. I'm having the plates checked out."

Outside, we walked quickly towards Michigan and Atlantic, passing a check-cashing store, two guys doing a drug deal in front of a massage parlor, a white pickup truck parked on the sidewalk, and a throw rug hanging over a parking meter. It was an area where you naturally walked quickly.

Kaycee said, "About Scurto, the Cleveland guy. He has a mortgage company that holds a second on Townsend's house. And Townsend has an option until May on raw land near the marina. I was out there yesterday and ran into a geologist on the property. He told me about plans for a high-rise casino, and said Townsend can't act on the option unless he gets his hands on a billion, the cost of the land plus the cost to build."

"The only way you get a billion in this world is to threaten to go to war with us."

I looked over my shoulder at street traffic. Not a yellow Audi in sight.

Chapter 28

My voice message to Kaycee said, "I'm having breakfast with Jordan in Philly. Going to escape from training Pico, making payoffs, and murder theories. Jordan wants to talk to me about something important. He can't drive to AC."

My eyes on the highway, I slid the FBI cell phone into the console and tried to make sense out of my message. My guess was that I was still attracted to the Kaycee that I met in the bar.

I got off Interstate 676 where the highway merged with another road in the city. I looked down at Jordan's instructions to the federal courthouse.

"Pass the first Starbuck's. Turn left at the second Starbuck's. Left at the next corner. Right at the next Starbuck's. Two blocks straight ahead. Park at the courthouse. The "Grounds for Divorce" coffee shop is on the top floor. "

Sunlight streamed through the windows and brightened the far side of coffee shop, which was cooled by an air conditioner set on North Pole. The room was jammed with dark suits holding serious conversations with tight-faced people. We wouldn't be noticed.

A coffee and a Danish in hand, I approached Jordan at a table on the sunny side of room. He was reading a newspaper that had a color photo of marshland. We shook hands. I read the headline upside down.

"POLICE RECOVER ANOTHER BODY IN ATLANTIC CITY."

Jordan looked up. "They dragged the marsh for Mansfield. Came up with a dismembered Black guy who worked at the marina. They can drag the marina from here to hell and gone and they'll never find him."

My FBI cell in my right pocket vibrated. I put it to my ear and said to Kaycee, "Hi, doll."

"Byrnes, can you talk?"

"Sorry, I can't make it."

"Here's the latest," she said. "The license plate on the rear car in Mansfield's photo is a phony. No record. So if you see a yellow Audi behind you, floor it."

"I love you too." Click.

I took a deep breath and tried to compartmentalize the information that was coming too fast. Jordan asked if the caller happened to be the woman I'd met in the Philly bar. I took a seat and said we were seeing each other, but left out a story that would turn him into a network talk-show guest.

Then the ever-probing Jordan asked, "Is it serious?"

Feeling edgier than when I walked in, I said, "She's got other things on her mind. But that's not what we're here for. You've got something to tell me. What is it?"

Jordan looked around, leaned towards me, and said, calmly. "My editor has assigned me to investigate the Sheldrake basketball program. I'm going to be in your jock for a while."

The more you dig, the closer we both are to dying.

My heart racing, I raised my voice louder than I wanted to. "So you brought me out here to tell me that you're Cain and I'm Abel? What the hell happened to family loyalty?"

"Look," Jordan said. "The fuse is lit. Get the hell out of Sheldrake before the place blows up."

I shoved my breakfast aside, leaned across the table, and calmly tried to keep the dominoes from falling. "Suppose you were on to something . . . and I'm not saying you are. But suppose you were and you were about to endanger your life. Would you keep going?"

"I'm media. They won't touch me. And this is front page. Mafia ties, a disappearance, and basketball indiscretions, all in one package. Don't you see?"

"And what about me? What if you find someone who's twisted. And they know we're brothers. We're both dead."

Jordan shook his index finger at me. "That's why I'm telling you to get out."

"I'm safer inside. And this is goodbye, brother. We can't see each other any more. I can't have any ties to you. Not a fragment." I pushed away from the table. "Get a larger insurance policy to cover your family."

CHAPTER 29

OCTOBER 10
FIVE DAYS BEFORE OFFICIAL WORKOUTS

My head was in my hands after I read an article at my kitchen table that began:

*NCAA TO INVESTIGATE
SHELDRAKE BASKETBALL.*
by Jordan Taylor.

Sheldrake College has received a letter of inquiry from the NCAA concerning the following potential violations: (1) Prohibitive expense-paid visits for prospective student-athletes who have not taken entrance tests, (2) Expense-paid visits to prospective student-athletes without presentation of an academic transcript, (3) Conducting a physical activity at which one or more prospective student-athletes reveal, demonstrate, or display their athletic abilities.

I reread the violations. They were coaching career-enders.

My Sheldrake cell phone went off. I picked it up.

DeCarlo barked, "Conrad, we've been hit. Hold on to your balls. NCAA investigation, man. Hammer got a letter of inquiry. He's called our staff in for an emergency meeting. You've got an hour to get there . . . and, Conrad, you know nothing and did nothing."

President Hammer's office was on the twelfth floor of the college. His conference room had a one-eighty of everything that made the town: the casinos, the boardwalk, and the beach.

Hammer was tall. His conference table was long. So was his face. He stood at the view end of the room holding a document in his hand. Our basketball staff sat motionless in chrome-armed chairs to Hammer's left, facing the Mardi Gras. Hammer read the allegations, sucking the air out of the room. Then he slapped the paper down on the table and said, "DeCarlo, I hired you even though you were one step from NCAA suspension. I hired you because you could get big players and big money. Now you've given the NCAA the sticks to beat us with."

A stone-faced DeCarlo said nothing.

Hammer boomed, "How our team performs this year is everything to Sheldrake. Winning it all equates to millions for Sheldrake and a $300,000 bonus for you, DeCarlo. But everything goes down the toilet if this inquiry turns into a full-blown investigation."

Hammer looked around the table as if he were searching for someone else to blame. His eyes landed on me. "Do you know anything about this?"

He doesn't even know my fuckin' name.

"We don't have that kind of program," I said. "We have a reputation. As long as I've been at Sheldrake, I have never seen or heard of anything unethical."

If Sheldrake gets away with this, they can get away with anything.

Hammer looked at Giranda. "How about you?"

"Dr. Hammer, we follow all the rules."

Hammer raised both hands as if he were about to lead us in prayer but said, " I've decided to satisfy the NCAA by having an internal investigation. When I was President of A&M, we had the same issue and this is the way I handled it."

I folded my arms and squeezed my biceps.

The A&M investigation was ugly. Does he have something else in mind?

Hammer went on. "I've retained Bob Tully, the Mardi Gras General Counsel and member of my booster organization to run the investigation. Tully will conduct an impartial investigation and report back to me. Then I will inform the NCAA that we are clean."

Hammer pushed away from the table and stood. Our staff rose in unison like we were puppets on his string. Then Hammer looking at us deadpan with his nostrils flaring, said, "Let the shredding begin."

*   *   *

As our staff waited for the elevator in the hallway, I wondered how Sheldrake was going to cover its tracks. I looked at DeCarlo, expecting him to renounce cheating with comments such as, "I'm clean," or "I've never committed an infraction." Instead, with shoulders slumped, he pushed the elevator button, and erupted, "They don't investigate unless someone leaked. Who was it?" He punched the button three more times. "The player who pissed me off about lack of playing time last season. The one we got rid of . . . what was his name?"

"Warren," Giranda said. "But we got him a scholarship at State so he wouldn't talk."

"Dean of Admissions and Records at Pago Pago?"

"No," Giranda said. "He's paid in full."

"Mansfield?"

"No."

There was dead silence as the archaic elevator door slid opened. We entered. Inside, DeCarlo turned down the directional handle. As the elevator descended, he said absently, "We're all going to hell."

Getting his analogy, I suppressed a smile.

DeCarlo went on, "I never paid any kid who wasn't the best person I could find for the position." Then he reached out and pulled up the control lever. We jiggled to a stop and he said, "I'm going to cut off the head of the dragon. Listen to this." He dialed his phone, held it head high, said, "Townsend . . . DeCarlo . . . just talked to Hammer. What are you going to do about Jordan Taylor? The guy that wrote the article . . .

the bastard that keeps digging into our program."

"I got him fired," Townsend said on speaker. "He was within reach. It's a good thing the publisher owed me big-time for taking care of all his fantasies at the Mardi Gras."

My gut knotted.

Jordan's out of work . . . Townsend may have saved his life by removing him from the story . . . That's good . . . And Jordan is farther away from Sheldrake basketball . . . That's better than good.

A short minute later, we stood across the street in the shadows of Boardwalk Arena and DeCarlo bitched about his imaginary enemies. Then he straightened, puffed his chest out. "Now we can really cheat. The NCAA will only pay attention to the last things we did."

My eyebrows shot up. *Look how straight his posture is now. Cheating gives him balance.*

DeCarlo continued, "So, I've got an idea, Byrnes. Bigger than anything you've done before."

I tried to block out all the possibilities that ran through my head. "You're right. Now is the time to strike . . . What haven't I done?"

DeCarlo didn't respond, as if he had aborted an idea, or the crazy side of his brain had just disengaged.

*   *   *

I called Jordan from the hallway of my apartment later that night, a safe distance from my desk-lamp bugs. His voice was on fire. "I got canned by the fuckin' guy who assigned me to investigate Sheldrake basketball. Somebody got to him. Somebody at your place. Who was it?"

"No idea."

"Well, I'm going to find out who got to my boss if I have to go to court. I got a wrongful termination attorney. I'll close the loop . . . find out who's really running the show at Sheldrake. And when I do . . . "

"Jordan, get another job. Write about someone else."

"I'm going burn their ass."

CHAPTER 30

ATLANTIC CITY
OCTOBER 14

The day before official practice began, Wheels met with DeCarlo in his office. I overheard their heated exchange through a half-opened door, despite the whir of Giranda's shredder in our shared office.

"The NCAA is going to nail you," Wheels said. "That's why I'm not planting Marquee Smith at Sheldrake."

DeCarlo snapped, "The NCAA isn't going to find anything. I'm covered. Don't back out now. Don't take my title away from me. I gotta have Marquee."

Wheels' tone spiked up. "This isn't about you. This is about me. I decide who plays where, who wins, who endorses our shoes. Your title's nothing compared to a world of people buying HotShoes with the name of someone I signed. I'm talking billions. You're talking titles."

"Cool down, Wheels. I've got everything in motion. I talked to Papa Joe and he's ready to do a deal. And you know that Marquee will go where Papa Joe tells him to go."

"You sure you're covered?"

"Nothing's going to happen."

Wheels mumbled something, then DeCarlo yelled, "Byrnes."

I gingerly walked into DeCarlo's office, not knowing why I'd been called or whom I was going to rat on.

DeCarlo sat comfortably behind his desk. "Byrnes, you and Wheels

135

are going to Philly tonight to close a deal for Marquee Smith."

His cell went off. He answered, agreed to something, and turned to me, "Let's go."

Wheels pushed away from the desk. "This is where I go to the sidelines. See you later, Byrnes."

Seconds after Wheels left, DeCarlo and I hustled down the long hallway towards the door to the parking garage. I pushed open the door, heard an engine running. The Topas Beer truck was parked in the middle of the structure, behind a couple of cars.

My mind flashed back to my first trip to the Cockatoo Bar.

Empty beer kegs being loaded into the Topas truck behind the bar. A keg dropped off the truck's platform didn't bounce. Empty containers bounce.

We approached the truck. The driver stepped down from the cab with a HotShoe box, handed it to DeCarlo, got back into the cab, and drove off.

DeCarlo and I walked back through the building, down the arena stairs, and around the bleachers. We entered a storage room between the visitor's and home team's locker rooms. Nothing but cabinets and a large wood table in the center of the room. DeCarlo placed the HotShoe box on the table, crossed the room, and opened one of the cabinets. He returned with a Payday shoebox, set it down on the table, and removed the lid. Empty. Then he opened the HotShoe box, exposing neatly stacked hundred-dollar bills. He piled the bills into the Payday box, edge to edge. "This is for Papa Joe, the AAU coach of Marquee Smith. You're going to hand him the Payday box filled with Sheldrake money. Anyone sees you carrying this in, they won't connect HotShoe or Sheldrake College."

"What's the exchange?"

"Thirty large to get a commitment from Papa Joe that Marquee will sign with us.

Wheels is also going to hand Papa Joe thirty grand. Papa Joe's AAU team will go HotShoe, and he'll tell Marquee to sign with us next month. After that happens, you guys will each pay Papa Joe 200K." DeCarlo gave me a wicked smile. "Can you imagine? Pico and Marquee in the same lineup. We're gonna tear ass?"

DeCarlo handed me the uncovered box.

Jeez, look at that. No, don't look at it. Look natural.

Caressing the box, I looked up. "Where's our money coming from?"

DeCarlo gave me a funny look. "Townsend. Where do you think?"

"And what does Townsend get?"

"It's about money. We buy the players, win games, fill the seats. Then the fans go next door to the Mardi Gras after the game to gamble. It's all about money."

So why did Mansfield die?

* * *

That night, I drove Wheels to Papa Joe's through North Philly's dark, mean-streets, avoiding large holes in the pavement where manhole covers had been stolen and sold for salvage. The temperature had dropped into the thirties. An uncommon snowstorm was expected. I wasn't surprised. Nothing was common about the world I was in.

I wore a peacoat. Wheels wore a Mackinaw jacket, like a woodsman in sneakers.

Suddenly, my headlights picked up the sheen from the outer rim of another manhole. I veered left for a second, then returned to the middle of the street.

Wheels said, "Papa Joe's not easy to work with. Mansfield tried it last Spring."

"What happened?"

"Mansfield made a delivery to Papa Joe. A door-opener. Fifteen large. But Papa Joe said it never happened. Next day Mansfield disappeared. I don't know if Papa Joe was holding out for more, or Mansfield took it. For all I know, Papa Joe took him out."

My heart did a drum roll. I shot Wheels a penetrating glance and said, "Which is it?"

"Don't know. Can't call the cops. HotShoe stock would drop fifty percent."

"Interesting business," I said, trying to play it cool, but heating up in my coat.

I turned a corner, rolled down another dark street.

"Slow down," Wheels said. "Papa Joe's place is the four-story at the end."

I passed an unlit building to my right, followed by a barely visible check-cashing store, then a trashed empty lot. At the corner, three Black guys warmed their hands over a flaming garbage can in front of a grocery store. Three stories of who knew what were above the store.

I pulled up next to the building's side entrance, ten yards from the flame. Heads turned our way. I took a shallow breath, tried and failed to come up with a positive thought.

Wheels dialed his cell, said, "Papa Joe, this is Wheels, we're out front in the Beamer."

Wheels hung up, looked at me, and said, "Gotta give Papa Joe a big hug. The neighborhood has eyes. They'll think we're okay as long as you hug him."

I focused on the building's dark entrance, waiting for Papa Joe.

Wheels, looking through the side window, fogged it with puffs of breath when he said, "Papa Joe used to be a voodoo doctor. Then he realized he could make more money by making friends with teenage basketball prospects and putting them on his traveling team. Next thing he knew, Payday was giving him shoes for his players and paying him a consulting fee to direct those guys to universities sponsored by Payday."

I took the breath I should have taken a minute ago, and mumbled to myself, "It's always about money."

A wide-body in an open, purple leather jacket emerged from the door. Bald head, full gray beard, big gut, walking toes-out as if he were carrying a hundred pounds in his hands.

We got out of the car, and I inhaled trouble.

Boxes on our hips, we met Papa Joe on the sidewalk. He was bigger up close. Miniature voodoo dolls hanging from his necklace caught my eye—especially the green and gold Sheldrake doll. "Papa Joe welcomes you," he said in a deep voice.

Wheels greeted him with a hug, then introduced me. Clutching my box, I wrapped an arm around him, feeling as though I were hugging a grenade that could go off any time.

Papa Joe turned and motioned to the guys on the corner. They came our way. At close range I figured them to be in their late teens.

He said to the short one in dark glasses, "You take care of this BMW, Papa Joe will take care of you. You don't take care of this car, Papa Joe will take care of you."

Stone silence. Not even a nod.

That could be a yes.

We entered the building. It smelled of cat urine. Papa Joe yelled upstairs, "Papa Joe, Marquee's coach, coming up . . . Papa Joe, Marquee's coach, coming up."

A few steps behind Papa Joe, I pinched my nose and poked Wheels. Meeting my eyes he mouthed "Meth Lab."

My nerves were wire-tight as we took the stairs.

On the second floor the smell was so strong that it pierced my sinuses. I tried not to breathe as Papa Joe unlocked the door nearest the staircase. Inside, in the darkness I couldn't hold out, sucked in a breath. The odors were similar to those of Pico's room: pizza and leather. The door clicked shut. Dim overhead lights came on. I expected to see human skulls and dried skins. Instead, my eyes jogged to a far wall that was banked with six layers of Payday shoeboxes. A shiny, white leather couch and matching chair took up the left side of the room. Two empty pizza boxes topped a black octagonal table in front of the sitting area. An open matchbox full of pins nestled next to the pizza box. Drawn louvered blinds, a locked door, and the voodoo man gave me a creepy sense of privacy.

Papa Joe gestured for us to sit down. We sank into the couch and placed the shoeboxes at our feet. He took off his leather jacket, displaying a red tank top and the handle of his best friend in a shoulder holster. He dumped the jacket on the floor, then settled back in the chair across from us.

I looked at Papa Joe's gun, then to the green and gold doll, and back to the gun.

My underarms leaked big time, and something told me not to take off my coat.

Wheels said, "Papa Joe, I know your agreement with the Payday Shoe Company is up for renewal. Now I want you to go HotShoe."

Papa Joe sat back with lips compressed, fiddled with a blue and white doll on his necklace. HotShoe colors. He said, "You didn't want Papa Joe when Papa Joe had no players."

Wheels, leaning toward him, said with all the sincerity of a pimp, "I've always been a Papa Joe fan."

Papa Joe's voice hardened. "What you got for Papa Joe?"

Wheels cleared the pizza boxes off the table, and placed the Payday boxes in front of Papa Joe. Removing the lid, he said with enthusiasm, "Payday shoeboxes, but HotShoe money."

As Papa Joe's eye's brightened, his tone turned friendly. "Papa Joe likes people who like Papa Joe."

"HotShoe likes Papa Joe very much," Wheels said. "Thirty grand now . . . Two hundred K when Marquee Smith signs with Sheldrake."

Wheels shut up and looked at Papa Joe, who nodded repeatedly as if in agreement. Then Wheels handed over the box. Papa Joe placed it on the floor, reached for the pin box, and picked one out.

If he sticks the pin in my doll, could he pierce my lung?

I took a breath, maybe my last, and repeated what I had memorized. "Sheldrake loves Papa Joe. Thirty grand as a down payment for Marquee. Two hundred K after he signs." I opened my box, poured the bills on the table, not coming close to the pins.

Papa Joe's curiosity wrinkles turned to smile wrinkles. "Ah hah. Papa Joe gets the picture . . . likes the picture. Marquee loves Sheldrake."

Thwak—thwak—thwak . . .

Something beating the air outside.

A spotlight shot through the louvered blinds.

"What's that?" I asked.

"Ghetto Bird," shouted Papa Joe as he sprang from his chair. "Get outta here!"

Doors slammed.

Steps thundered.

Papa Joe grabbed the moneyboxes, pushed us out the door. Wheels and I sprinted downstairs, bumping shoulders with other people on the scramble. On the street, we ran for our car, started it up. People scattered in all directions. A spotlight washed past us and beamed up the wall. A distant siren became louder each second.

I pulled G's, cornering right, running on rims. My left foot on the brake, right on the gas, I swung a right at the next corner darker than hell. Skidded. "Slow down," Wheels yelled, "you're going to smoke the tires! There's no one behind us."

"But the sirens . . . "

"The cops want the meth lab upstairs."

I sped through a yellow. "Is this really worth it?"

"You got to know what counts in life."

"What counts for you, Wheels?"

I entered a main street and weaved through traffic.

"Marquee counts," Wheels said. "He's our fourth-quarter guy. He could make our year-end look good to investors. And I'm talking two years down the road. We plan ahead just like you do when you recruit ninth and tenth graders. Want to stop for a cup of coffee?"

"Yeah, in Paris."

CHAPTER 31

The next morning, climate change hit Atlantic City as gale-force winds blew snow sideways, beating the hell out of my street. Wearing heavy cotton sweats, I turned on the kitchen light, moved the thermostat to seventy-five, and found my cell phone.

By 7:00 a.m. all the Sheldrake players had received my wake-up calls. Forty-five minutes later, I would shepherd them to class, one of my responsibilities as team academic administrator. But the Papa Joe thing was wearing me thin. And the deception of my college basketball experience had morphed into shades of gray.

A half-hour later, I leaned into a punishing storm that stung my face. I sloshed two blocks to the dorm, pissed that the players couldn't get to class on their own, pissed that my ski gear didn't keep me warm or dry. Inside the dorm, I headed to the twelfth floor and the rooms of eleven guys who were genuinely committed to learning as little as possible.

"Let's go," I said loudly, banging on the first door. "Time to go to class."

Nitro yelled back, "Don't go off, man."

"It's time. Let's go, Pico."

"He's already in class."

"What? A student in our midst?"

"He read the assignment."

I continued down the hall, rattling each player's door as the clock ticked down. Returning to the first door, I was about to knock on it again when it opened. Fully dressed, a notebook under one arm, Nitro gave me a foul look, snapped, "Why don't you guys fix our classes? You fix everything else."

I erupted. "Someday basketball's going to go away and you're going to have to wipe your own ass."

"We all play the game. Mansfield understood that. You don't."

"I think you should be responsible for yourself."

"Watch me play and see if I'm not responsible."

"Okay. Let's go."

Our conversation didn't change the drill. I had to lead the players from one class to another, making sure no one ducked out the back door.

I escorted them across the street to the college, no one uttering a word about the NCAA inquiry. Psych 101 was a sure "A." The professor, Dr. Ames, was crazy about basketball, and our coaching staff was crazy about him. "A" for Ames. At nine o'clock, the players would attend History. The history professor, Dr. Better, would give our players B's. B for Better. All of our "go along, get along" professors received four, midcourt tickets to our home games, including parking privileges in the arena garage. All that for the Mardi Gras bottom line.

*   *   *

At two p.m., I attended a team meeting in the locker room that reeked of chorine bleach on the floor too prevent athlete's foot. In fifteen minutes we would have our first workout of the season. Two rows of bodies wearing reversible green and gold shirts filled up the folding chairs in front of me. In the first row sat our seven-foot center Americus Hart, who revealed gold incisors with each smile. Next to him was Nitro, then the bald six-three shooting guard, Illinois Jackson. At the end of the row, sitting on the edge of his seat, was power forward Pepe Gomez, a six-seven redwood tree stump. To his right, thin shooting-forward

Willard Penn, whose droopy eyes made him look half awake. Pico sat tall in the second row with the second string.

DeCarlo stood at the head of the room in Sheldrake sweats. His look said *"I'm going to rip you a new one."* Giranda and I were two paces away from him waiting for his blast furnace mouth to open.

DeCarlo, holding a paper in one hand, turned and wrote on the built-in white board, "Nothing will stop us. Not the NCAA. Not nobody."

Pepe Gomez turning to Willard Penn, said, "We doomed, man."

Penn spoke to Gomez out of the side of his mouth. "I don't know nothin'."

DeCarlo barked, "Focus, Penn." Then he wrote, "This is our year." He turned back to the players. "Fuckin' media and the NCAA are doing their best to ruin us. Not gonna get away with it." Then he paced and spoke louder. "If you're caught breaking NCAA rules, you can't play any more. Not here. Not anywhere. You got that?"

"Bad news, man," Americus said, hanging his head.

I felt no different than I did the previous night when the helicopter spotlight was on me. There was no place to hide. Not here. Not anywhere.

DeCarlo went on. "I'm not going to tell you what to say to the NCAA. Let your eligibility be your judge. Remember, Sheldrake has always run a clean program. No under-the-table-money." Then he startled me by saying, "So raise your hand if you're guilty of breaking NCAA rules."

Americus held his hand high.

Jesus.

"No, Americus," DeCarlo said. "You're not guilty. Not guilty of anything. Nitro, you better talk to him later."

DeCarlo paced again. "Reporters are waiting in the hallway to draw blood from us . . . but remember, we only bleed green and gold."

Americus said to Nitro, "They found something else in my blood."

"I told you to use a condom," Nitro said.

DeCarlo continued, seemingly oblivious to the front-row exchange. "It's my policy," he said, "never to have my players talk about an on-going investigation."

DeCarlo's been through so many investigations, he has a policy.

"Only one player will speak to the reporters. And that's you, Nitro." DeCarlo stepped forward, handed him a one-pager. "Nitro, as captain, you read this statement to those fat-ass, blood-sucking reporters. I'll go out first. Give me a minute. Then everyone except Nitro heads for the court."

DeCarlo looked at me with a twisted face. "I'm not going to give those assholes anything to chew on. Watch me, Byrnes. I've been through this before."

I followed DeCarlo out of the locker room and into the hallway where a handful of men in down jackets and turtleneck sweaters gathered around him. Cameras and tape recorders pointed at his face, as questions were hurled hard, fast—one on top of another.

"Is it true the NCAA is going to bury you? Is the NCAA drawing a line through your name? Did Mansfield have anything to do with this?"

DeCarlo's face tightened. He pushed past reporters, shouted, "Fuck you guys!" as cameras flashed, and recorders spun.

"Thanks for the quote," someone said.

Players emptied out of the locker room led by Nitro. The media surged towards them like termites drawn to wood.

Nitro stopped, held his statement up, and read slowly, "The players know nothing, and did nothing wrong. We wish the public would respect our privacy and let us attend class and get our degrees. College is about education."

CHAPTER 32

I stood next to DeCarlo and Giranda on the baseline as players took the court under the glare of overhead lights and tracking media eyes. Reporters scurried around the court and trudged up the long bleacher staircase to take seats just below the walkway. There they hovered like hawks sensing the death of our program.

My heart skipped a beat.

There's Jordan upstairs. He snuck in. Still after the Pulitzer.

My eyes moved down, from green-and-gold seats to green-and-gold uniformed players.

They're moving slowly. Hung-over from discussing NCAA infractions. Pico missing free throws. Team shots aren't going down. Walking, not running. DeCarlo should have set the tone in the locker room. The first day of practice should be intense.

DeCarlo said to me, "Gotta get their minds on basketball." He blew his whistle.

Players racked their balls on the sideline, then walked to the baseline like they were strolling down the beach. DeCarlo grunted, glanced down at the three-by-five card in his hand that held a minute-to-minute, two-hour workout schedule. Giving the players a sour look, he yelled, "Get your ass in gear! This is our year. Let's go . . . 'change of pace, change of direction.'"

I shook my head

I would have gathered them around and said, "The NCAA won't apply penalties that will affect this season. This is our year. We're going to March Madness. That's all you've got to think about. NOW LET'S GO!" But I'm not the coach.

The players took off down the court in four lines of threes, running, faking, cutting. But their shoes did not squeak as they foot-faked. A dispassionate sign. Then the players spread out in the half-court and DeCarlo led them in hands-up sliding drill, an exercise to build endurance and discipline.

He barked instructions. "Back! . . . Forward! . . . Right! . . . Left!"

The players responded with quick movements. Fifteen minutes later, they were grimacing in pain when DeCarlo threw up his hands and stopped the drill. As the players caught their breath, he raised his voice. "We don't have much time to get in shape. Every minute counts. Right now your opponents are getting ready to kick your ass."

He should train tigers.

"Before we split up to run offense," continued DeCarlo, "I'm naming the starting five. Same five that started last year. I will call you guys the 'Sons-of-Bitches' and I will refer to the second team as 'Bastards.' There should be no mistake who you are."

DeCarlo loves basketball, but he hates the players.

Pico, standing at the top of the key, blurted, "I'm no Bastard."

Shit. Mr. Ford said he'd go nuts if anyone called him a bastard.

DeCarlo said, "Pico, that's the name of your team."

"I'm no B-a-s-t-a-r-r-r-d," Pico shouted..

Players took on the bewildered look of a police station lineup.

My mouth opened to speak out, but I closed it again.

Take Pico's side and you'll be out of a job, off the case, and in prison.

"This isn't about you, Pico," DeCarlo said. He looked at Americus. "All you Sons-of-Bitches, take your positions in the front court." Then he looked at Pico. "You Bastards-and that includes you, Pico, watch our offensive motion from mid-court."

The first team SOBs took their positions spread across the half-court.

These players don't care what he calls them as long as they wind up in the NBA.

Every Bastard except Pico jogged to the centerline. He remained at the top of the key, arms folded with a look that said, "I dare you to move me."

DeCarlo and Pico are glaring at each other. The Bastards can't run the offense with four players.

Feeling like a jerk for not defending Pico, I pointed to the Bastards at mid-court, saying, "Over here, Pico."

Pico shuffled to mid-court.

The SOBs ran their offensive motion without a shot, a series of off-ball screens just above the baseline, on-ball screens above the key. The center, Americus Hart, set off-ball screens when the ball was below the free-throw line, on-ball screens when the ball was above the free-throw line. After a screen, he would slip to the free-throw area for a possible reception and shot. It was smart offense. He was a good mid-range shooter.

At the other end, Giranda taught the Bastards Sheldrake's motion while I coached Pico. In a week they would learn the comeback motions—what to do when the defense stopped the offense.

More physical conditioning followed. Five-on-five, fast-break drills, then a full-court twenty-minute scrimmage where Pico dominated. He showed his anger at DeCarlo by swatting away SOB shots within eight feet of the hoop like King Kong batting away attack planes.

Near the end of the scrimmage, I watched Nitro dribble up court and pictured a Topas Beer keg bouncing off the pavement outside the Cockatoo Bar months earlier. Everything clicked into place. I had to call Kaycee.

"I'll be right back," I told DeCarlo. "Have to go to the head." DeCarlo nodded, not moving his eyes from the scrimmage. I jogged to the locker room. There, standing at the far corner of the urinal trough, I called Kaycee and scheduled a meeting in 3 hours.

When I returned, DeCarlo ordered the team to run lines, a drill you didn't want to run right after a meal. Sprinting from the end line to the nearest free-throw line and back, twelve players progressively touched each line that crossed the court with their fingertips before returning to the baseline, only to take off again and touch the next nearest line. Twenty repetitions.

When the team completed the drill, they stood on the base line, their shirts wringing wet, tongues hanging out, sucking air, and dotting the floor with sweat.

"Is anyone tired?" DeCarlo asked with an ornery smile.

Taking deep breaths, Americus Hart raised a hand.

DeCarlo's face dropped. He said, "That means we aren't in shape. Ten more lines for everyone." The players took off again, this time running a step slower than in the last round.

Halfway through the drill, Nitro stopped at mid-court, bent, and heaved white cream that spread on the floor like pancake mix on a griddle. Then he straightened, wiped his forearm across his mouth, jumped over the vomit, and continued his sprint like nothing happened.

He won't quit no matter what. No wonder he's an All-American.

* * *

Twenty minutes later, the players were still dripping sweat as they departed from the locker room, leaving behind steam from long showers.

I waited at the exit door to console Pico.

He approached with fire in his eyes, said loudly, "Fuck DeCarlo!"

My eyes jogged across the room to DeCarlo. His head spun our way.

I looked back at Pico. "Coach didn't mean anything personal."

"Fuck him!" He flung the door open and marched into the hall.

A step behind him, I said, "He didn't mean any harm."

"Bullshit!" Pico said, his words echoing down the cold hallway.

I re-entered the locker room and approached DeCarlo. "Pico believes he *is* a bastard. He can't be on that unit. You know his story."

"I'm running this fuckin' team. Not him and not you."

I'm talking to his child.

Emotion twisting in my gut erupted and I went into my parent. "That's wrong."

"You're out of line."

I snapped, "There's got to be a better answer than driving away a future All-American."

"We'll see."

CHAPTER 33

Night had fallen by the time I arrived at the first floor elevator of the Polynesian Casino in the Marina area. Kaycee was waiting for me at the Island In The Sky bar on the top floor. My nerves were still frayed from a DeCarlo moment. I needed a drink.

A hunched-over man wearing a tattered black overcoat, tennies and no socks approached me from the casino.

Serious face. Maybe down on his luck. Wants a contribution.

I reached into my pocket.

The man said, "You know why we're all here?"

"No."

"Because we're not all there."

I acknowledged my imperfections and said, "I am flawed."

"We're all flawed," the man said.

The elevator door opened. I got in.

Dark windows on three sides flanked the Island in the Sky. A small stage occupied the far end of the room where a three-piece band played "My Girl." A parquet dance floor separated the stage from surrounding tables. A few couples swung to the music. Tall palm trees in large planters were scattered between twenty small tables where gray heads sipped Happy Hour drinks.

Kaycee waved me over from a corner table to the right of the stage.

As I was about to take a seat, she raised her glass and took a sip of clear liquid. "A hundred and eighty proof," she said. "Best there is."

I smiled, gave her a once-over lightly. She wore her favorite attire, a dark blue pants suit. Her blonde hair shimmered under the overhead lights. Her coat was buttoned. She was packing.

"I'm glad you called," Kaycee said. "But don't get any ideas."

I took a seat. "Something bugging you about me?"

"Your eyes. They're all over me. So what else is on your screen, Byrnes?"

I lowered my voice and told her about the keg that had fallen off the truck months ago and didn't bounce, the tunnel from the Cockatoo Bar to the Mardi Gras, and the guard with the bad job.

She took another sip, set it down, and shook her head. "Farfetched."

"Listen. The kegs are light when they're unloaded. Heavy when they're loaded. They're packed with something—drugs, diamonds, something. They could go through the tunnel and up to Townsend's penthouse where they're loaded, then returned to the truck."

"Look, Byrnes, I'm not the kind of person who's going to bet if there will be a rainbow tomorrow. Give me some proof."

A balding man sat down at the next table and eyed us.

Kaycee gave him a glance and said to me, "Let's talk on the dance floor."

As we walked towards the other dancers, I said, "Give me a half-hour at the Cockatoo. I'll buy you dinner if I'm wrong."

"I'll give you fifteen minutes."

"You're on."

My hand on the small of her back—I brought her close. She didn't resist. Then, about eight two-steps later, she asked, "You ever been married?"

"Once. It didn't work out."

"Any children?"

I took a breath. My voice lowered a notch. "A boy. He's gone."

We continued to dance and my mind drifted.

It's was all your fault. He played well that night. Eighteen points. But he made some poor decisions. At home we argued. He ran out. Took the car. Head-on crash. Dead on impact.

I felt a sudden mix of emotions: regret, loss, sadness, fear.

My feet stopped. I dropped my hands.

"What's up, Byrnes?"

"I have to see if Pico's all right. Come with me."

I talked about Pico's dilemma on the elevator. Slightly agitated, I tried to explain DeCarlo's coaching methods. That was harder than explaining Pico.

A short time later, we were on the top floor of the dorm. I left Kaycee at the end of the hall and passed by a couple of students in their underwear who gave her lengthy appraisals.

I knocked on Pico's door. No one answered. I knocked again.

He finally opened the door, gave me a wide-eyed look as if I were naked.

I pursed my mouth, said, "Hey, I'm Conrad Byrnes. I coach Pico Rimpau. And I came by to see how he's doing."

Pico gave me a long look before responding with, "Pico's all right. He thought about whacking DeCarlo, but he's all right now."

"I want him to know that I understand what happened and I'm trying to change things."

Pico's eye's narrowed. "He needs somebody on the other side."

"On the other side of DeCarlo?"

"Yeah."

"Is Pico going to practice tomorrow?"

"He'll be back."

CHAPTER 34

The next morning my spine tingled against the kitchen chair when I read a wire-service story written by Jordan. Sooner or later he was going to touch Townsend, the third rail of Sheldrake basketball.

His story began:

EVERYTHING ON THE TABLE
IN ATLANTIC CITY

Sheldrake College basketball's starting team consists of transferees from Pago Pago Community College in American Samoa. They are one of the subjects of an NCAA inquiry into recruiting violations. With Coach Babe DeCarlo one violation from being suspended by that governing body, it is logical that they would ask the following questions: Why would this South Sea Five enroll at Sheldrake? The college has no campus, is miles from the nearest city, offers nothing but gambling, and has an amusement park that is closed during the winter. Could it be because DeCarlo had something to do with boosting the recruits' grades from ineligible at all NCAA institutions to clear-admit at Sheldrake? Or could it be that the players fell in love with DeCarlo because he calls his first team "Son-of-Bitches," and his second team "Bastards"? Or could it be because Sheldrake is undefeated at home because they have "Frank, Jesse and Butch" officiating those games? As we dig deeper into the mysteries of the program, more questions and some answers will arise.

That afternoon DeCarlo ranted about the article during practice like I knew he would.

An hour into our workout, we went through a block out drill on the bright, shadowless floor. Defensive players were supposed to get their backs between the offensive players and the basket on a shot attempt, then rebound the ball. There would be contact.

DeCarlo shot the ball from three-point range in a corner. The SOBs pounded the backs of the defensive Bastards as they went for the miss. But Pico did not wait for contact. He went skyward, rebounding the ball high above the square like no other human I ever saw.

DeCarlo screamed, "Some of you Bastards aren't paying attention! For shit's sake, follow directions." He paused. "Let's go again."

The defensive players assumed their positions between their man and the basket. Then DeCarlo put up another errant shot. The ball bounded high above the cylinder toward Pico. Again, he didn't wait for contact on his backside, leaped skyward, and ripped the ball down.

Is Pico showing up DeCarlo for placing him with the Bastards?

"No!" DeCarlo yelled. "You Bastard. *Block out* means block out."

Players froze.

Pico pivoted toward the bleachers and put his foot into the ball. The ball shot off his HotShoe and sailed above the scoreboard. It finally came down against a chair-back about thirty-five rows up, then ricocheted from chair to chair like a pinball.

"Get the fuck out of here!"

"I quit!" Pico screamed. He tore off his workout jersey and threw it to the floor, then ran towards the locker room.

I shouted, "Wait a second."

He kept going.

I went after him.

A short minute later, I sat silently on a bench across from him in the locker room and waited for him to cool down. He avoided eye contact, stripped down, threw the remainder of his workout gear on the floor, and hurriedly started to dress without showering.

When he was almost completely dressed, he looked at me and exploded. "I am not a bastard!"

"Of course not. But you set off DeCarlo by not following his direction . . . . You were pissed about yesterday."

Sweat leaked down Pico's forehead. Saying nothing, he flung his leather jacket coat over a shoulder and kicked open the locker room door.

"Pico, let's talk in an hour. I'll be finished with practice and you'll be cooler. We'll work this out."

*   *   *

After practice, I hurried to Pico's room. The door was open. His ball and luggage were missing. He was gone. His cell phone lay flat on top of the television.

I froze for an instant.

Shouldn't have left him alone. Gotta find him.

Nitro entered, wearing a heavy blue sweater and dungarees. As he looked around he shook his head. "Gone again. He shouldn't have went off. When DeCarlo recruited me, he said he loved me. Now he calls me a son-of-a-bitch. But I know I'm an Awe-Star." He paused. "Pico can't go very far . . . Pico loaned money to everybody. Gave money to the homeless until there was no money left under his mattress."

My heart pounding, I said. "Can he get his hands on a car?"

"He drives a car like he drives the lane. Out of control. Believe me. No one would lend him a car."

"So where would he go?"

"Maybe he went home."

"He has no home. No parents. He came from the streets . . . All this time, you never knew."

Nitro's dark eyebrows edged up. His voice lowered. "That's rough, man . . . So that's what the bastard thing is." He looked down. "We're screwed, man. We can't start the season without him."

*   *   *

I searched hours for Pico, feverishly covering the same tracks that I had when he disappeared months earlier. Local markets, storefronts, playgrounds, cardboard boxes. About ten, I called Kaycee and told her what had happened.

At midnight, DeCarlo called me. I didn't answer.

He left a message. "Don't come back without that Bastard."

CHAPTER 35

*W**here the hell is he? Two fuckin' hours of sleep. Missed practice. Got to keep going.*

Driving slowly down Pacific Avenue, I looked everywhere for Pico. It was mid-afternoon, and dark clouds over the Atlantic were heading towards shore.

I picked up my FBI phone after one ring. It was Kaycee.

"Meet me across the street from Cockatoo Bar," she said. "I'm waiting for the Topas Beer truck. And, Byrnes, Topas Beer went out of business six months ago. That's what I'm looking for—something that seems right, but isn't."

"Look, I'm still searching for Pico and I'm beat."

"I don't care."

*   *   *

I showed up minutes later. The Cockatoo Bar looked a hell of a lot better than Attica.

Half-awake, I slipped into Kaycee's dusty car. It was snuggly parked between two SUVs, across the street from the pot-holed alley and the brick-faced Cockatoo. She was slouched deep in her seat, a baseball cap pulled down just above her eyes, a black leather jacket over a sweatshirt.

Scattered about were packages of snack food, binoculars, a camera, coffee thermos, Starbuck's cups, and paper towels.

Just as I said, "Watch for the keg exchange," rain began to pound her car like a drum roll.

Above the clatter, Kaycee said, "While we're waiting, let's see if Pico took a plane."

Her fingers walked on her cell.

My eyes shut down.

Then her cell beeped bringing me back. She put it to her ear, grimaced, said, "There are no current plane records for Pico Rimpau." Then she nudged my shoulder. "Stay awake, man!"

"I'm with you. He's got to be close by."

I picked up a paper towel and wiped the dew off the windshield. When I settled back in my seat, I glanced at her long legs. I looked up and caught her gaze and blurted the first thing that popped into my head. "You ever been married?"

She gave me a divorce-court look. "He didn't like the fact that I came home late at night and couldn't tell him where I was or what I was doing . . . Clean settlement. No children. You?"

"Basketball consumed me . . . Her friend became her lover . . . Then our son died."

"Coaching did that to you?"

"And the FBI did that to you?"

The white Topas Beer truck rolled down the street. It turned into the alley and parked behind the bar. The driver in a red and blue Phillies jacket stepped out into the downpour and pulled open two cellar doors on the sidewalk. Another man in a dark sweatshirt climbed out and opened the truck's rear loading door. He hopped up on the truck's platform and then chest passed the silver beer kegs down to the driver.

"Either he's tossing light beer or the kegs are empty," I said.

"Your jock brain is working, I'll give you that. There's nothing in those cans."

The silver cylinders were stacked on the metal cellar platform. Then the driver lowered himself into the cellar with half the kegs, and lifted himself back for the remainder.

Minutes ticked by and our stakeout became more of a drag than a drama.

I inhaled the damp, stale air and said, "Do you date?"

Her eyes on the alley, she blurred the driver's-side window with her breath, "Let's say I never see the same man twice."

"So you get all the good stuff and none of the bad."

Her head jogged to me and back to the window. You could say that."

All of a sudden, rain distorted our visibility like a curtain of crystal beads, and Kaycee rolled down her window.

My thoughts of her sex life were interrupted when I saw the driver straining to load the kegs back onto the truck. "See what I mean?" I said. "Each keg gained a good twenty pounds. My bet is they're transported through the tunnel, and up to Townsend's penthouse where they are packed with something."

A flash of lightning darkened Kaycee's profile but brightened the alley. She quickly rolled her window up.

My cell rang. I hoped it was Pico. It wasn't. I pressed *talk*. My eyes on the truck, I said, "Papa Joe, good to hear from you."

Papa Joe said, "Payday wants to give Papa Joe three hundred large for Marquee. Now Marquee is thinking about a Payday school. Papa Joe wants to hear your latest offer."

"Three hundred for Marquee? I'll have to get back to you." Click.

I told Kaycee about the recruitment of Marquee Smith, as the Topas Beer men returned to their cab.

"Byrnes, the hypocrisy in your game is unbelievable."

"Hypocrisy is a virtue in this game. Coaches are trapped. If they don't cheat to get the best talent, they don't get to the NCAA tournament and they'll be fired. And if they cheat, they'll eventually be caught and be fired. There are few untouchables in this game."

"Bad business model."

"Worse than you can imagine."

Kaycee's spun towards the alley. The truck driver had stepped out of the cab once more and entered the Cockatoo bar.

Two stakeout hours later, the driver returned to the truck. Then his assistant went into the bar.

"What the hell are they waiting for?" I asked.

Kaycee threw her head back to the headrest. "Darkness."

CHAPTER 36

Kaycee moved the car down the block under a blinking yellow Mardi Gras sign. There we waited under a dark sky. Ahead was a sliver of the white truck sticking out of the alley.

My cell rang. *Maybe it's Pico.*

I hit DeCarlo's number and cleared my throat. "This is Coach Byrnes."

"DeCarlo growled through the phone, "Have you found that bastard?"

"Pico's not a bastard and I haven't found him. I've looked all over the city and I'm still searching."

"Where are you?"

"Uh, walking down Atlantic, near Mississippi."

The truck backed out and stopped traffic. Then it came forward, its lights on us, but turned left.

Kaycee started her engine.

"What's that noise?" DeCarlo asked.

"I got in my car and started it up."

"Find him. Nobody walks out on Babe DeCarlo." Click.

Kaycee pulled out. We were immediately stuck behind a car trying to park. She veered left, crossed the double yellow, came back, blowing through a four-way, then headed south.

"Stay with me, Byrnes. We normally tail with two or three cars, maybe a copter. Now we're on our own."

"You're on your own. I have to find Pico. Let me out."

Kaycee said nothing and shot through a yellow. In seconds we were half a block behind our target.

"Look," I said, leaning forward. "DeCarlo's all over me about Pico and I'm worried about the guy. I'll give you thirty minutes, then I gotta go."

"You're my date. If we get caught, you're my alibi."

I let my head fall against the headrest, stared in the distance at nothing in particular.

What happened to taking roll and assigning squad games? The life I once hated, now longed for.

The Topas truck continued south on Atlantic. We maintained our distance one car behind, made every light, passed blocks of dark houses and storefronts. Then we weaved from lane to lane, shielded by one car, sometimes two.

The sky opened up. For a short minute it was like driving through a car wash before it suddenly cleared.

Passing through the town of Ventnor, we rushed by several houses on tiny lots and a few storefronts. A light here and there.

When we entered Margate, the truck swerved left onto Jackson.

Kaycee doused her headlights, and seconds later took the same corner.

"Townsend's place," she said. "I should have known." She guided the car slowly down a dimly lit street and stopped behind a parked car about seventy-five yards from the gate.

The gate slowly swung open. The truck rolled in.

Kaycee turned left, drove down the block, swung around, and parked next to Townsend's ten-foot-high brick wall. We got out. Checked it. Nothing to grab onto.

I looked the other way, pointed, and whispered, "A walkway."

We quickly walked down a narrow path, damp and sandy, darker than hell. Where the path ended, the beach began, greeting us with heavy surf and moist, chill winds. Our backs to the wall, I peeked around the corner. On the beach, thirty yards away, a tall man in yellow raingear walked away and passed Townsend's balcony. Probably security.

I looked at Kaycee's darkened face. "Don't we need some kind paperwork for this?"

She pushed my back. "It's a gray area. Let's go."

"You told me there are no gray areas."

She said nothing. We eased around the wall and saw a steep hedgerow running from Townsend's house to the walkway wall. Then we hurriedly found a break in the hedges and scraped through.

We stayed low, darting from bush to bush, heading towards a distant light. No barking dogs. No security lights going on.

If we get caught they'll bury us right here.

A doublewide garage became visible.

Within a wedge shot of the building, I saw beer kegs being unloaded from the Topas truck. Then headlights from a moving van swung past the entrance to the house, turned left, and lit up the tangle of bush in front of us. I froze as the van pulled up next to the Topas truck and backed toward the open garage.

Two men slipped out of the van and unloaded two large wood crates into the well-lit garage loaded with silver beer kegs. The Topas men began unscrewing the tops of the kegs, then poured stacks of bills into the crates, filling them to the top.

I whispered, "Laundering . . . shit, send some my way."

The crates were screwed shut, wrapped with plastic sheeting, then loaded back onto the van.

Kaycee tapped me on the shoulder, pointed to the beach. She took a step and suddenly went down with a thud. I took a slow breath, looked towards the workmen. No eyes our way.

"Gopher hole," she whispered. "Cracked something."

I pulled her up gently, and wrapped her arm around my shoulder. Kaycee limping all the way, we worked our way back to the hedge, waited a minute for security to make his rounds, then got the hell out.

Back at our car door, Kaycee standing on one leg, I said, "Give me the keys. I won't lose the van. Put your foot up and keep the swelling down."

"I'll drive," she said.

The van veered right as it shot out of the driveway. We ducked down to avoid its headlights.

"Give me the keys," I said. "You're not driving."

Her FBI spirit on hold, I took over the wheel, and we trailed the van that rushed towards Atlantic City. I forgot about Pico for the moment and focused on the money.

With only two vehicles on the road, I kept my distance, maybe seven car lengths behind. Approaching Atlantic City, the van turned onto the Atlantic City Expressway. An hour later, after exiting and re-entering the highway several times, I trailed the truck by a quarter-mile, coming off I-95 in Philadelphia onto Broad Street, then contining towards the docks.

I passed a cruise-terminal sign, wound up on shadowy Admiral Perry Way on the waterfront and stopped short of Pier 3. I parked behind a shed. Seventy-five yards ahead, the van pulled up to a triple-tier cruise liner, *The Dolphin*. The crates were loaded into the hull.

Kaycee placed a call to check on the destination of *The Dolphin* and the licenses of the trucks we'd followed. She hung up, said, "I'll get someone to follow the money. Townsend can be charged with laundering, and income tax evasion. But Mansfield wouldn't have called me about that. He said it was big. Townsend skimming millions isn't the *big* he was talking about. There's got to be something else out there, partner."

The closer to tip-off, the heavier my chest. There's no way out. If I run, it's the end. If I stay it's the end.

Across the hallway, Giranda says to me, "Can't get any more exciting than this."

"No. It can't."

The hallway was silent as he stares at me for a moment. Then he says, "You ever think back to your first coaching job? Think about why you got into this business?"

I stare back as my mind rewinds to my first day as a high school coach.

Walking through the halls of the main building to sign in. The air was fresh. There was a bounce to my step. My mission was clear.

"I wanted to be like my old high school coach—caring, supportive, make men out of boys, coach winners. And I felt good about having a secure job, something my father never had. We lived from hand to mouth."

Giranda checks his watch, then says, "But you left that secure job."

"My life changed. I needed to grow. Be all I could be. I never dreamed . . . I mean things happened fast. It's not like I planned."

CHAPTER 37

ATLANTIC CITY
OCTOBER 18

Bob Tully, Townsend's fixer and Sheldrake's General Counsel, sat at one end of a long glass-top table in the president's conference room. He pushed a tape recorder away from a short stack of papers. DeCarlo sat to his left, tapping his foot against the carpet, while Giranda sat to his right, strumming his fingers. I sat next to Giranda. The clear view of the beach through tall windows interested no one. We focused on the mikes in front of us that were wired to the audio recorder in the center of the table.

DeCarlo sneered at me.

He's either pissed at the NCAA, pissed at me for not finding Pico, or pissed at his offense. Take your pick.

I blew warm air into my cupped hands. The thermostat on the wall in front of me said seventy. It felt like fifty.

Tully, who operated somewhere between the unethical and the criminal, said with a half-assed smile, "Let's get started." He reached out and hit "record," introduced himself and our casually dressed staff, then said, "This is Sheldrake College's internal investigation of NCAA allegations against its basketball program. Thus far, I have interviewed the Sheldrake players and found no NCAA infractions." He pushed the pause button, then provided some handouts.

"Ready?" Tully asked.

I nodded. Giranda sat motionless. DeCarlo waved his hand as if to say, "Bring it on."

Tully clicked "record" again, swore us in without a Bible, and said, "Coach Byrnes, I'll start with you. Have you ever been involved with the fixing of SAT scores for Sheldrake College?"

Everyone smiled except me.

I saw myself handing over an SAT payment to Washington at USC. I squeezed out a "No."

Tully's head swiveled to DeCarlo and back to me. "Has anyone in the Sheldrake Basketball Department ordered you to fix grades of incoming freshmen?"

I looked down as my heart thumped. "No."

"Coach Byrnes, have you or anyone in this department ever been involved with academic fraud?"

"No."

Tully went on to ask me about illegal tryouts for prospects, my knowledge of the Division One recruiting rules, and under-the-table payments from boosters.

I denied everything. After the first lie, the rest were easy.

Tully thanked me for my time. I sat back and waited for the second act.

Tully's first question to DeCarlo was, "Have you ever paid under-the-table money to a Sheldrake player?"

DeCarlo's face turned ugly. He pounded the table with his fist, said, "I've never paid a player more than he was worth. The NCAA has been on my ass since I left All-Saints University. Following me around, tapping my phone. What the hell do you expect me to say? Fuck them."

"Jesus," said Tully, reaching out to rewind. "DeCarlo, you've got a script right in front of you. All you have to say is 'no.'" Tully took a breath. "Okay—once more with feeling."

Tully asked the same question and DeCarlo said, "Fuck no."

He feared no one.

Tully raised both hands, palms up as if to say, "What the fuck?" Then he said, "DeCarlo, just say 'no.' It's the only word on your script."

Tully continued. He asked DeCarlo the same questions he asked me. DeCarlo responded accurately.

Fifteen minutes later, our 'in-depth' interrogation ended, and I made my way to the elevator, followed by DeCarlo and Giranda. While we waited for the ride down, my cell vibrated. I pulled it out, which could have been a big mistake.

"Hi Kaycee."

"Can you talk?"

I looked at DeCarlo. After a deep breath, said, "No, I heard that's a bad movie."

"Then listen. The beer truck and the moving van are owned by Joan Augustus. She's in the truck-leasing business in Philly. She has no criminal record, no connections to crime."

"And who's the star?"

"The beer truck and the moving van are leased to the Palm Abrasives Company in Atlantic City, a company owned by Townsend."

"Could be a winner."

"And the cruise liner stops in the Caymans. That's probably the drop-off point." Click.

DeCarlo gave me a somber look. "You're not going to the movies until you find Pico."

CHAPTER 38

TWO DAYS LATER

Rain pounded the street below my kitchen window. Six inches yesterday and it wouldn't stop. Scanning for basketball news on my computer, I read the first paragraph of Jordan's morning briefing on Sport.com.

> *Pico Rimpau, a freshman basketball player at Sheldrake College, is missing. Despite denials from the coaching staff, Pico Rimpau is not on campus and no one has seen him for two days. The six-nine Rimpau was brought up in an orphanage and did not play high school basketball. He defied the odds and earned his way to the position of second-string center of Sheldrake.*

As I sat at the edge of my kitchen chair, my eyes jogged from the computer screen to the window.

The rats are going to come out of the woodwork.

My cell rang and I picked it up.

"Coach Byrnes?"

"Yes."

"Ace Hutchison from NYU. We met at the HotShoe Camp. How the hell are you?"

Son-of-a-bitch. I'm being hustled by the guy who applied for my job.

170

"Other than my job, what do you want, Ace?"

"Hey, this is a friendly call. I just read Jordan Taylor's blurb about Pico Rimpau. Listen, if there's a problem Pico can come over here. We have a scholarship open. And we'll find a spot for you."

"Pico took a couple of days off."

"Look, we'll take him—no questions asked. At least let me talk to him. Give me his cell number."

"You're on the wrong trail, Hutchison." Click.

Seconds later, I received another call from a coach at some college I had never heard of. He also wanted Pico. I fended him off, but couldn't dodge the next call. It was from Wheels. He ranted about Sheldrake basketball getting the wrong kind of attention from Pico's disappearance and that the story was going to lead back to him. Then he blasted Pico for having a street-guy mentality, finishing with, "My private eye will find him." He slammed his phone down.

My heart pumping a little faster, I read the last paragraph of Jordan's article.

> *Michael Mansfield, an assistant coach at Sheldrake, who disappeared from the program in May, is still a missing person. Who's next? What the hell is going on at Sheldrake?*

I moved to the window wondering where my search for Pico had gone wrong. I stared through a rain-streaked glass at people below scurrying under windblown umbrellas, and wondered if Pico was staying warm.

*   *   *

I arrived at the Hall an hour later. DeCarlo was meeting with Giranda in his office. Next door at my desk, I surfed the Net and wrote down the address of every college and community basketball court in Philadelphia. I bet Pico was on his island of familiarity and freedom.

But he could be in danger.

My mind turned more negative than it was already.

The phone rang. My heart in my mouth, I picked it up.

"Basketball Office."

"May I speak to Babe DeCarlo?"

A man's voice.

"Coach DeCarlo is in a meeting. This is his assistant. I'll take a message."

"This is Francisco Saenz from the Northern Lights Mission in Philadelphia. I read that you have a missing player. We have a very tall, young man who came to our mission last night. He has a thin face, wispy beard, sparse mustache, and a long nose. I wonder . . . "

My heart quickened. "What name did he give?"

"He said his name is Conrad Byrnes."

My mind spun. "That's me . . . I mean that's him. What's he doing there?"

"You wouldn't believe it if I told you."

"Don't let him out. I'll be there in an hour."

* * *

My wipers were on high-speed all the way. In the city, I followed Francisco's directions. I drove north on gray, uninviting streets, over manholes without covers, past pawnbroker shops, bail bonds stores, and a car flat on the pavement without wheels. After ten minutes, I got that empty feeling that comes with being lost.

I swung to the curb on Spring Garden and Eighth, rolled by a few stores trying to get a number. No luck. But I suspected I was close to the mission when I passed a man in a tattered yellow jacket pushing a cart draped with a shower curtain.

I circled the area and found the mission a block away—a two-story gray building on a corner. A green canvas awning covered the courtyard entrance where scores of people stood shoulder-to-shoulder in the cold, their belongings in shopping carts and garbage bags. Rain streamed down the edges of the awning forming the outside boundary of their world.

I parked in a damp underground garage. My stomach turned with anxiety as I took the elevator to the first floor. Down a narrow foyer I found the reception counter. There I asked for Francisco. While waiting, I turned and gazed through tall windows at the homeless crowd hovering under the awning.

"I'm Francisco."

I pivoted. Francisco Saenz was Black, bald, a few inches shorter than I and closer to forty than he was to fifty. He was dressed in Levi's and a gray sweatshirt with the imprint "Northern Lights Mission." His friendly eyes said that this was a good place for him.

"I'm Conrad Byrnes. The guy who gave you my name is Pico Rimpau."

"I thought so," Francisco said. "No one gives their real name around here."

We shook hands, and I pointed outside. "Can't these people come in?"

Francisco relaxed yet in command, said, "If they come in, they have to hear our pitch and give up their drugs. Right now they don't trust us . . . but you're here about Pico Rimpau. I was curious why a healthy, six-nine, young man would show up here and want to get in our program. Something told me to take him . . . I didn't think he would be here long. Then, I read the blurb this morning. I'm a basketball addict, uh, fan. And I knew he had to play somewhere."

"I really appreciate your call. Can I see him?"

Francisco gestured for me to follow him. He ushered me down a short hallway with cold white walls, continued through a dining room full of adults of all ages in clean clothes. Some with hopeful eyes. Some with blank stares. So distant from my world.

When we entered another hallway, I asked, "Where have you got him?"

"He's out here. Follow me."

At the end of another corridor, Francisco pushed open a door to the rainstorm and had to speak loudly to be heard. "See him? He's shooting baskets across the court."

Grainy images of someone shooting hoops. Like the first Edison film.

"Barely."

"I wouldn't go out there." Francisco pointed down at the basketball court that had turned into a wading pool because of a two-foot high, cement border that rimmed the entire court.

I stepped into a foot of ice-cold water, the top of my head stinging from the downpour, water streaming down my face and irritating my eyes. Then I sloshed across the court with shoes that felt like sponges.

Pico, wearing a matted T-shirt and dungarees, put up a short shot that caromed off the rim and splattered on the pond.

I approached him, raised my voice, and called his name. He turned with wide eyes and blurted, "What are you doing here?"

My voice cracking, I said, "Do you think after all we've been through, I wouldn't come after you?"

His look became a stare.

I stepped towards him, reached up and put my hand on his shoulder. "Let's talk inside. I love basketball. But not this much."

The rain still drenching us, Pico asked, "How'd you find me?"

"You're not exactly invisible."

He turned away and took another six-foot shot. This time the wet ball slipped off his fingers, hit the side of the metal backboard, and splashed down. He waded a few feet to the floating ball, scooping it up with two hands. Then he straightened and looked my way. His voice unstable, he said, "College ball ain't what I thought."

"Not what I thought either. Let's talk inside."

He slumped slightly, cupped his eyes with a hand to avoid the down-pour and cried out, "I'm not a bastard . . . I have a name!"

My teeth now chattering, my voice choking, I said, "I know." I sloshed towards him, placed my hand on his soaked back. "Let's go inside."

Pico hugged the ball to chest, and we splashed back to the door Francisco had held open. We dripped our way to a packed dining room, where, ringing wet, we sat on opposite sides of a plastic table, drawing no attention from the bundled-up guests with whom we sat shoulder-to-shoulder. Francisco brought us wool blankets to stop our shivering, towels for our heads, and hot coffee. We toweled down and

MADNESS OF MARCH

wrapped ourselves in the blankets. Then Francisco left us alone.

"Pico," I said. When you escaped from the St. Andrews, you were running to something. Basketball. Now you're running away from something. It's better to run to something than run away from something."

His hand shaking, Pico took a careful sip of coffee. "I had to think things out."

A bearded man sitting next to him, looked into space, and mumbled, "There's no going back."

"So, what have you figured out, Pico?"

"I don't have many friends."

"I'm your friend."

"I know. And DeCarlo's not anyone's friend. And he treats all the players the same. Like shit."

The bearded man mumbled, "People are no damn good."

My eyes not wavering from Pico's, I said, "You've got a room, money, and you can play ball. Everything you ever wanted. DeCarlo's strange. But he's a good coach. Just what you need."

"It's not the money," Pico said. "I just want to be respected as a human being."

"I understand. Give me a chance to straighten this out. I'll call him. Stay here."

As I started to engineer my way out of the bench seat, Pico said, "There's something else."

I froze with one leg curled over the seat. "Girlfriend? Better offer?"

Pico dropped the blanket from his shoulders and pulled up the sleeve on his T-shirt. My eyes widened. There. plain as day was a white, five-inch, number fifty, tattooed on his deltoid in block letters. A statement that would rock DeCarlo.

"I'm not going back unless I'm number fifty," he said. "When the press takes my photo from the side, they'll know who I am. Numbers on the front and back of the jersey won't give the identity I want. They will know my name."

I broke out in laughter. "So number fifty is your way of getting back at DeCarlo, putting him against the wall. Let me solve this thing. Be right back."

I walked to a far corner and dialed my cell.

"Babe, this is Byrnes. I found Pico and here's the thing . . ." I told DeCarlo that Pico would come back if he were the sixth man on the Son-of-a-Bitch team and that he was never to be called a bastard again.

"Okay," DeCarlo said, "but I'm going to ignore him. He needs to learn a lesson."

"Fine, but there's another issue." As I tried to explain the tattoo, I didn't need a telephone to hear DeCarlo yell, "I'm the fucking coach! No one tells Babe DeCarlo who wears what. And fifty is Americus Hart's number."

I waited a long moment for his wrath to subside, before saying, "You don't want Pico's fouls charged to Americus, do you? An official would see fifty on Pico's arm and think it was Hart's number."

"Everyone has a tattoo—I can't believe it . . . How 'bout he wears a T-shirt under his uni?"

Silence for a long moment before DeCarlo growled, "Okay, but that Son-of-a-Bitch better win for me."

CHAPTER 39

It took three days for Pico's story to die down outside the hallowed walls of Boardwalk Hall. But inside, DeCarlo's dislike for Pico increased. During our workouts, DeCarlo called every member of the team by name except Pico, whom he referred to as, "Hey, you." And he did not applaud anything Pico did well.

I took a positive approach, walked the sidelines, and yelled, "Way to go, Pico. Good job." Then I would sneak a look at DeCarlo who said nothing, but distorted his face. I finally realized that DeCarlo wouldn't fire me because I was connected to Pico. I could say almost anything and get away with it. And I was responsible for Pico. I put him in this crazy 'funhouse.'

DeCarlo stopped berating Pico one day, as the team moved quickly from drill to drill. Half-court defenses, half-court offenses, full-court transitions. But during a thirty-minute scrimmage, things began to pop again.

I was the lone official and Pico was the only substitute on the Sons-of-Bitches. During the first half of the game, DeCarlo didn't sub-in Pico. With ten minutes left and the ball out of bounds, I yelled, "Sub-in. Pico, take it for Americus." DeCarlo gave me a nasty look but said nothing.

Pico clapped his hands, sprinted to the SOB's defensive end and positioned himself as a one-man zone, waiting to be the monster within six feet of the hoop. The Bastards brought the ball up the court quickly and went into their offense. Then a pass down low, a six-foot shot attempt, and up went Pico, swatting that shot into the first row of bleachers. Then another inside attempt and another Pico rejection.

I ran behind Pico to officiate play at his offensive end of the court and shouted, "Good job. Keep it up."

But Pico got lost on offense. He would have been okay if the offense were static, one pass and a shot. But the ball would ping-pong from one side of the court to the other in concert with player movement, causing Pico to lose sight of the ball and wind up on the wrong side of the court.

Then DeCarlo yelled, "Hey, you, screen the right guy!"

But then Pico's defender, a nice kid who had run the offense for two years, talked him through the screen sequences.

Standing at mid-court, a whistle in my mouth, I wondered if Pico could make two transfers in a New York subway, and if he would ever be ready to play for Sheldrake.

CHAPTER 40

The next morning, I joined our staff in the small conference room adjacent to DeCarlo's office to schedule every minute of our two hour workout that afternoon. Giranda sat next to me and DeCarlo stood a couple of paces away at the white board, our usual formation. DeCarlo began the meeting by calling Pico by name, a positive sign. And it appeared as though things had been settled until President Hammer suddenly broke into our meeting. With sweat dripping down his forehead, Hammer said, "They've got us now, The NCAA rejected our internal investigation and they're bringing someone in to interview all of us at the end of this week."

"Relax, Hammer," DeCarlo said, "I'll handle it. They've been chasing me for years."

"You better come out unscathed," the president said. "We've got a lot of money riding on this."

* * *

A few days later, Tully and our staff milled around Hammer's glass-enclosed conference room awaiting a frontal attack by the NCAA. Finally, a bald-headed man with a face like an owl appeared in the doorway. He looked familiar. He was shorter than average height, in his forties, and wore a dark suit. Following him in were a middle-aged woman holding a stenography machine and a man in a Mackinaw jacket carrying video equipment.

We took seats facing each other across the table like opposing forces on a battlefield.

The irony of it all was that suit-guy had his back to the Mardi Gras, the source of our cash. In the next moment, my heart thumped when I recognized suit-guy as the man who had taken photos of Pico and me on the boardwalk last summer. I strummed my fingers on the table wondering what else I could do for a living.

"Still after me, Burnett?" DeCarlo fired a warning shot, giving me shortness of breath. "You chased me out of All-Saints; now you want to bury me? Bastard," he mumbled."

Burnett smiled and said, "DeCarlo, if you can wait, the stenographer and the cameraman are setting up to take your confession."

I hoped Burnett wouldn't look my way. But Burnett was about to pull out all stops to bury DeCarlo, while our head coach would try to prove his innocence against all odds.

Burnett set his briefcase on the floor and fished out a yellow pad with my name scribbled across the cover. He placed it on the glass tabletop. Below my name were neatly printed questions. I held my breath. Then with his chin out he seemed to forget me and turned to DeCarlo. "You should have told your players not to wear their Rolexes to my interview."

DeCarlo's face twisted, and Tully pounded his fist on the table.

The room was cemetery quiet.

Burnett then looked at the cameraman and stenographer and nodded. We were on. Burnett introduced himself, stated his business, and said, "Coach Conrad Byrnes."

I tried to look cool. After all, I was the road to DeCarlo.

Burnett asked me my full name, position, and birth date. After I responded, he said, "And what is your responsibility at Sheldrake?"

I said calmly, "As assistant coach, I do what DeCarlo tells me to do, mostly help with practice, some recruiting."

"And how did Pico Rimpau get to Sheldrake?"

My armpits dripping cold sweat down the side of my body, I said, "He wanted to play at Sheldrake. I recruited him. He signed."

"Isn't it true that Sheldrake gave Pico Rimpau something to sign here?"

"Objection," Tully said. "Leading. Trying to put words into Mr. Byrnes' mouth."

I ignored the guilty signals that my heart sent to my head, and deception took over. "I can answer the question," I said. "The answer is absolutely not."

"Aren't you in charge of paying off players?"

"Objection," Tully said. "Accusation. Leading."

Burnett scratched a line through that question, rebounded with a sharp tone.

"You ever paid a Sheldrake College player?"

I stared at Burnett. "We don't pay our players . . . why don't you tell me what you've got so I can respond?"

Burnett leaned across the table, "I promise, I won't disappoint." He opened the folder and carefully pulled out an eight-by-ten black and white and shoved it towards me.

Boardwalk photo. I'm sitting on a bike with a brick in one hand. Pico standing next to me in shorts and shoes staring down at the brick in his hand.

"You want to tell me about this photo? Looks like you're training Pico Rimpau out of season."

My eyes on the picture, I said, "It's unethical to coach our players during the summer."

"That's a non-denial denial. What was Pico doing with the brick?"

I looked at Burnett and tried desperately to come up with an answer. "Huh. Pico wanted to show me how many things he could do with a brick."

"Seconds later you were riding your bike next to him as he ran down the boardwalk with a brick in both hands. You were training him."

"Pico showed me that running with bricks is one of the things he could do with the objects. He also said bricks could be used as chalk, doorstops, bug squashers, paperweights." I chuckled. "Siding for a house, a walkway, and an outhouse."

"Very funny," Burnett said. "Maybe this won't be as funny." He slid another glossy my way. "Let the record show that Coach Byrnes is looking at a photo of himself and sports writer Jordan Taylor."

Shit—the coffee house meeting.

DeCarlo screamed, "What the fuck!"

I forced a breath, scanning the faces at the table. Accusatory looks everywhere.

"Why were you talking to this investigative reporter?" Burnett asked.

I took a deep breath and looked at DeCarlo. Squeezed out, "Jordan Taylor is my brother."

DeCarlo erupted, threw up his hands, "You're a fuckin' mole! That's what you are, a fuckin' mole."

This isn't the way I planned my life.

I put up my hand to buy time. "Let me explain."

DeCarlo cut in, "I got your explanation up my ass."

Burnett said, "Why don't you explain to all of us?"

I folded my cold fingers on the table. Inhaled. Looked squarely at Burnett. "When I took the job at Sheldrake, I knew Jordan was an investigative reporter. But I didn't know what he was investigating. When he asked me about Sheldrake basketball, I told him to talk to other people in our program. That photo was taken when we had an argument over his investigation of Sheldrake. We aren't speaking now. That's all there is to that."

God help me.

"So you fucked me," DeCarlo blurted.

Tully said, "Let Burnett handle this."

Burnett spread his hands. "Coach Byrnes, what did Jordan Taylor's investigation uncover about Sheldrake basketball?"

"I read the paper just like you." *He's not going to buy that.*

Burnett gave me an odd look and thanked me for my cooperation with a wave of the hand, like I was of no help. I sat there stunned that he let me off the hook.

Burnett took a five-minute recess to let the stenographer make corrections, and DeCarlo went to the end of the room and made a call with his eyes on me. As Burnett continued to speak to the stenographer, DeCarlo returned to his seat and whispered to me, "Everything's okay. Don't worry about a thing."

I started to worry, staring at DeCarlo longer than I wanted to, but refrained from wiping the bead of sweat that rolled slowly down my forehead.

He had to talk to Townsend. Townsend gave me a reprieve. He made Mansfield disappear. Had Jordan fired. Why was he saving me?

During the next forty-five minutes, Burnett was soft on Giranda, hard on DeCarlo. But DeCarlo, blaming everything on a dead man, responded by telling Burnett that Mansfield was responsible for all of Sheldrake's recruiting infractions. That led Burnett to conclude, "You're saying that you aren't in charge here, that the program has no controls. Is that correct?"

"That's right," DeCarlo said.

Eyes wide, my back straightened.

Other schools had gotten a slap on the wrist for the "lack of control— the I don't know what the hell happened defense." But Burnett wants to blast DeCarlo. This program's going down. So is your career.

CHAPTER 41

"I was always a bumper-car gal," Kaycee said, "but this is a great place to meet if you're insane."

Kaycee and I rose slowly in the Ferris wheel above Atlantic City's Steel Pier amusement park, the boardwalk below as cold as our chairs. On this last day of the park, a few bundled-up amusement park lovers walked the midway, bucking chill ocean winds that blew wrappers in every direction.

Dressed in a black leather jacket, a black wool turtle neck, tight-fitting pants with knee-high boots, Kaycee was a knockout.

I felt her shoulder touch mine and instantly slid my arm around her back.

She said, "Too bad this is just a ride and we have to come back to earth."

"So let's talk about you and me."

Kaycee's body shifted away ten degrees, her mind did a one-eighty, and she said, "What makes you think I'm looking for a boyfriend? You don't even qualify for life insurance."

I withdrew my arm. "What are you afraid of, Kaycee?"

"I'm just careful."

"Of what?"

"The future."

"Then I'm not going to tell you what I think of you."

"Don't . . . why did you ask me up here? Let's get to it."

"Okay, you want business. Here it is . . . Yesterday DeCarlo told Townsend that Jordan's my brother. But Townsend didn't have me fired. I'm telling you the walls." A roller coaster with a couple of screaming passengers shot by, about fifty feet away. "The walls," I repeated, "are closing in. I know Townsend is saving me for something, and he's not a 'live and let live' kind of guy."

"This is what we've been looking for. But you better be very careful."

"Careful of what? I don't know what I need to be careful about. I have no scouting report. It's a dark hole . . . Have you told me everything?"

"You know everything I know."

As we began our descent, the tall Taj Mahal across the way dropped from view; then the boardwalk appeared. At ground level I heard laughter and clanking ride-chains. I looked out at the mid-way and mumbled, "Step right up, folks. See the headless coach. If he had a head on his shoulders, he wouldn't be here."

When we rose again, Kaycee said, "Hang in there, Byrnes. I've been down this road before and it always works out."

"Oh, yeah. Mansfield took that road. He's not here anymore."

"Mansfield wasn't a case. He was a phone call. You're a case. And I haven't lost one yet."

Suddenly, I had the feeling that I was in midair, about to take a fall. "Tell me about your successes."

Kaycee hesitated as if it were an FBI secret, cleared her throat, said, "Okay, so this is my first case. But I've been through the training."

I erupted. "So I'm tied to the tracks, a train's coming at me and you're turning the pages of your manual. That's what you didn't tell me. You're a rookie and we're running on luck. Well, I'm definitely not lucky. I've lost a wife, a son, and I'm looking at ten to fifteen. Get somebody in here with experience."

Descending again, she shot back, "I know what I'm doing. And you're the last person I want to lose."

"Look, I need a gun . . . someone's going to come after me and I need a gun."

Kaycee crossed her legs away from me. "I'll take your request upstairs. Now if you can suck up your guts, I'll bring you up to speed with my side of the investigation."

"My guts, your manual."

"You know, Byrnes, I like you. And I can see that there's enough asshole in you to be a great coach. But you're not coaching me. So save your nasty. You're going to need it." She paused. "You ready for your briefing?"

"Go," I said with a tinge of indifference.

"The two crates of bills wound up in a Caymans bank. No telling where the money went from there. Electronically, it could go anywhere. Second, I've been by the Palm Abrasives Company. It's on the east end. It makes scouring-powder, and it looks like any other low-rise industrial building. But the question is, 'What is Townsend, a casino gambler with mob ties, doing in the scouring-powder business?'"

"Someone needs to get inside those walls. Find out what's really going on and get me out of this hell hole."

"I don't have a good reason to get a warrant." Kaycee said.

"Just get me a gun."

CHAPTER 42

In a warm windproof jacket, I did a speed walk down Atlantic, passing Kentucky and New York Streets. I didn't notice barren trees, drug handoffs, or speeding cars. In shop window reflections, I was looking for a slow moving car and a pedestrian who came to a stop when I did.

Comfortable that there was no tail, I entered a food market, wheeled a cart down an aisle and called Kaycee where the nuts met the jam. For the last three weeks, Kaycee had been on the road and our only exchanges were voice mail.

She answered right away.

"Kaycee, you sure left at the right time. Nothing's been happening. But I still need the piece. Did you get it?"

"Hold on. I have to move away from this boarding line. I'm in the Vegas airport." Seconds later, she said, "Can't do it. But I have information. Someone who worked for Townsend in Las Vegas may be in the mix. A guy named Williams, AKA Willams. Conrad, this guy doesn't know the difference between losing his temper and killing someone. He did five years for serving up an acid cocktail to Townsend's Realtor, then ten for electrocuting a guy who owed Townsend. Inmates called him Weird Harold. He's been back on the street for some time, but I can't locate him."

"Why do you think this guy is in the mix?"

"Because he carries out Townsend's death wishes."

"What does he look like?"

"Sixty, full head of hair, big nose, bushy eyebrows."

"No one with that description has doctored my Gatorade or put my hand in a wall socket."

"No time to be funny. I have to get back in line. How are things at your end?"

"DeCarlo's calmed down about Pico. And Pico is more fluid on offense. DeCarlo also told Americus that if he wore number 40, he would retire the jersey after the season. So Pico is number 50 front, back, and deltoids. Now we're ready to play."

"You open at home tomorrow. It would be great if I could be there."

"Yeah ... oh, one more thing. DeCarlo is going to talk with me tomorrow about something else Mansfield was responsible for."

CHAPTER 43

"This was Mansfield's job," DeCarlo said as he clicked open the door next to the visitor's meeting room. A second later, fluorescent light flickered and dressing room furniture revealed itself to my right. To my left was a television monitor, a remote and a headset on a heavy table from which a wire shot up the wall to a vent near the ceiling.

DeCarlo picked up the remote off the table and pressed a button. A bright picture of a white board and fifteen chairs in the visitor's meeting room appeared on the monitor. "We're on channel 4 now," he said.

A bugging operation. He wants me to spy on Temple.

"Is the camera in the vent?"

"Yeah, and we're almost soundproof."

I glanced at the carpet on the walls, ceiling and floor, looked back at DeCarlo. "So I'm the analyst?"

"You got it."

Stick me in this place for two hours—I'll go crazy.

"At their pre-game meeting you'll learn their strategy," DeCarlo said. "Text me anything we haven't practiced for. Then hit channel 3 and watch our game. When Temple returns to the locker room for halftime hit channel 4 and scout them again."

"You want me to do this for every home game?"

"Yeah. Comes with the territory."

"Well, at least I'll be on the floor when we travel."

"No, you'll be scouting our next opponent."

Is this what Townsend saved me for?

* * *

I managed the shoot-around at eleven a.m. with Giranda. Standing on the sideline, I watched our players loosen up with three pointers and free throws.

Giranda said, "This one's in the bag."

"Because of our TV system?"

"That and we've got insurance. As an independent we hire our own officials. If the game is tight with two minutes left, they'll homer Temple. Three seconds, palming, fouls. You watch."

"What do these Boy Scouts get?"

"A fixed roulette wheel at the Mardi Gra."

"Sweet," I said. "But we can't do this stuff on the road."

"We play teams that just returned from Hawaii. They have island fever and more jet lag than we do. We've also scheduled teams that are one game away from playing a tough matchup. They all look past us."

* * *

An hour before the Temple game, locked in the storage room, I stared at the door, felt the temperature rising and my shirt dampening. I checked my watch. Two more hours and I was out of there.

Over the dressing table, I studied my face in the mirror, then murmured, "Spy . . . stool pigeon . . . pimp. You've really advanced in life."

At the sink in the corner, I threw some water on my face, but couldn't remove the guilt.

I crossed the room, got channel 3. Nothing going on. I got channel 4 just when Temple entered their meeting room. They were tall, taller, and tallest. Impressive in street clothes. In minutes, they emerged from the locker room in cherry-and-white sweat suits, then charged out the door for a pre-game shoot-around. When they returned ten minutes later, I had paced the floor more times than I could remember, thinking about getting caught.

My Sheldrake cell vibrated. The screen read, "Restricted."

"This is Coach Byrnes," I said in a half-whisper.

"Conrad Byrnes, Mark Swift here. I sat next to you at Winning Dynamics. I'm working for them now."

Shit.

"Look, I-"

"I'm calling you about our next seminar, 'Winning Can Change Your Life.'"

"Winning Dynamics has already changed my life. Take me off your list."

I hung up just as the Temple coach stood ready to do battle in front of his players with a marker in his hand. "Listen up," he said. "We're going to beat Sheldrake by going to the zone. Sheldrake won't be ready for our 1-3-1. His red marker squeaked out the positions of his players on the white board. Then he enlarged an X on the left wing and said, "Poncho, this is you, the big X."

Six-nine Poncho Cruz on the left wing. Big, agile, quick. Difficult to get a pass by him.

I quickly texted DeCarlo, who according to my watch would be giving the players last minute instructions in our locker rom.

I switch channels and watched the teams go at each other while I stayed in the audio-visual room.

Temple's in the zone . . . Nitro brings down the ball . . . recognizes the 1-3-1 . . . we go 2-1-2. Nitro drives a seam . . . in the air . . . hits Willard Penn in the corner . . . jumper . . . that's three . . . let me out of here.

The Temple coach looked down the sideline at DeCarlo, probably wondering how we made the adjustment so fast.

Standing in front of the tube where I'd been since the game began, I said softly, "Hey, coach, I'm the reason you're screwed. I see you. I hear you. I put it to you."

Cheating gave us a six-point lead, and there was nothing to report to

DeCarlo about Temple's half-time.

Before the second half began, I crossed the room and put my hand over the knob and froze. *I can't go outside for a breath of fresh air. Someone would see me. Stay put for the last act.*

With five minutes remaining in the game, I watched Pico spring off the bench and entered the contest. "Go get 'em, Pico," I said, shaking my fist. "This is your moment."

The game streamed by.

Pico blocks a shot . . . another. A fly swatter . . . whoops. Came down on the center.

We're ahead by four . . . Temple fouls Nitro on a jumper . . . The guy didn't touch Nitro . . . Frank and Jessie will be rewarded . . . Nitro sinks two . . . up six. Palming on Temple. Ball into Pico low.

"Do what I taught you. Fake and go."

He fakes a shot . . . travels. . . not called . . . dunks. Fouled. Hits one. Up eight . . . fans boo. Are they booing Pico? Why would they do that?

One minute before the game ended I ducked out of the audio-visual room. Feeling like an escapee, I slipped inside our locker room, still hearing the boo-birds.

After the horn sounded, players entered. Smiling, joking, yelling.

"Hey, Coach Byrnes," Americus said, covered in sweat. "Where you been?"

"Scouting."

I went around the room shaking players' hands, then found Giranda alone in a corner reading the stats. "Hey, nice going. But why the boos after Pico hit the free throw?"

"The fans had Temple and four," he said. "We won by five."

"So we're not bringing in seven thousand fans—we're bringing in seven thousand gamblers?"

"Welcome to Atlantic City."

LUCAS OIL STADIUM
INDIANAPOLIS, INDIANA
APRIL 5
MINUTES BEFORE TIP-OFF: 25

I lean against the cold hallway wall outside our locker room, wondering what might have been. *I had no idea during the regular season what was planned for me. If I'd known, I would have disappeared on my own.*

I flash on December, January, February. A myriad of thoughts surface.

Townsend and Wheels never contacted me during the winning season that drove me crazy. Sequestered in a room, I couldn't touch the game. Miserable, I spied. Scouted. Paid-off.

Jordan hammers away.

Who knew it was going to be sphincter-tightening time?

And the Palm Abrasives Company . . . remember that night . . .

CHAPTER 44

"They wanted me to quit, Kaycee. That's why they put me in that room."

"They could have fired you," she replied. "But they didn't. Now the regular season is over and you can stop asking yourself that question . . . Turn right."

I swung Kaycee's car onto a dark, narrow street. an industrial park with low-rise brick buildings and bars on every window.

Whizzing through blackness in the dead of night, I said, "It was my dream to coach college ball. Winning Dynamics said it was my destiny to be all I could be. But I discovered my shady side . . . High school coaching was better. I was on the floor, made all the decisions. Now I've been locked into cheating. Sidelined from life."

"I hear you. But soon it will be over and you can get another high school job."

"If I live that long." I let off the accelerator. "Where the hell is the Palm Abrasives Company?"

"At the end of the block."

As I gently touched the brake, Kaycee picked up a pair of blue latex gloves from the floor and slipped them on.

"Byrnes. Stop bitching. You're not in prison, and Sheldrake's having a great year. You cheated your way past NYU, Seton Hall, and Rutgers at home in December. Went 8 and 0. Now you're 25 and 5."

"And rated sixth in the nation—amazing what you can do when you have an edge."

We rolled up to a building at the end of a cul-de-sac.

"Go down the driveway to the left," Kaycee said. "Shut off your lights. The dumpster is probably around the back."

At the end of a long driveway, I turned a corner and was blinded for a moment by a security light. I pulled up to a dumpster under the light, we got out, and I took a breath of very cold air. Then I quickly slipped on latex gloves and an old dress shirt over my sweater and hoisted myself up and over the dumpster's ledge.

"Hit that light," said Kaycee.

"Yes, Ma'am." I grabbed a short two-by-four off to the side, stepped up on a pile of trash, and smashed the light. I ducked as fragments of glass showered down in front of me.

Kaycee, in dirty khakis and a tufted jacket, climbed up on the dumpster's ledge. The moonlight silhouetted her body.

Even climbing into a dumpster she looks good.

She didn't take my hand, jumped in with a flashlight, and said as she rummaged, "Remember, we're looking for company materials . . . They laid off some people today . . . Plenty of things had to be thrown out . . . Someone here is connected to Townsend. We're going to find out who it is."

I gave her a hard look, "I never thought I would wind up in a dumpster with a blonde."

"Focus, Byrnes. Focus."

I bent, uncovered boxes of shredded paper, lunches, bottles, and smelled rot. "Nothing here. They shredded paper. They shredded employees. They shredded everything."

Her flashlight brightened a half-eaten tuna on rye. "Keep looking."

Minutes later, I said, "Hey, a pamphlet."

I handed it across the dumpster to Kaycee, who brightened its pages.

"A five-page company directory. This is it. Now let's get the hell out of here."

As we climbed out of the dumpster, I held my hand out to her, but again, she rejected it.

We drove back to her apartment on quiet city streets emitting an odor that would draw wild animals. Kaycee contacted her office and read the list of employees to someone at an FBI computer. A few minutes later, she said, "Wills was the only name I'm interested in. Could be Williams."

CHAPTER 45

B abe DeCarlo spun around in his office chair, his ear to his cell. "So it's done, Wheels. Who do we play in the first round? . . . Saint Augustine . . . from where? . . . Southeast Gulf Conference. And we got a number-one seed although we have five losses. Thank you, HotShoe. Who do we get in the second round? Cal. You know I'll pay you back, Wheels." Click.

Sitting on the other side of the desk with Giranda, I asked DeCarlo, "How did Wheels know who we play in the tournament before the country knows?"

DeCarlo turned his palms to the ceiling. "What are you, naïve? The majority of selection committee members, including coaches, are HotShoe consultants. We're a HotShoe team, man. Do the math."

"Don't you think the media will figure this out?"

"Investigative reporting is rare. We're safe."

"How many number-one seeds are HotShoe Teams?"

"All of them. But forget about shoes. We've got a number-one seed in the West bracket and we open at UCLA against Saint Augustine. That's what counts."

Standing over me now, Giranda said, "We should win by a hundred. St. Augustine is a nobody."

"That's dangerous thinking," I said. "That's how you set yourself up for an upset."

"They're not in our league," Giranda said. "There's not one player on their team that could make our squad."

DeCarlo pushed off his chair. "Let's go downstairs and watch our team get the news."

We followed DeCarlo around the bleachers to our meeting room, where our players in green-and-gold sweats sat hunched over, their eyes on the large screen. A short white guy in front of our team aimed a camera at our players. Just inside the doorway, DeCarlo stood next to a young woman with a taut face.

Giranda and I slipped behind the players to watch the gleeful draws in the West displayed on the tube one by one. Chosen teams in every school color imaginable came on, cheering and waving. A short minute later, the announcer said, "And seeded number-one in the West bracket, from Atlantic City, Sheldrake College."

The camera's light brightened our players, as they sprang from their seats, cheered wildly as if they had just won the lottery.

I glanced at DeCarlo. *He looks miserable. Maybe it's the predicament he's in.*

The woman stuck a microphone in front of his face and light swung our way. "Congratulations, Coach DeCarlo. Its been a great season for you, but your team hasn't played as well on the road . . . Do you have any reservations about playing on the road in the tournament?"

"I've been to more tournaments more times than you've been to Starbucks. No problem."

"How about last year's first-round game when you lost? Would you hazard a guess as to the outcome of this year's game?"

You're asking the wrong question.

DeCarlo's eyes narrowed. "Yeah. You'll know as little about basketball at the end of our game as you do right now."

The reporter's mouth dropped and she froze for a moment before coming back with, "You're a sixth-ranked team in the AP poll. How do you think you got a number-one seed?"

DeCarlo turned and stormed out the locker room. The reporter gave the cut sign to the cameraman. Then she turned to me with a long face. "I heard he was a tough interview."

"He doesn't disappoint," I said."

The reporter wiggled her head like she was shaking off a fly, handed her mike to the cameraman and turned back to me. "How is Pico Rimpau progressing?"

With Pico and Americus standing behind me, I said, "He's blending in well, averaging double digits off the bench in scoring and rebounding."

"Will DeCarlo ever go with Americus and Pico in the same line-up?"

I glanced at Americus, who shot Pico a dirty look.

"You'll have to ask Coach DeCarlo. That's not my department."

The reporter stared at me for long moment before saying, "I'm not asking that guy anything."

CHAPTER 46

No one saw us off at chilly Atlantic City Airport. Probably because our fans couldn't get odds on whether we would crash upon takeoff.

Six hours later, we registered at a cylindrically shaped hotel off LAs Sunset Boulevard and the 405 Freeway, a few minutes from UCLA, one of the sites of first-round regional play. Prior to getting on a chartered bus at two-thirty for a brief workout, I entered DeCarlo's room through his wide-open door, Across the room, Wheels and DeCarlo argued in front of a large window that framed Santa Monica and its beach in the distance. Wheels, in green sweats, said sharply, "You're forgetting who you answer to . . . Pico needs more visibility. You have to play him at least twenty minutes tomorrow night."

DeCarlo wearing a white T-shirt over black skivvies said "I've changed my mind. Winning is the most important thing. It's not how many future shoes Pico can sell."

I shut the door behind me, stepped into the living room, and stopped when Wheels blasted DeCarlo with, "You screw with me I'll take you out!" Then he turned to me. "What the fuck you looking at?"

I said, "The tourists on top of the red buses know more about basketball than you do."

Wheels said, "Rookie coach . . . shit." His cell phone rang to the chimes of "Here Comes Santa Claus." He put it to his ear, and only said, "Papa Joe . . . Yeah, I'm fast-tracking your man Marquee Smith." With that Wheels hung up and walked out like nothing happened.

"Was he serious?" I asked DeCarlo.

"Just part of the game," he said seriously.

* * *

At mid-afternoon, we bused past multi-million dollar estates on windy Sunset Boulevard to the northern entrance of UCLA's roman-esque campus. We parked in an underground garage a short walk to Pauley Pavilion, a multi-tiered building that housed memories of John Wooden's ten national titles.

Inside, Pico stood at the top of the key and gazed at banners hang-ing from rafters all around. I approached him. "You'll have your own pennant on Boardwalk Hall. It will hang from the rafters, be green with gold, and people will remember."

"Do you think?"

"I know."

* * *

That night, at the beginning of the game, DeCarlo yelled, "Check the defense," the first thing Nitro is supposed to do when he brings the ball down the court the first time. As Nitro slowly dribbled across the mid-court line, our wings crossed from one side of the court to the other, and Americus sprinted to the high post checking to see if a defender was attached to him. If the defense was stationary, it was some kind of zone. Three defenders ran with our guys. It was man-to-man. And twelve thousand fans waited for something to cheer about.

Nitro took a hurried shot.

"Run the offense!" DeCarlo yelled, as if he thought the players were in shock and couldn't remember what they had practiced and employed for the past five months. But it was DeCarlo who was unnerved.

We're bigger, quicker. St. Augustine is methodical on offense. We're anxious—throw up a hurried shot after one pass. Impatience spells trouble.

If I were coaching this team . . .

"Call timeout," I blurted to DeCarlo. "We're out of sync."

DeCarlo, his eyes fixed on the game, said, "Shut the fuck up."

Minutes passed. We got behind. The crowd began cheering for St. Augustine.

DeCarlo sprang from his chair, walked down the sideline to mid-court, and yelled at Nitro, "Run the damn offense!"

Nitro puts up an errant twenty-five footer. Returning to defense he shakes his head as he glances at DeCarlo.

I reposition myself in my chair.

Get down ten and we'll lose. No championship game. I can't take this.

"Call time out," I repeated. "Settle our team down or we'll be out of it."

DeCarlo turned to me. "If I want your fuckin' advice, I'll ask for it."

We try to intercept each pass. They backdoor us. How many times have they done that? I can't count. We're screwed.

I glanced up at the scoreboard.

Seconds left. 30–20. Not good. We've got 20. Fans are still rooting for St. Augustine. The horn blares ending the half.

I followed jogging players across the court to a meeting room. DeCarlo trailed. In seconds the team was in front of a corked wall, a white board to the side.

Players are silent. Eyes on the door. Fear of DeCarlo is alive.

Thunder!

DeCarlo kicked in the door. Wrapped his hands around a folding chair. Swung it back, came forward like a hammer throw. Let it fly.

"Oh, God!" shouted a player.

Heads ducked. Chair legs pierced the cork wall, then vibrated.

The only sound in the room was a ticking clock.

Wild-eyed, DeCarlo made his way toward the head of the room and yelled, "Is there anyone in this room who would like to have a St. Augustine scholarship tomorrow? Anyone who'd like to go home tomorrow and not play Saturday? Anyone who'd like to remember losing to St. Augustine for the rest of their lives?"

DeCarlo stared down all the players. They were as still as museum statues. Then he walked to the back of the room and threw open the door, which had a splintered hole in the bottom panel.

Players flushed out the room, yelling the unprintable.

Seconds later, they received polite applause on the court.

I took my courtside seat next to DeCarlo, whose eyes were two deaths.

"Okay," I yelled to the players warming up. "Twenty minutes to settle the score."

Play ensued. Each player playing for a memory of a game that would never fade.

We're a different team. Energetic, focused. Intercepting passes . . . Our shots go down . . . St. Augustine looks like St. Augustine, not the L.A. Lakers . . . Where's Pico? He's not playing. DeCarlo is getting back at Wheels.

The final horn blared.

I look up at the scoreboard. Sheldrake 61, Saint Augustine 47.

The final score between Wheels and DeCarlo is yet to be settled.

CHAPTER 47

The phone on DeCarlo's bed stand rang. He jumped up from the cushioned sofa and scooted around the bed, leaving Giranda and me to watch Cal's tournament win on the computer.

"DeCarlo here . . . yes, Dr. Hammer . . . What? . . . What?" DeCarlo's voice grew taut. Blood drained out of his face. "So they fucked me good . . . what paper?" He slammed the phone down, circled back and opened the hallway door. He returned with an *L.A. Times*, leaving a trail of sections behind him. Then he stopped in front of us holding the edges of the Sports Section.

I leaned forward and cautiously asked, "So what do the words 'fucked me good' mean?"

DeCarlo said, "Listen to this headline, asshole. 'SHELDRAKE BEATS ST. AUGUSTINE, LOSES TO NCAA. The NCAA Infractions Committee, upon an in-depth investigation of Sheldrake College Basketball, has leveled the program. Beginning immediately after the NCAA Basketball tournament, and for a period of two years, Sheldrake will lose seven scholarships and return tournament money.'

"That's the good part," he said. "Now hear this: 'Sheldrake shall disassociate from boosters and cancel the booster program. Furthermore, Coach Babe DeCarlo, under NCAA probation for breaking recruiting rules at All-Saints University, will receive the death penalty. After

tournament play he will be barred from employment by all NCAA basketball programs.'"

"Oh shit," I uttered under my breath.

DeCarlo discarded the section as if he were tossing a playing card
into a hat. As it sailed to the floor, he said, "I knew those bastards were
coming for me."

*It's all about DeCarlo. What about Pico? The rest of the players?
Giranda? Me?*

I suddenly had visions of being at the end of a very long unemployment line.

The bedside phone rang again, breaking my thought pattern.

DeCarlo marched over and snatched it. "Yeah!" Silence. Then, "I
don't care if you're AP, UP, or peed all over yourself—you don't know
the whole story. The NCAA fucked me. They ripped my heart out and
ate it. Sure, you can quote me." He side-armed the receiver against the
wall denting the plaster with a thud.

DeCarlo isn't going to crawl off the stage.

He turned to us. "It's not over. We play tomorrow. We're still in the
tournament. Giranda, get the players together for a meeting downstairs
now."

"Balls to the wall," I said.

"Balls to the wall," DeCarlo repeated.

A half hour and much uncertainty later, we met the team in a room
near the lobby. The room was large enough for a lot of attitude and
twelve chairs around a long table.

I sat across from Pico and listened to the mumbles and grumbles that
come with a crisis.

DeCarlo pounded the table with his fist, then stood and softly sum-
marized the newspaper story. The room went silent. DeCarlo tried to
fire up players who had vacant eyes. "We're going all the way," he said.
"The NCAA wants to see us lose. But, we're going to screw them by
winning."

During the chalk talk, I couldn't help but look across the table at
Pico's hand. Flat on the table, his ring finger was adorned with a gold

piece that had a ruby setting.

Gold band. Ruby setting. Inscriptions around the setting. Looks like a championship ring.

DeCarlo said to the team, "You all came to Sheldrake to have a chance at winning the title. Well, here we are . . . and we play tomorrow. Now tell me about the man you're going to cover, Americus. Tell me about Hansen."

The stone-faced center said, "Coach, he can drive to his right or his left. He's amphibious."

Looks, giggles, then laughter all around with the exception of DeCarlo.

DeCarlo's hard gaze unchanged, he said, "Apparently, Americus, you're ready to play. All of you need to be ready. Study your assignments. Cal is tough. We're favored by three. That tells you how tough they are."

After the team was dismissed, I stopped Pico in middle of the hallway, pointed at his ring.

"Pico, that's an interesting-looking ring. May I see it?"

He smiled, took it off, and handed it to me. "NCAA Championship," he said.

I examined all sides. "Wow, NCAA Champions, St. Johns, 1995. Where did you get it?"

"Pawn shop in Atlantic City."

"What pawn shop?"

"O'Reilly's. Why?"

"This could have been Mansfield's ring. He played on that team. There can't be more than twenty of these rings when you count players, coaches, and administration. Let me borrow it when we get back to Atlantic City. And Pico . . . don't tell anyone you loaned it to me."

"I don't know nothin'."

"Thanks. Now be ready when called upon."

"I was ready two nights ago. The man never called me. Now I'm going to bring a mystery novel in my jock so I'll have something to do."

My eyebrows shot up. "You got to be kidding."

"Yeah," he laughed, "just wanted to see your face."

After leaving Pico, I headed for an empty men's room, took a far stall, and called Kaycee about the ring.

*   *   *

That night, above the noise of twelve thousand screaming fans, DeCarlo yelled, "Get the ball into Americus. That's it . . . Take him, Americus . . . way to go . . . Don't gloat . . . get back."

The crowd and the cameras don't bother me tonight . . . five more games and we're in the finals.

Ten minutes to go in the first half. DeCarlo pointed down the bench at Pico who quickly slipped off his warm-ups and crossed in front of me to report to the scorer's table.

Players sprint back and forth. Green on gold one way, navy and gold the other . . . Shots go up . . . Whistles blare . . . Free throws go down.

Pico is a one-man zone on defense. Here comes 23 of Cal. That's A.C. Johnson. Drives past Nitro . . . in the air in front of Pico. Pico coils. Johnson lofts one above the rim. Pico springs, reaches, swats it out of bounds. Deafening crowd noise . . . Jeez, what timing.

I looked up at the clock. A minute left in the first half. We were down two.

Johnson fouls Nitro above the key. 26-foot shot. That's stupid. Nitro makes two of three free throws. Horn sounds. We're tied.

Deep in the second half, I turned left to Giranda and pointed at my clipboard stats. "Number 23, Johnson. Zero for six from the field. Seven turn-overs. And this guy is going to be a draft choice?"

His eyes on the flow of the game, Giranda said, "Johnson's an All-American idiot."

The horn sounds, ending the game. I stood, looked up at the score-board. 60-56. Four wins from the title.

Our team bumped fists and gave Cal some half-hugs. We jogged toward the locker room, passed long tables just outside the sideline boundaries where the media and dignitaries were seated.

A tall man dressed in a dark suit with a headset clamped on his shiny bald head and a mic in his hand blocked DeCarlo's path. "Coach DeCarlo," he asked, "how does it feel to lose to the NCAA and beat Cal on the same day?"

DeCarlo growled, "I have a file on the NCAA which I'm going to reveal next week. They fucked me. Now I'm gonna fuck them." He brushed away the mike with a hand and loped to the locker room.

The reporter blurted into his mic, "Are we on a seven-second delay?" *What-the-hell file is DeCarlo talking about?*

CHAPTER 48

ATLANTIC CITY AIRPORT
MONDAY, MARCH 14
5 P.M.

There was a bounce to my step when I exited the plane behind our team. Thoughts of Townsend, NCAA penalties, and DeCarlo's suspension were overrun by visions of playing in the Sweet Sixteen. But my nerves turned raw when a wall of reporters closed in on DeCarlo shouting questions about the NCAA secrets he was going to disclose.

DeCarlo, who left the plane with Wheels, plowed through the paparazzi creating a wake of talking heads. Then he crossed the border from folly to preposterous when he said over his shoulder, "I'm going to bury the NCAA."

Seconds later, reporters pursued DeCarlo from the baggage carousel to curbside. There a valet brought up Wheels' Mercedes and they both got in. Surprised me. They were at each other's throats in L.A.

I was waiting with the team for my luggage to come down when someone tapped me on the shoulder. I turned and came face-to-face with a flat-nosed man with deep-set eyes, and yellowed teeth.

"Any injuries?" the man asked in a voice that sounded like pebbles and Brooklynese thrown into a blender.

Injuries change point spreads.

I chose my words carefully, said, "Fuck off."

He did.

I spotted Kaycee striding towards me from the street entrance. My heart jumped. I gave her a wide smile. Wearing a short black skirt, spike heels, and a red ski jacket, she smiled back. Then she closed in, gave me a hug, and whispered in my ear, "Let's see Pico's ring."

A relationship of biblical proportions popped like a balloon.

I glanced at the other side of the carousel where Pico shot me a smile suggesting I had something going. I did. We were going to trace the ring. But not then. I had a coachs' meeting at seven. Our staff had little time to prepare for Colorado State before we were back on a plane Thursday.

Giranda and the players boarded two green Sheldrake vans in the white zone for a ride back to the college. I got into Kaycee's car and showed her the ring. She shrugged, seemingly unimpressed. In thirty minutes we arrived at my apartment. But she wouldn't come in. The mini skirt must have been for the crowd.

At seven, I approached DeCarlo's office with Giranda. The door to the office was wide open. So were my eyes. File drawers were pulled out. Papers strewn all over the place. The computer gone. Our casually-dressed secretary was on her hands and knees picking up the mess.

"What the hell?" I said.

The secretary straightened as if hit by electricity. Her eyes flitted from Giranda to me. Her voice unsteady, she said, "Somebody called me for Coach DeCarlo. The guy said I didn't have to work Saturday—so I didn't. Then I felt guilty about not picking up Saturday's mail. LOOK AT THIS!"

"Did you recognize the guy's voice?" I asked.

"No."

I peeked into the assistant's office. Everything was in order. Then a light went on in my head. I swung back to Giranda, and said sharply, "Someone was looking for the dirt DeCarlo said he had on the NCAA."

"No. DeCarlo popped off Saturday night." He pointed absently at the secretary. "She said someone called her on Friday."

"Someone had the keys to this place," I said, "or knew how to pick the lock."

Expecting DeCarlo to show up any minute, we collected all the files and piled them on the cabinet. The secretary would deal with it. We didn't call the police. We didn't need questions about our business. The burglar may have known that.

I waited patiently at Giranda's desk while studying a DVD of our next opponent, Colorado State.

Seven-thirty.

No sign of DeCarlo.

Eight-thirty.

We had more scouting notes than we needed. I turned to Giranda. "What do you think?"

Eyes peeled to the monitor, he said, "Colorado State has a player we can't stop."

I said with an edge, "We're missing a coach who mouthed off about the NCAA."

He smiled. "The full moon get you?"

"Look what happened to Mansfield. Missing person. I think we've got another one."

I crossed the room and called DeCarlo's cell from my desk. Left a message. Called his home. More voice mail. Then I dialed the president. Dr. Hammer said DeCarlo was scheduled to meet with him in his office at eight the next morning.

I told Giranda.

He said, "There's probably a good explanation."

"Or a bad explanation."

I remembered my first meeting with Kaycee, and her suspicions about Mansfield's disappearance and my tenuous status. Again, I thought the worst. The room turned cold, or was it just my hands and feet?

I took a breath and phoned Wheels. All I got was, "I dropped DeCarlo at the garage at six. No one else around. I wouldn't worry. He probably has a girl friend you don't know about."

"I don't think DeCarlo would confuse preparing for the biggest game of his life with prom night."

I called the hospital. They'd heard of DeCarlo but hadn't seen him.

Hoping that DeCarlo would still show up, I joined Giranda and watched Colorado State's last game, tapping my pen on the desk from tip-off to the horn.

Ten o'clock.

I pushed away from Giranda's desk, said, "I'm going home. If DeCarlo doesn't show up tomorrow morning, I'm calling the cops."

I stepped out onto the boardwalk and met a whipping wind. My neatly combed hair blew in every direction. I zipped up my black leather jacket and dialed Kaycee. Heading towards my apartment, I said, "Kaycee, DeCarlo was a no-show this evening. I think he's *adios*."

"If he doesn't show up tomorrow morning, call ACPD, but don't tell them about our arrangement."

"You covering me?"

"Make sure you're not followed."

"That's not a cover." I clicked off, looked over my shoulder. No one around. The only sound was the roar of a crashing wave on the beach.

CHAPTER 49

DeCarlo's absence and the big tournament game made me toss and turn all night.

When I showed up at the office at eight, Giranda was at his desk reviewing Colorado State reports. I paced the room until eight-thirty, then called Hammer. He said DeCarlo was a no-show.

I suspected that a line would be drawn through DeCarlo's name when I called Missing Persons at nine. A guy working the desk listened to me, then said, "We don't act until forty-eight hours after a disappearance. But since it's Sheldrake basketball, we'll send someone right over."

A half-hour later, I heard a commanding voice: "You Conrad Byrnes?"

My eyes snapped from the game plan on my desk to a man at the door. Medium build, unwrinkled, cheap blue suit, short brown hair, erect posture. He was the kind of guy who would never miss a belt loop.

"I'm Byrnes."

"Detective Horst, ACPD." Stepping forward, he flashed a badge and I.D. card. "You reported the disappearance of Babe DeCarlo. Have you heard from him since you called?"

"No."

"No, huh?" He lowered himself into a hard chair on the other side of my desk. "I've been working the Mansfield case. Looks like someone doesn't like Sheldrake coaches."

I couldn't put two words together. Finally said, "Yeah."

Horst took out a pad and a pen and flipped a page. Then he air-balled questions about ransom notes, enemies' list, death threats, and girlfriends. Not stopping there, he said, "We checked DeCarlo's credit card. He last used it in L.A. So who was the last person to see him?"

"Jimmy Wheeler," Giranda said from across the room. "He said he was going to drop DeCarlo here from the airport. That was yesterday about six."

"Wheeler?" Horst said. "The HotShoe guy who runs college basketball?"

"The same," I said, reaching into my desk drawer to fish out a press guide. I turned to page one and handed it to Horst. "Here's a photo of DeCarlo." Then I told him what DeCarlo was wearing on the flight and the look of his carry-on bag.

Horst leaned forward and lowered his voice a fraction. "Was DeCarlo suicidal? I mean the NCAA just cancelled his career."

"No. He was excited about getting this far in the tournament."

"Do you know of anyone who would like to see DeCarlo dead?"

Do I know!

"Every player non-starter on our team at one time or another. Then you can add several thousand fans . . . but that's basketball."

"Yeah, I played high-school ball. Didn't see much action." He glanced down . . . "Hated the coach." He scratched something on his writing pad. "So, Coach Byrnes, what else can you tell me about DeCarlo?"

I thought for a moment, said, "He only saw basketball, never saw life."

"Tell me about it."

I walked Horst past DeCarlo's file cabinet towards the hallway. Suddenly he stopped and asked, "Where were you between six and seven last night?"

"In my apartment. My girlfriend dropped me from the airport. You don't think . . ."

"Just asking." He continued walking, said, "We'll have a crime-scene guy come by for prints." He stopped again. "And what was in DeCarlo's computer?"

"We have no idea."

"Anything else you want to tell me?"

Yeah. I'm working with the FBI.

"Nothing you'd be interested in."

CHAPTER 50

We met with the players after lunch in the locker room. My arms crossed, I stood before twelve sets of dark inquisitive eyes in Sheldrake sweats. They sat quietly in two rows, maybe anticipating my words. Other than having been Pico's tutor and team scout, I didn't know them very well. And I was unsure of what to say.

DeCarlo was ugly. Took you to the Promised Land . . . Odds are good for you, bad for me. I could be next. Could be at death's door.

Giranda and I spoke at the same time.

I said, "DeCarlo's not coming."

Vying to take over the reins, he said, "Let me have your attention."

Nitro, sitting directly in front of me, said, "Coach Byrnes, where's DeCarlo?"

Looking at Giranda, I said, "I'll handle this." I faced Nitro. "DeCarlo disappeared."

There was a babble of negative confusion. I heard, "Gone? Not coming back? Did he do a Mansfield?"

With Giranda staring daggers at me, I said to the team, "You guys come from neighborhoods where people disappear all the time . . . where people face all kinds of problems . . . where some people quit on themselves . . . But you're here because you have a habit of battling through the impossible . . . This is one of those times, when you need to suck up your guts and defeat the monster in your head."

"Okay. So who's gonna coach?" Nitro asked, as if I was just another community organizer trying to break through years of 'no way out' situations.

Pico, sitting behind Nitro, said, "That's cold, man."

"That's President Hammer's decision," I said. "But no matter who coaches, we have the players." I pointed at each player, looked into their eyes, then said, "You can't win without players. And you guys are the toughest bunch that ever played in the tournament." I swallowed. "So nothing is going to change." I held up my palms. "Same offense, same defense. Unless Hammer says otherwise, Coach Giranda and I will be with you all the way. So it's on to Portland and let's win there."

"Are we going to workout?" Nitro asked..

"We're taking today off. Next workout's tomorrow at two. And don't talk to the media."

"Who's going to disappear next?" Americus Hart asked.

"Colorado State, Friday night."

I thought my comment was timely. But all I got were looks of resignation and uncertainty.

"Hang in there," I said. "I know this is difficult. But if we hang together, everything will work out."

I followed the team as they filtered out of the room. Some mumbles, some grumbles. In the hallway, they passed five reporters in casual attire who quickly closed in on me like I was good ink.

"Where's DeCarlo?"

"Was DeCarlo fired?"

"Is he connected to the Mansfield disappearance?"

"How do the players feel?"

"The players will do what they need to do," I said. "The police are investigating. And I can't comment on the case."

"Do you think there's a chance of DeCarlo returning?"

"I don't know. But my thoughts and prayers are with him."

What I really mean is *My thoughts and prayers are with me. He's gone.*

CHAPTER 51

By the time I arrived at Kaycee's office, DeCarlo's disappearance was all over the news. Sitting behind her desk, she asked me the same questions as had Detective Horst. After getting nowhere, she said, "Hold on to your balls, Byrnes; this is going to be a rougher ride than I thought. I hope you're not the next coach."

"Will it ruin our relationship?"

"Might mess up your face."

*   *   *

I drove Kaycee's car towards O'Reilly's Pawn Shop where Pico had purchased the ring. It was on the south end of town. A real shit hole. Bad bars, bad vibes. If someone was looking for the scene of a crime, all they had to do was come here and wait.

I pulled up in front of O'Reilly's and we got out. The shop window was full of guitars and cheap watches strung with small price tags. Inside, it was money under glass. The counter to our left showcased Tiffany stuff, Patek Phillippe, Constantin, and Cartier watches. The long case straight ahead displayed enough handguns and automatics to take the town. We were the only customers.

A man behind the counter said in a raspy voice, "If we don't have it, you don't want it." He was unsmiling, short, bald as a light bulb, and had a prune-face.

We approached him. I dug the St. John's ring out of my pocket and handed it over. "A friend of mine bought this ring here ... See the inscriptions? St. John's, NCAA Champions . . . I'd like another."

The man looked me over, not unusual for an appraiser. Then, studying the ring, he turned it slowly so that the round ruby caught the overhead lighting. "Let me see what we have," he said. "Be right back." He went into the back room.

Kaycee gave me a shrug as if to say, "Maybe we're on to something."

Within seconds, the man returned with an assortment of rings on a red velvet pillow and placed it on the counter. Wedding, birthstone, graduation rings. He said, "The gamblers brought these in recently." He pointed to an encrusted diamond wedding band. "How 'bout it?"

Kaycee gave me a sideways smile, then said to the man, "Thank you. We want to know who pawned the NCAA ring. Maybe they have another just like it."

"Hey," the man exclaimed. "That's personal stuff."

Kaycee reached into her wallet, pulled out two crisp Franklins, and placed them on the counter. "This should cover personal stuff."

The man snatched up the bills as if he were going to make a run for it. "Give me a moment." He returned to the back room.

I heard the soft tapping of computer keys. Then he reappeared and handed Kaycee chicken-scratches on notepaper. I looked over her shoulder and made out A. Wills. 1025 Pacific, Atlantic City.

My mind rewound. Vegas. *Townsend's man Williams AKA Wills.*

Kaycee turned back to the man. "Do you know what Wills looks like?"

"You might find out by going to that address."

*   *   *

The Pacific address turned out to be a field of weeds next to a two-story, clapboard house. A dead end. I stood on the sidewalk with Kaycee, dumfounded. Unperturbed, she turned to me and said, "Wills must be Williams. My initial search of Wills didn't turn up anything, but I'm going to keep checking. And I'm also going to look for DeCarlo on a slab. He could be under a John Doe."

I took a step towards the car and stopped. "So what's the connection between Mansfield and DeCarlo? Two basketball coaches at the same school disappear. No motive. One suspect in Townsend. No prints."

"Townsend wants the new casino. That's all we know. But the answer could be right in front of us, and we don't see it."

"Or right behind me."

Chapter 52

In the office with Giranda the next morning, I stopped answering the landline. One more reporter wanting an update on DeCarlo was one too many.

Another ring. My cell. A familiar number. "Coach Byrnes here."

The words, "This is Townsend," sent chills down the length of my spine.

When he said, "I want to talk to you about DeCarlo's job," I didn't bubble over.

"It's nine, " he continued. "Be in my office in a half-hour. You're interested, aren't you?"

I cleared my throat, glanced at Giranda, who also was a candidate, and said softly, "I'll be there."

"I've got to go," I said to Giranda. "Be back soon."

Giranda shot me a suspicious look, like he knew why I was leaving. But he said nothing.

* * *

Twenty-five minutes later, I passed through security at the Cockatoo Bar, avoided the puddles in the tunnel, said "Hi," to the man with the bad job, and took the elevator to Townsend's penthouse. When the elevator door slid open, Townsend was there to meet me in his ever-present black and white attire.

He was as cold as an ice sculpture with a twenty mph wind chill. He didn't shake my hand. But he didn't have to. It was shaking on its own.

"Conrad, your time has come."

I faked a smile.

He motioned me over to one of the parallel couches. I sank into a pillow-back and sat across from him.

He leaned forward, placed his elbows on his knees, and went "Brutus" on me. "DeCarlo was a good man," he said. "DeCarlo broke rules and dishonored the college. We aren't going to operate like DeCarlo any more. This is going to be a straight program."

Fuck you too.

"Since DeCarlo isn't coming back," Townsend continued, "I want to appoint you head coach. There's a tough game coming up, but I think you're ready." He paused. "Now the only question is . . . do *you* think you're ready?"

I could hear my heart pounding and thought Townsend could hear it too. Nothing like signing up with someone who may be a serial killer. I swallowed hard. An affirmative could mean I was closer to death than I ever had been, and closer to coaching the NCAA champion. I took a deep breath and exhaled, "Yeah, I'm ready."

"Good," Townsend said, "We have to move on this. It will be good for all concerned. You'll be on DeCarlo's pay schedule—per day of course. Now go see Hammer and sign the contract."

"Why per day?"

"We're going to see how you work out."

"You mean if I win, I continue to coach?"

"Something like that." I walked towards the elevator, Townsend close behind, my world running at thirty-two frames per second.

"One more thing."

I stopped dead in my tracks thinking he was going to deliver the kicker.

But he said, "When the reporters drill you, tell them 'You're just a high school coach trying to do a job.'"

He hit a nerve. "I don't want my team reading that."

"Tell the press what I said. We're softening up the opposition."

*   *   *

I waited in the president's conference room for ten minutes, the first five picturing myself making coaching errors, the second five seeing myself disappear.

Finally, Hammer entered wearing a dark suit and holding a red folder. He immediately took a seat at the head of the table, one chair away from me, glanced out the window at the Mardi Gras, then opened the folder on the table. "I want to tell you," he said, "that I feel very bad that we've lost DeCarlo. But now that he's gone, we're going to appeal the NCAA penalties. After all, it was DeCarlo who brought the NCAA down on us."

Bullshit.

Hammer wasted no time placing the document in front of me. "This is our agreement. One thousand per day until it's over. Sign here."

The words "until it's over" gave me mixed emotions, all bad.

He handed me a pen that my clammy fingers quickly dampened. I looked at the number, then scratched my signature above my printed name. I was more anxious than eager, more frightened than thrilled. The job was everything I'd ever wanted—and less.

We stood. I wiped my wet palm on the back of my pants, shook hands with Hammer, and walked out of the office feeling dazed.

Downstairs in a first-floor men's room, I called Kaycee. "You're talking to the new head basketball coach of Sheldrake College. Townsend gave the word."

"That's a zinger. I thought Giranda would get the job. Be careful, Byrnes, and keep me up to speed."

CHAPTER 53

I strode into the basketball office, stopping in front of Giranda, "They appointed me head coach."

Giranda peered over his computer monitor and said with dripping contempt, "DeCarlo's car is in the fuckin' garage."

I barked back, "You're pissed about not getting the head job . . . That's not my fault."

"They should have talked to me—I've got seniority."

"Look, this isn't the post office. It's the crazy game of college basketball—and I only got a day rate. How good is that? If I lose Friday, I'm out of a job. You want to help me until then or don't you? If you do, we have to prop up the players, develop a game plan, and keep away from the invisible hand of death. You can have the fuckin' car. Are you in or out?"

"I'll take the car, and I'm in, but I don't know why."

"Well, neither do I."

Giranda's landline rang.

"Don't pick it up," I said.

"What if it's a player?"

"They have our cell numbers. It's the press. We don't have time for them."

We spent the next half-hour devising a simple plan against Colorado State that could work if our players weren't disoriented and I could coach. CSU had Sky King, a six-nine, two-thirty kid. He was good enough to hurt us. He could hit the three or drive for the slam. But he didn't have a mid-range shot. We planned to pick him up on the perimeter with our big forward, Willard Penn, and force him to drive into Americus or Pico. Then he'd go for the hoop and we'd give him a leather sandwich.

Giranda and I walked onto the proscenium end of the arena floor at two o'clock to see the players warm up. They were loose. Too loose. Acrobatic shots and drop kicks—just as I feared. They were as disoriented as I was. I tried to remember how I coached in high school under difficult conditions and blew my whistle. I yelled, "Okay, all you circus performers, on the baseline."

They took their sweet time lining up.

I walked down the line peering intently into their eyes, got back to the middle, and said, "I've been appointed head coach."

My words were greeted with dead silence.

I continued. "Some of you may be thinking 'Let's see if he can coach us.' Well, there's no time to test each other. This is most the important game of our lives. A win Friday and we play Sunday to get into the final four." I walked slowly to my right, eyeing each of them, stopping in front of Nitro, where I said, "I know I can coach. You know you can play. So you have to trust me to make good decisions, and I have to trust you to carry out those decisions. But you still have a choice. Walk away from the greatest playing opportunity of your lifetime—or go for it . . . I say we go for it. What do you say?"

To my delight, Nitro threw up a fist and barked, "Gofur it."

There were instant shouts of agreement.

I put the back of my hand out. It lingered there a moment. Then the players gathered around and laid their hands on top of my cold one like the spokes of a wheel.

"Ready?" I said.

The players yelled, "SHELDRAKE," and withdrew their hands.

"Okay," I said. "Ten minutes of concentration on our game plan. We are going to stop Sky King. And there are no more Bastards or Sons of

Bitches on our team. That's over."

That was greeted with a round of applause.

The players took the floor and we walked through the plan. Minutes later we went full-tilt, both teams going after one another. During the next half-hour we ran five-on-five break drills and three-man shooting drills. Then I ended practice. Our late season legs were tired legs, and we weren't going to leave our game on the practice floor.

I dismissed them with, "We leave from the parking garage at nine tomorrow morning. Although we play in Portland Friday, I want you packed for five days. Don't plan on coming home Saturday because we're going to have another game to play on Sunday."

I stand next to the opening of the participants' tunnel, fans streaming into the stadium all around. I unroll my game program and flatten it out against the cold cement wall to my right, then write in the margins of a HotShoe ad on the inside back cover.

> *I, Conrad Byrnes, being of sound mind and poor judgment, knowing that I will die at game's end, will the following to the Northern Lights Mission in Philadelphia: One bike, One Corvette that needs an oil change, One Atlantic City National Bank checking account that needs to be balanced. I wish to be buried at the entry to Lucas Oil Stadium. My tombstone to say, "Conrad Byrnes. He was sold, went for the gold, now he's cold." I also want my brother, Jordan, to know that I loved him to the end.*
>
> *Conrad Byrnes*

CHAPTER 54

During the long flight to Portland, Giranda reached across the narrow aisle and handed me a sports page with a large photo of Pico blocking someone's shot. The beginning of the article read:

SHELDRAKE SEEKS TO PART NCAA
WATERS WITH ROOKIES IN PORTLAND
By Jordan Taylor

Two potential heroes, Pico Rimpau and Conrad Byrnes, combine their talents for tiny Sheldrake College when its quintet faces off against Colorado State in the Sweet Sixteen of the NCAA tournament tomorrow night in Portland. One year ago, center Pico Rimpau was on skid row in Los Angeles, a runaway from St. Andrews Orphanage. On the move, he had a dream—to be a college basketball player. He wanted to be like the players in the big arena that he saw when he slipped in to gaze at TVs in skid row bars. One year ago, Conrad Byrnes was a high school coach in Los Angeles watching the national tournament on TV. As far-fetched as it may seem, his dream was to coach the NCAA Champion. Today,

Rimpau is an emerging 6-9 star, who comes off the bench to clear the way for Sheldrake victories. And Byrnes has been thrust into the Sheldrake head coaching position after the mysterious disappearance of Babe DeCarlo. When interviewed outside Atlantic City's Boardwalk Hall after a workout, Rimpau said, "I'm excited. Today people stop to ask me for autographs. One year ago, the only people who stopped me were cops. I owe it all to Coach Byrnes." Regarding the Colorado State game, Rimpau said, "They're good. But like Coach Byrnes says, 'This is our time.'" Although Conrad Byrnes declined to be interviewed, it wouldn't surprise this reporter if he said he was overwhelmed by the veteran coaches in his path, and glad that Pico Rimpau is on his side.

I finished the article, pissed about Jordan's comments regarding me. Then I squirmed out of my seat, stood in the aisle, and located Pico halfway back in the full plane. I held up the paper and pointed to the article. A wide grin crossed his face as if he had read it. The good, the bad, and the ugly eyes of basketball would be all over him now, and it was my responsibility to protect him from the ugly eyes.

CHAPTER 55

We landed in Portland, Oregon, on Thursday, oblivious to every thing but our game. When a reporter stopped me at the baggage carousel to ask about our agenda, I replied, "Eat, sleep, and warm-up." At least that's what I'd planned.

We checked in at the upscale Nomah Hotel a few blocks from the Rose Garden, the site of our regional Sweet Sixteen game. The hotel was in lock-down. The only way someone could get to us was through the registration desk, and they had blackout orders.

No sooner did I settle into a soft chair than my phone rang. It was Bob Roberts, assistant at Colorado State. I asked him how he got through. Like a good recruiter who was capable of anything, he said, "I told the desk that I was your brother, who just got back from the war."

I thought, *anyone that good deserves my attention.*

"Go on."

Roberts said, "I have something that's very important to you."

I told him to come up, because in this business you never know.

A few minutes later someone pounded my door. I swung it open to a tall white guy in yellow PayDay sweats. His hair was disheveled, and his green Polo collar was up on one side. Wild eyes indicated he was a smash-a-beer-can-to-the-forehead kind of guy. After quickly checking the hall both ways, he said, "Coach Byrnes . . . Bob Roberts. We need to talk."

"Two minutes."

He stepped inside and perked me up with, "Sky King wants to transfer to Sheldrake. You could be number one in the polls next season with him even though you're on probation."

"Go on."

He opened a palm. "Colorado State isn't renewing my contract, and I'm looking for a new home. I'll take Sky King with me. I brought the son-of-a-bitch to State and I'll take him out. Sky King wants to be a lottery pick. Forty million. Not going to happen this year. He's only averaging twenty. But at Sheldrake it could be thirty."

"So you want five percent when Sky King goes pro?"

He gave me a knowing smile. "Wouldn't you? Listen, Sky King is from Philly. He will be eligible right away."

There was another knock on the door.

Roberts said, "I told Wheels I'd be here. He's in on the deal."

"Whose fuckin' program is this anyway?" I muttered as I reluctantly stepped toward the door.

Wheels' long head appeared in the peephole. I opened the door a crack.

"Is he here?" Wheels spapped. "Is Roberts here?"

I opened the door all the way. Wheels entered the short entry and shook hands with Roberts, then went to the half-hug. Wheels and Roberts sat down on the living room couch. I took a chair across from them and steamed. Then, no small talk, just numbers. Roberts would get two-hundred-K when King enrolled at Sheldrake. Another two hundred when King signed with HotShoe.

Roberts stood, and said to Wheels, "Sky King is as good as in a Sheldrake uniform."

I raised my voice. "Sky King may be a great player, but this is my program for the moment and I decide who stays and who goes."

As if he were hard of hearing, Wheels held up a hand to me, and said, "We'll talk."

I shut up until Wheels let Roberts out. Then turning back, he said excitedly, "If you stay at Sheldrake, you can have Marquee Smith,

Rimpau, and King in the same lineup."

Wrong.

Simmering, I said, "You may run college basketball, but now you don't run me. Who the fuck is Roberts, anyway?"

"Calm down, Byrnes. Roberts used to run the travel team New York United. Payday bought him and Sky King. A package deal."

"Talks like a guy with a rap sheet."

"He's clean. Beat a drug rap and a child-molestation charge. What's important—he delivers."

"Oh, that's great," I said, dripping with sarcasm. "And what about Sky King's character?"

"He was innocent of the drive-by."

I paused a moment to reflect. "Count me out. I'm not playing slime ball for a damn shoe and high poll numbers."

Wheels' eyebrows shot up. "Every guy on your team except Pico has a sheet."

"I inherited those guys."

"That's basketball."

"Look, I've had enough."

"Hey, Byrnes, there's no room in this game for a coach who's had enough."

Wheels exited just as my landline rang. I answered.

"Something's going on," Pico said. "I need you to come down to my room."

"What is it?"

"You wouldn't believe it if I told you."

A few minutes later, I came to Pico's room where the door was wide open. Pico was standing in the middle of the room. The smile that he brought to Portland was gone. My eyes shot over to a Black man sitting in a sofa next to a rain-streaked window.

"Who's that?" I asked Pico.

Pico, his ball clamped against his hip, pointed at the man but didn't smile. "This man says he's my father."

The man stood. He was of average height. Pico was six-nine. Pico had long fingers. The guy had stubs. Pico's face was long. The man's face was round, unshaven. Offering a smile, he said, I'm John Darby. Pico's father. Pico told me a lot about you."

His voice was ragged, like he'd smoked his way through life. He wore stained black pants, HotShoes and a tattered jean jacket over a T-shirt.

No likeness. Fraud father. Money in his pocket.

I clenched my teeth.

He stuck out his hand.

My muscles tensed and I did not shake it.

Darby withdrew his hand and glared at me.

I gestured to the sofa. "Sit down, Darby. You too, Pico."

Darby returned to his seat, and Pico took to the sofa, his ball on his lap.

I remained standing a few feet from them. "Okay, Darby, let's have it. How did you find Pico?"

"I read an article on the AP. Called around."

His tone was matter of fact but with an edge now.

"How did you find his room?"

"One of the players told me."

I shook my head. "You from L. A. or just a guy passing through?"

"I lived there for many years," Darby said. "I left shortly before Pico was born. Hey, this is my son . . . don't you believe me?"

Pico began to rub up the basketball's pebbled surface.

I said, "You better downshift, Darby. You've got a big hill to climb. Tell me, what's Pico's real name?"

Darby folded his arms. "John Darby Jr. What else?"

I tried to gain some more ground with, "You have a birth certificate?"

Darby ignored me, turned to Pico, and said, "John, you are my son and I've come back for you."

My voice hardened. "So you have no proof that Pico is your son."

Darby turned back to me, said calmly, "Look, my wife left him. But I am his father."

My ears pricked up and I began to pace. "Why didn't you search for him when you learned that she dumped him?"

Darby went silent.

Pico pushed off the sofa and crossed the carpeted floor with the ball clamped to his hip, blocking my view of Darby for an instant. Then he looked daggers at Darby. "So I've got to be SOMEBODY before you can claim me? What am I to you—a horse?"

Darby said, "I didn't know where you were until today."

Pico snapped, "You fenced me in for eighteen fuckin' years. Gave me a shit life. Fucked me over. NOW you want to play father."

Darby pushed off the couch and stood. "I've made some mistakes. But I'm here now." He drew out a bill from his wallet and held it out. "Here's a hundred. Go have some fun."

Pico didn't reach for it, shot back, "I'm not a piece of meat!"

Darby put the money back but didn't take his eyes off Pico.

I said, "Pico, if you want proof, we can get a DNA test."

An irate Pico turned to me. "DNA? What does that shit mean? Did Not Appear? That's what that's all about isn't it? Did Not Appear." He turned to Darby. "I don't care if you are my father. Get the fuck out of here. I don't want to ever see you or hear from you again."

Darby froze.

"Go on." Pico said. "Get out of here."

I said to Darby, "You better leave before this gets out of hand."

Darby walked toward the door without looking back. "It was your mother's fault." He slammed the door behind him.

There was an awkward silence in the room.

After I took a deep breath, I said, "Darby gave up easily because he's not your father."

"No. My father was good at walking away. He walked away nineteen years ago. He's a guy who walks away. But I don't want to have anything to do with him." Then Pico looked out the window. "Funny," he said, "I always wanted a parent. Then one shows up and I don't want him."

"I'm sorry this ever happened, Pico. You won't be bothered any more . . . and you know what? I would be proud to have you as my son."

CHAPTER 56

By mid-afternoon Thursday, the pressures of my life clamped around my head like a vice. I needed an aspirin or a new job. I settled for an aspirin—probably a bad choice.

The concierge in the hotel lobby directed me to a pharmacy across the street. The team bus was leaving in twenty minutes and I was in a hurry. When I exited the gold-framed glass door it was raining and I quickly weaved my way through a handful of people standing under the hotel's beige awning. At the curb I looked left. No cars. I stepped into the street. Someone grabbed my shoulders from behind and threw me backwards onto the wet sidewalk. As I landed on my butt, a car breezed by me, right to left. A one-way street. I'd looked the wrong way.

Momentarily stunned, I looked back over my shoulder and caught a glimpse of the man in a black raincoat who saved me. About my size, he was a bald Abe Lincoln. The man darted toward the hotel entrance as if he didn't want to be seen. "Hey," I yelled, "you saved my life!" The man disappeared inside. I didn't chase him. I had things to do.

Ten minutes or so later in the back parking lot, a pain reliever causing my stomach to ache, I hoisted myself into our quiet bus. Standing next to the driver, I counted heads and then said, "Where's Americus?"

Pico, sitting in front of me, his ball on his lap, said, "Some kind of meeting. Got a lot of meetings today."

"Too many for my blood."

I rang Americus. "What's up?"

"Coach, I've got a situation."

"Glancing at the driver's expressionless face, I said to Americus, "This bus is leaving in minutes. You better be on it."

"Come to my room, Coach. Something's goin' down."

Can't I just coach?

On the tenth floor, Americus opened his door. His grandmother, Mrs. Hart, sat straight ahead in triple X green slacks, white blouse, and black leather jacket, taking up every inch of her chair. She welcomed me with a surly face. "You stay out of this, Byrnes. We got a family thing."

My eyes jogged to a white guy standing next to her with a pen in his hand. Tall, three-day beard, beige slacks, white sport shirt open to his navel. He looked condescendingly at me as if he were a member of a club I desperately wanted to belong to.

I thought about saying, "What's the fuck's going on?" but eased into it with, "Why am I here?"

Americus pointed to the man, said, "This guy wants to be my agent."

Shit. Every oddball is coming out of the woodwork.

I followed Americus a few steps to the middle of the room, my mind spinning all the way. My eyes managed to focus on an unsigned agreement spread across the cocktail table that had a lot of *'here too*'s and *wherefore's*.

Son-of-a-bitch. Americus is going pro before the end of the season.

Wanting to hit somebody, I barked at Mrs. Hart. "We're playing for the national title. What are you playing for?"

"A house," she snapped back. "And I'm going to get it."

I turned to Americus, "You sign now I'll report you. Ineligible. No title, no visibility, your team pissed at you . . ."

Americus pointed at his grandmother and blared, "See. I told you."

Mrs. Hart glared at me. "Byrnes, you and I were month-to-month. Now I'm going for a long-term deal." She turned to Americus. "Basketball is about the money. You lose tonight, your stock ain't worth shit. And Sheldrake is only favored by one. Tells me you can lose your ass."

"We win," I said, "his stock goes up and we ARE going to win."

"Byrnes," Mrs. Hart shot back, "You're a rookie coach going against guys who been there. You ain't been there. You ain't been anywhere. I want my house in the country with the flowers. Only flowers I see now are on caskets."

I looked hard at Americus, who began to pace with his head down. "Americus, your stock goes up with visibility. You gotta make it to the finals. Let me make this easy for you. " I brushed by him, snatched the agreement, tore it up one side and down the other, then threw it on the carpet.

Mrs. Hart sprang from her chair and got down on her knees trying to piece the contract together. "You bastard, you tore up my house."

"He gets hurt," the man said, "it's all over."

I gave the man a hard look. "Why do you want to sign him if he can get hurt at any time?" I motioned to Americus. "Come on. We got a game to win and a bigger house to buy. And Mrs. Hart. Trust me. This will all work out."

She tilted her head back and shot me a "Fuck you" look on my way out.

* * *

Americus and I sprinted toward the team bus just as rain began to spray us down like a cheap carwash. Next to our ride my FBI phone went off. I motioned Americus to board while I put the phone to my ear. Water dripping down my face, I listened to Kaycee.

"I went to the Atlantic City morgue," she said. "No sign of DeCarlo. Then I went through the death certificates . . . looked for bodies identified by Townsend, Tully, Wills, Williams, or Willams . . ."

I cut in, "What'd you find?"

"Nothing. Then I went back to O'Reilly's Pawn Shop and found the broker who handled the ring transaction. He said Wills is about six-foot, bald, has bushy eyebrows and a big nose with a wisp of a beard."

"How old?"

"Late fifties, early sixties."

"Hey, that guy saved my life today."

"Come on!"

After telling my story, I asked, "What the hell is Wills doing in Portland? And why did he save me? People are disappearing and he saves ME."

"He saved you because you're Townsend's man. Appointed and anointed. And they know you're not a rat-fink."

"What are you going to do now?"

"Find Wills and track him. Good luck tonight."

CHAPTER 57

We received deafening applause from twenty-thousand fans who were eager to get their money's worth.

I followed the team onto the Rose Garden floor, headed for our row of chairs down the sideline, passed a long line of tables used by the media and VIPs.

Forget deaths, suspensions, and player problems. Wipe everything out of your mind except the game.

Six cameras positioned around the arena—all focused on me. Bands blaring, cheerleaders wiggling, balls pounding, my mind spinning.

Focus. Damn it, focus. This is it! Everything you ever wanted.

I took a deep breath, listened to the national anthem, then the PA announcer who said, "Now let's have a moment of silence for that great American, Coach Babe DeCarlo of Sheldrake, who has been missing for several days."

My players, wearing a small, black BD stitched above their numbers, bowed their heads. Total silence in the arena, with the exception of a white-coated vendor across the way spewing, "Mister, five bucks . . . pass it down the aisle."

After player introductions, the head coaches names were mentioned. I walked in front of the scorer's table to shake hands with Pat McGee, the veteran Colorado State coach who swaggered my way. I shook hands with the tall, fleshy-faced man, thought about getting a level playing field, and said, "Take it easy on us."

In a throaty voice, he responded kindly with, "Fuck you, Rookie."

I gave him a look that would shatter glass.

What would you say if I told you Sky King wanted to transfer to Sheldrake? "Fuck you and a half?"

*   *   *

Our game plan worked wonders the first half, but I couldn't tune out the sounds of cat- calls—a coaching detractor. We hit a good percentage, and six-eight Willard Penn limited Sky King to twelve shots, much more than we had planned. But King released seven, errant twenty-five footers in apparent frustration. His poor shot selection and our ability to make open shots gave us a 30-24 lead, at the half.

In the second half Willard Penn was effective on defense, forcing the long-legged King farther outside his reception area, then influencing him to drive down the lane into Americus at the hoop. Americus then picked up King about one giant step from the hoop letting King shoot a series of shots that clanked off the rim and into our hands.

With five minutes remaining we led 52-47. It was then that Coach McGee jumped off his bench to berate a passing official. "I'm being robbed!" he roared. He reached into his back pocket and plucked out his wallet. Then he held it out to the official. "Here take my wallet, you've got everything else." Our fans booed, his fans cheered.

I recognized it as a reenactment of what McGee pulled on TV last year against BYU. Drew a technical, fired up his team, got a "make-up" call, and went on to win.

Don't let that happen. Do something.

Going into my own act, I lashed out at the officials with any words that popped into my head, no matter how incoherent. "See," I yelled, "there he goes again, and it's not him, it's me. I got rights. It's the rule. You know that . . . but him . . . so there. Don't you know? See. It's him. Wrong. Very wrong."

The ball reversed course, and the trailing official ran by me at mid-court, shooting me a weird look. "What's wrong, Byrnes?"

The focus was now on me, not McGee—just what I wanted. I kept making non-sensical comments until McGee gave up and just glared at me, probably wondering if they were going to take me away.

The official I had just ignored blew his whistle and called a foul on Colorado State. Nitro went to the line. That same official came to the scorer's table to report the foul. He asked again, "Coach Byrnes, what's wrong?"

I pointed to McGee. "That joker's trying to draw a technical so he can turn the game around."

The official shook his head.

At the two-minute mark, with the score tied at 68, King drove by a tired Americus for a slam that banged off the rim. Upon returning to defense, King glared at his coach with narrowed eyes and a pushed-up chin.

I said to Giranda, "That was impossible for him to miss."

He said, "McGee just called him an asshole."

"There's something going on between them."

We exchanged baskets in the waning minutes; the game slowed as both teams took high percentage shots and did not foul. With one minute remaining and the score tied at 60, I inserted the six-nine Pico for a panting Americus Hart. Pico had seen limited action in the first half and had not taken a single shot.

The moment of truth for Pico came seconds later when Sky King received a pass in the corner and drove the baseline right at Pico. Pico jumped out to meet him in front of the basket. Seemingly startled, King passed the ball across court to a teammate in the corner, but it sailed high over his head and landed in the fourth row.

I yelled out, "Thank you, Sky."

He didn't look back.

Down the court, Coach McGee stood with hands on hips staring at King as he came back on defense. King didn't hesitate to glare back.

At my end of the court, Nitro scored on a drive when Sky King failed to help from the corner. A few seconds later, State brought the ball down and I yelled. "Let the ball go in to King." *He's self-destructing.*

King received the ball at the top of the key, took a long step toward the hoop, and pounded the ball off his shoe. It bounced directly into Pico's hands as the horn sounded giving us a 62-60 win.

I sprang from my seat, applauded our team, who were busy applauding themselves. Then I wondered if it was Sky King who pulled us through. Too many misses in the first half, self-destruction in the second half. He wasn't that bad and I wasn't sure we were that good.

CHAPTER 58

From the tip-off, fans stood, applauded, yelled, and waved fists after every score. I was living my dream of coaching in the final eight. Then my mind spun with thoughts of death and imprisonment, then a myriad of negative basketball thoughts. As a result, I froze in my chair and watched the game as a third party.

Missouri, in black, answered every one of our field goals with a monster dunk or a drive. Then momentum swung to Missouri when "Big House" Johnston, a mountain of a post man, began handling Americus down low like he was a toy. Then Junior Mason, a point guard who could run through the raindrops without getting wet, drove past Nitro as if he had waved a checkered flag. Missouri pulled ahead by six. But then momentum swung back to us when Junior Mason missed a series of off-balance shots and threw a number of errant passes into the stands.

Control your mind. Focus. Take deep breaths.

When the horn blared ending the first half, I tilted my head up and looked at the scoreboard. The bright lights said, Missouri 33-31. Somehow I missed the first half.

Moments later I stood at the head of the locker room and read the faces of twelve young men, some ready to play, others bewildered. I wondered if I could get them to follow my directions one more time, if I could draw upon my high-school coaching experience for a big game.

I raised my voice. "We've got to get some controls. The way it's going, Mason will win it or lose it for them. We need to make sure that he loses it." I stared into Americus's eyes and said, "You lean on Johnston when he's away from the ball. Keep him from meeting Mason's pass when he drives." I turned to Nitro who was having little success defending Mason. Sitting next to Americus, he leaned forward and stared at the floor, beads of perspiration pouring down his forehead, draining onto his cheeks. "Nitro," I said. "Look at me. Give Junior Mason more room out front. Make a jump shooter out of him. Trust me one more time."

He said, "You sure?"

"I'm sure."

In the second half, my strategy worked surprisingly well for the first ten minutes. "Big House" handled the ball only a few times, scoring once, and Junior Mason missed everything he threw up from a distance. With that, we pulled up to Missouri at 52, then built a four-point lead.

Everything went our way for the next five minutes until Americus went up for a defensive rebound and came down on the inside of his ankle, collapsing on the shiny floor as if a puppet master had let loose of his strings. He lay on the court prone, wiggling in pain. With timeout on the court, the fans were quiet as church mice, as our trainer helped Americus hobble off to x ray.

At that moment, Americus's grandmother, sitting close by, stood and played him like a cash register with, "Come back, Americus, I need you. You're my house."

I waved Pico over. He sprang from his chair and sprinted to me. I looked up and said calmly, "Keep your knees bent . . . don't take Johnston's head-fakes. You'll be fine."

Seconds later, the tempo of the game faster than I liked, Junior Mason again drove by Nitro. But Pico stepped up the lane and crouched, readied for a takeoff. Mason stopped short of Pico and lofted a shot three feet higher than the rim. Pico shot up like a rocket and caught the ball at the top of its arc with one hand. The crowd came to its feet and roared as Pico, in one motion, tossed the ball to Willard Penn at the other end of the court for an easy lay-up.

Mason tried to answer with three 3-pointers—all of which could have chipped paint off the rim.

Nitro, a head taller than Mason, got into the action outside the top of the key when he banged home a three-point jumper over Mason, giving us a three-point lead, 66-63.

Missouri called time-out.

As the players hurried towards me, I felt the nausea that comes with thinking "what ifs?"

What if we fouled? What if we turned the ball over? What if we missed free throws?

My stomach churning, I got up cigarette-length to each sweaty body and barked, "Tough and no fouls. Here comes the press. Keep your head up and meet the pass. This is our game and they're not gonna to take it from us."

After Nitro penetrated a half-court press and hit a short jumper, Mason retaliated by driving past him. But seeing Pico in his way, he tried to rifle a sharp pass to Johnston down low. But the ball landed in the fourth row. I felt elation and surprise at the same time. I enjoyed the break but new Mason was better than that.

Six seconds left and somehow we led, 71-63.

"Take it down, Nitro," I yelled. "Let 'em foul you."

Mason peeled off his man at center-court as his teammate came up the sideline to clamp Nitro over the center stripe.

"Trap, trap," I yelled to Nitro. "Hit Pico. Top of the key. Pico, meet the pass."

Three seconds.

My heart sped.

Two seconds . . . one.

Pico met the pass at the top of the key.

The horn blared.

All of a sudden my nauseous was replaced by exhilaration, and I shot off the bench and ran around looking for a player to hug. They were piling on one another at mid-court, not interested in me. Someone stuck a microphone in my face, asked me how I felt. My mind spinning, I said

"Perfect," as I ran to the locker room.

Minutes later, I stood on a chair in a wild, butt-slapping, towel-snapping locker room trying to get the team's attention. "Pipe down," I yelled. The noise dialed down. "Great team effort. We're one game away from the big top. No workout Monday. Workouts Tuesday and Wednesday. Then it's on to Indianapolis for games Saturday and Monday. Get a good night's sleep and dream on."

I got down off the chair and made my way to a corner where I asked the trainer how Americus was doing.

"It's broken," he said with a long face.

My stomach dropped. *I lose an All-American and Pico has to play forty minutes. He's never played more than fifteen. We better believe the impossible is possible.* "Where is he?"

"In the training room getting a cast.

The unexplainable also crossed my mind.

Why didn't Missouri foul? Why was Junior Mason ineffective coming down the stretch? Did I have an angel on my shoulder? Or did Mason have the Devil on his?

CHAPTER 59

The next day I gave my team a day off, temporarily disconnected the bug in my BMW, and took a leisurely drive with Kaycee to the Philadelphia Medical Examiner's office at 321 University. I liked being with her, even though we were heading to a place where death was welcome. And maybe, just maybe, DeCarlo would have passed through this facility.

We made the hour-long, straight-away drive to Highway 76, crossed a river, then rolled onto University and 38th. I parked behind a row of SUVs in front of the modern brick building.

Down the first floor hall of the Medical Examiner's offices we stopped at Records. Inside the small office, a thin man hunched behind a tall counter, his eyes glued to a computer screen. He wore a starched white shirt and a tie with hand-painted amoebas. Behind him was a metal door marked "Authorized Personnel Only."

Kaycee displayed her badge to the thin man, whose name tag said "Foster." His colorless face turned ashen, like we were on to something.

"I'm looking for someone who disappeared," Kaycee said. "Bring up death certificates for March, 15, 16, and 17 of this year, and tell me if any of those bodies were identified by Williams, Willams, Wills, Townsend, or Tully." She drew out a small writing pad from her coat pocket, scratched out the names, and handed over the paper.

"Yes, ma'am."

We hung over the counter that separated Foster from the living and watched his fingers dance on the keyboard. Minutes later, the man looked up. "Sorry. Nothing for those names."

I said out of the blue, "Try March 14, the day before DeCarlo disappeared."

"DeCarlo?" Foster asked.

Kaycee snapped, "Just match bodies with the names I gave you for that date."

More clicking before Foster looked up again. "On March 14th, A. Harold Wills identified a body as Adolph Rupp. Says here, 'Wills was Rupp's half-brother.' Says below, 'Rupp, a six-two, two-hundred-forty-pound man, was found in Swann Memorial Fountain at 19th and Logan at 2 a.m. He was face down. Police recovered the body. Cause of death—accidental drowning.'"

I said to Kaycee, "Maybe someone conked him, then dumped him." Then I turned to Foster. "Was there a blow to the head?"

"Yes. There was a blow to the frontal lobe. But there was no autopsy. Rupp had no identification or valuables. And Karstars, the Medical Examiner, signed it off."

Kaycee said, "Doesn't make sense that he climbed into this fountain and took a head-first dive into three feet of water. Someone dumped him in the fountain so the cops could pick him up and bring him here."

"Just reading the record, ma'am."

I said, "If this is DeCarlo, why was the death certificate signed by the medical examiner a day before his disappearance?"

"That's premeditation," Kaycee said. "Could get the death penalty."

"Jesus," Foster said as he shifted in his seat.

"So where's the body?" I asked.

"Look. I'm new here."

"For all I know, you're part of this."

"Not me."

I raised my voice. "So where's the body, man?"

Taking a deep breath, Foster said, "Wills authorized the body to be

248

transported to the Franklin Crematorium the next day—which is odd because regulations state the body can't be moved for three days."

"Crematorium?" I said. "So Wills had an agreement to get the body out fast. What else you got?"

"Wills identified the residence of the deceased as 1025 Pacific, Atlantic City."

I exchanged a quick, knowing look with Kaycee. She said to me, "Empty lot. We've been there. Wills gave that address at the pawn shop."

"Do you have a photo of the deceased?" I asked.

"I'm scrolling . . . Hey! There's something's wrong here. Here's a photo of the last corpse I went past. The man died twice. Same guy."

We scooted around the counter and saw a photo of a man with a wrinkled face, black hair, about fifty. Then Foster scrawled back to the same photo on the previous record. They both were DeCarlo.

Foster tilted his head back to Kaycee. "These records don't seem right. But again they're signed off by Karstars."

Kaycee said, "Karstars, huh? Keep going. What do you have on file for May 12, 13, and 14 of last year? I'm looking for another guy who disappeared. Look for the same names identifying the body."

"No," I said. "Look at May 11, the day before Mansfield disappeared. There may be a pattern."

After a minute, Foster squirmed. "Here's another body identified by H. Wills. Found at Swann Memorial Fountain, same reporting information. Oh, jeez. Says here the deceased was black, but here's a photo of a white man. Someone may have been in a hurry to change this record and botched the job."

Kaycee said, "And who signed off on this? Karstars?"

"That's correct. And the paper work of the toxicologist and pathologist have been doctored. I can see the smudges. This was scanned in."

"So Karstars is the last one to sign off on the form?"

"That's correct."

I pointed to the metal door. "Is Karstars in there?"

"In there somewhere."

"Kaycee said, "Tell him the FBI wants to talk to him. Don't say anything else."

Foster sprang from his chair, pushed open a spring-loaded metal door flushing out cold air, and entered.

"Kaycee, let's just go in there."

"We haven't been invited and I don't have a warrant."

Foster rushed out with a disturbed look. "Karstars took off running when I told him . . . "

I burst by Foster into a cold-storage room, Kaycee right behind me. We sprinted past people with masks and cutting instruments, entered another room that smelled of road kill where bodies had been cut up like Thanksgiving turkeys. No Karstars. In the next room, bodies were stacked like logs in plastic bags. Still no Karstars. We shot back to the first room and I thrust open an exit door and ran down a ramp to a two-lane alley. An ambulance was parked against the wall. I looked the other way at a leafless wooded area behind the employee parking lot. No one in sight. Then the sound of peeling rubber of peeling rubber swung me around. About twenty yards from the boulevard, a shiny, red 1960 Corvette did an Indy takeoff, the driver in a white coat.

"That's him!" I yelled to Kaycee. "That's Karstars!"

We ran toward the Vette. It braked at the driveway's edge, then wedged into traffic.

Seconds later, we jumped into our car at the curb.

The Vette screeched south on University. I spun my wheels into traffic, narrowly missing a truck's bumper. Four cars and a good fifty yards behind the Vette, my accelerator to the floor, I pounded my horn at the car in front of me.

At the next corner, the Vette blazed through a red light, edged left before squeezing between a car and truck. I held my breath and went for it, cutting off another truck's tail.

"Son-of-a-bitch!" I yelled.

I narrowly made it through traffic, only to be stopped at a light two cars behind Karstars, who gunned his engine then shot across the intersection.

"Bastard," I cried, stamping on the gas, but jerking forward when I hit the brake in the intersection to avoid a car.

The Vette continued to sprint down University and swerved right onto Baltimore Avenue. I followed, sharply cutting right about fifty yards behind him. He skidded left into a cemetery. Still a couple of seconds behind, I took the entry full throttle, gaining speed all the way.

Ahead, the Vette sped down a tree-lined road.

My accelerator to the floor again, our car shot straight ahead, holding the road, then almost losing it on a turn.

The Vette took a left on a dirt road between tall monuments. I spun a brodie on the corner enveloping us with a cloud of dust, then sped behind him, concrete structures whizzing by. Approaching a mausoleum, he tried to make the Vette turn left, but couldn't pull it off and smashed its grill into a marble wall. Metal crushed, fiberglass ripped, wheels spun.

I skidded to within four feet of the Vette. We scrambled out. Kaycee snapped her pistol from its shoulder holster and aimed it with two hands at the Vette. I ripped open the crumpled door and looked inside. A mess. The lower portion of the white plastic steering wheel was embedded in Karstars's chest, the top of the wheel was in his mouth. Blood oozed out of his mouth, down and around the wheel, finally dripping onto his beige slacks. His eyes were closed. He wasn't moving. He wasn't going to.

Kaycee said, "Special Agent Brewer, FBI. Get out with your hands up."

I got out and turned to her. "Not going to happen."

She ducked in and checked his pulse, edged out and said, "We just lost a co-conspirator. But at least he didn't have time to tell Wills that we're on to him."

* * *

I was at downtown's FBI headquarters when the day's sun was a distant memory. I leaned against a cold hallway wall just as Kaycee asked me, "So who's Adolph Rupp?"

"Adolph Rupp coached Kentucky Basketball for decades before he died. His star players were guilty of fixing games in the early fifties. The NCAA barred his team from playing for one season."

"So Weird Harold is a basketball historian?"

"Historian, electrician, murderer—and don't forget lifesaver. It's the last part that has me worried. Why did he save my life?"

CHAPTER 60

On the dais with three other Final Four coaches, I was the first to field questions from a roomful of reporters at the Indianapolis Marriott. I was prepared for questions about Pico defending Charles, game strategy, and how it felt to coach the semifinals. Instead, a man with a bad dye job in the first row waved a newspaper at me wildly, and said, "What did you think of this article?"

I reached out and clamped my fingers around the mike. "What are you talking about?"

As my voice rebounded off the walls, my FBI phone rang. "Excuse me," I said, "it's my mother."

Some giggles. Mostly silence.

I put the cell to my ear and looked out at nothing. "Yes, Mom?"

"So you can't talk?" Kaycee said.

"How many tickets do you need?"

"Listen. Wills paid for the cremation of Mansfield and DeCarlo and walked away with the ashes. I rang a frequently called number on Karstars's cell. It was the Palm Abrasives Company. I did some fancy footwork and learned that Wills is Director of Operations and Chemical Components. I don't know why I didn't do that earlier. Wills oversees the setup for the elements of scouring powder and one of the elements is ash. He's been working there for three years."

"So?"

"So from time to time he pours in ashes."

"You mean . . ."

"Yeah. Think twice before using scouring powder in your sink . . . you're probably washing down Mansfield and DeCarlo."

"Jesus!"

"Another thing," she said, "Wills is on vacation. I'm betting he's in Indianapolis. I'm coming out there. And don't worry, we're watching your back." Click.

I slipped the phone into my pocket, tried to clear my brain, and said to the reporter, "What was your question again?"

He pointed to the newspaper. "What are your thoughts about Jordan Taylor exposing your program? Haven't you read it?"

I raised my voice louder than I wanted to. "I got out of bed and ran over here. What are you talking about?"

The man walked to the makeshift stage. "Here," he said, "top of page one."

I read the first paragraph to myself.

> *AP writer, Jordan Taylor, who broke the NCAA investigation about Sheldrake College Basketball, is going to reveal that program's connection to the underworld on Monday, the day of the championship game, he told other reporters on Friday evening. Taylor, who has suggested underworld ties to Sheldrake in the past, said he will name names.*

I felt like Jordan had punched me in the gut. I dropped the paper on the table and thought,

The article alerted Townsend and Wills . . . screwed up the FBI investigation. What does Jordan know?

"Family emergency," I said into the mike. "Got to go." And hustled off the stage.

As I headed for a far door, I ignored "What does Jordan Taylor know?" coming from footsteps behind me.

A few minutes later, I scurried down the sidewalk away from the Marriott and left a message on Jordan's cell. "Jordan, this is no Pulitzer. You're touching some wires you don't want to touch." I hung up and called Kaycee and briefed her about the bomb Jordan was about to drop. Things were going to explode.

CHAPTER 61

4:25 P.M.

Our bus circled Lucas Oil Stadium, then angled into a fenced-off parking lot as the window wipers feverishly brushed aside falling snow. Outside the giant stadium, tens of thousands of fans were packed like sardines waiting for the doors to open. Vapor clouds drifted briefly over their heads then disappeared.

Seated behind the driver, I looked down at my newly pressed, pin-striped slacks. I didn't remember putting them on. I reached out and slowly ran my fingers down the crease. Parallel lines, straight, manageable, unlike my life.

I stared out the window at nothing in particular, and for the hundredth time, reworked the DeCarlo—Mansfield mystery and thought, *I'm still the puzzle piece that doesn't fit. But all I did was take the jobs of two dead men.*

Concentrate. Only one game from the finals. No time to solve the mystery.

* * *

When we took the floor an hour later, a small portion of fans erupted with an enormous cheer. It was like they had just broken out of prison. But that sound was nothing like the cheers that exploded for Notre Dame a minute later when they sprinted out of the tunnel. You'd think that almost everyone in the stadium was from Indiana.

I watched All-American Robert Charles of Notre Dame warm up. Slashing through the air. Cutting and rebounding.

But great warm-ups in basketball mean nothing. The game means everything. And I was asking a lot of Penn and Pico. Penn would defend Charles tight outside, while Pico, filling in for Americus, would pick up Charles on a drive inside. It would be the difference between winning and losing. And Pico had never played forty minutes. The only thing that would save him from wearing out was TV time-outs. Each delay was given at sixteen, twelve, six and four minutes left in each half. And I could extend some automatic timeouts by calling my own.

Feeling nervous-normal, I paced, clear-headed in the first half, the action in front of my face. For the first time in the tourney, I was in the zone, calling plays, calling timeouts, and calling out officials without being in a fog.

Everything worked. Pico forced Charles to miss inside again and again. And Penn repeatedly forced Charles to change his shot outside with a hand high above his shot.

All in all, we made eleven out of twenty field goals, and a couple of free throws and led 35–30 at the half.

But in the white-walled locker room, Pico, who never played an entire half, bent over his chair gasping for air. He was done. Spent. Drained.

Standing at the head of the room, I called to the trainer across the way. "Wrap Pico's quads in iced-cold towels to get the acid out of his legs. Then, recharge him with some Gatorade."

Pico," I said, "twenty more minutes we're in the finals. Can you make it?"

As the trainer wrapped his legs, Pico sucked air and squeezed out, "Count on me."

While I was paying attention to Pico, conversation in the room picked up. Ready to give my best half-time talk, I yelled, "Listen up."

Nitro, sitting at the end of the first row, turned back to a few play-ers sitting behind him, blurted. "Shut the fuck up. It's halftime. Game's not over."

Dead silence. Then Nitro said, "Ga-head, Coach."

I gave them a hardboiled look. Revved up. "Take a deep breath. Concentrate—because when you leave this room, you're going to play like your life depended on it. The team that controls the first five minutes of the second half will win it . . . That will be us."

As I reviewed our second-half strategy, several narrow-eyed players nodded in agreement. Too bad they were kids that hadn't played. Then Willard Penn said to me, "What if we get in trouble?"

I looked around the room at each player. "If I get you into trouble, I'll get you out of trouble. That's my job. You do your job. I'll do mine."

* * *

In the second half, Charles, operating on offense in the far court, was unstoppable. Fall aways, leaners, bankers, scoops—all went in against tired Penn and Pico. I paced in front of our bench, muttering to myself, "Too bad Charles didn't hear my halftime talk."

With seven minutes left, Notre Dame led 57-54 and we were gassed.

I called timeout. With the players huddled around, I said, "Seven minutes is a lifetime. Take your time on offense. Save your energy. Everything's going to be okay . . . Let's go to work."

Back on the court, Nitro responded, by hitting three threes, pointing at his defender each time as if to say, "Back at you, sucka."

We exchanged buckets for the next five minutes. Then at the two-minute mark we were tied at 78, and it looked like the last team to have possession of the ball would win.

Charles threw up three consecutive, twenty-five foot shots that only drew iron. And each team hit four free throws and we were looking at 64-all with one minute left. Drenched in sweat, I took off my jacket and threw it down on my chair without missing the action.

Charles, usually a great player in the clutch, missed two free throws. And on his team's next possession he traveled. At the other end of the court, Pico made two dunks, giving us a narrow 68-64 win.

The stadium rocked with applause. Rushing to Pico, the team encircled him for a monster hug. Arms around each other, the players jumped up and down like they were in their bare feet on hot coals. I wedged my way inside the circle, yelling, "You son-of-a-bitches and bastards. Great effort! We're a team now!"

*   *   *

Pandemonium in our locker room. Screaming, towels thrown, heads soaked with soda.

My heart beating like a runaway train, I hoisted myself up on a long table and lifted my hands. "Let me have your attention."

Nitro yelled, "Quiet. Coach has something to say."

I smiled. "Let's enjoy this one, but don't forget about Monday night against NYU. We owe NYU and, fortunately, we get them for the title. They beat us in December, and they'll be over-confident. We have the edge. Believe me, we got them right where we want 'em."

Chapter 62

In my hotel room an hour after my team had a thirty-minute shoot-around in the stadium in front of twenty thousand fans, I tried unsuccessfully to take a nap. Fully clothed, I watched a local newscast coming from the TV atop the chest of drawers. As soon as I settled in, the phone on the hotel bed stand went off. It was Bob Finney, president of the coaches association. He asked me to speak about Babe DeCarlo at the luncheon on Monday. They needed me to stand in for someone. I accepted. Hanging up, I threw my head back on the pillow and smiled.

Everything is coming my way.

There was a knock at my door. To my surprise it was Townsend and Tully. In dark suits they stormed in without a word, walked past me, then lowered themselves onto the sofa. I took an adjacent stuffed chair, letting the newscast play.

"Well," I said, "you guys have to be satisfied—I've taken us to the final."

Townsend's eyes now slits, he said with an edge, "This isn't your time, Byrnes."

I took an uneasy breath. "What do you mean? This is my game to win."

"No," Townsend said, "You lose."

Trying to understand what he meant, I heard myself breathing.

"Look," Townsend went on, "I fixed all your games . . . All those missed shots . . . bad passes. All those games when you beat the spread. The fix was on . . . Now you're going to lose the big one and we all win."

My brain went off like a fire alarm. *Fixed! . . . Fixed! . . . Fixed! Me—a piece-of-shit coach. A patsy.*

I opened my mouth, but nothing came out. Suddenly, coaching at Sheldrake was like going to Tijuana for a weekend and coming back with a tattoo and a dead girl in my trunk

"I picked you to coach Sheldrake," Townsend said, "because I thought you'd cooperate when the time came. The time is now. NYU is favored by two because they beat you last winter. But after I spread a significant amount on Sheldrake, the odds will be plus one, Sheldrake. Then shortly before the game I'll put a small fortune on NYU to win. Then you lose."

His words seared my ego like battery acid.

I took a breath, a hard-to-come-by breath. "If I'm a loser, why won't my team lose on their own?"

"This game is too important to let the players decide the outcome. Your job is to keep them from getting hot, getting momentum. You're a good coach. You know how."

For a long moment Townsend's icy demeanor didn't change. He looked through me like I was meat on a hook.

"Townsend, you couldn't have fixed three tournament games so fast. You didn't have enough time to sell the players on the deal."

Townsend said, "Don't be naive. They've dropped games for me during the season. Now they're set up to win."

Mansfield found out! DeCarlo had a big mouth. He had to go too.

I folded my arms, took another breath. "How do you know I'll go along with you?"

"Townsend opened his coat, pulled out a cell, and said calmly, "Because I have a life insurance policy." He dialed, listened, and said into the phone, "This is me. Get him to the phone." He got up, stepped across the plush carpet, and put the instrument to my ear. "Say hello to your brother."

My heart dropped. "Jordan?"

"Conrad," Jordan gasped, "do what they tell you."

"Jordan, where are you?"

Hearing background noise on the phone, my eyes shot over to the TV. The newscaster's voice in my room was the same voice coming through the cell. Indianapolis TV. Jordan was in or near Indianapolis. "Jordan! Jordan!" The line went dead.

Townsend took the phone back as my mind gyrated.

Jordan had my back in elementary school. Taught me basketball. He was there for me. Asshole! He's still my brother.

Townsend said, "A little life insurance can go a long way, Byrnes. You talk to anyone about this, Jordan dies . . . Lose and your brother lives . . . Lose and I'll appoint you full-time coach . . . Lose and nobody gets hurt. Losing is the only thing."

Sinking into my chair, my chest felt like someone was sitting on it.

"Just in case you hate your brother," Townsend continued, "I'm going to sweeten the pot. You lose and you'll get five million. It's all set. Swiss bank. Numbered account. All you have to do is make the wrong substitutions, call the wrong timeouts, and draw the wrong plays."

"I understand," I said, thinking of my options.

Townsend said nothing.

I walked them to the door as if I was part of the action. Then I made my way to the bathroom where I splashed cold water on my face, looked into the mirror and I saw nothing but fear. I turned away from the mirror, thought about calling Kaycee. *I have to trust her. Can't trust Townsend.* I dialed. She was en route to Indianapolis. I left a voicemail. Laid out Townsend's plan—the fix and the kidnapping.

Then I went to my laptop on my desk, turned it on and in horror, watched the last few minutes of my tournament games. Terrible shot selection, unforced turnovers. All at the right time. Townsend had perfected the fix.

I went to the window like it would solve all my problems, and stared out at a flat city.

I could win it all . . . No. Win and Jordan dies . . . Lose and they'd kill him anyway . . . Then me.

CHAPTER 63

MONDAY
NOON

Following a sleepless night, I took a cab to the Marriott, pushed through a revolving door, and saw a sea of coaches in the lobby. Maybe a thousand of them. Tall, taller, and tallest. Coaches on the way up, on the way down, or on the way out of the profession.

I searched for the escalator leading to the mezzanine where the banquet would be held and shuffled past clusters of black faces and white faces in sport coats, collared T's, Hotshoe and Payday sweats. I heard, "I had a bad contract," which meant, *"I just got fired."* I also heard, "Please make that call for me," which meant, *"Get me that job."*

I kept moving through the crowd, saying under my breath, "Nobody dies . . . not Jordan . . . not me."

"Excuse me." I squeezed between two men in HotShoe sweats.

One of them stepped aside, gave me an inquisitive look, and said, "Hey, aren't you—?"

I cut in, "No, I'm not."

My head down, I moved on.

Would Jordan fix a game for me? I have to fix this one for him. Mom said Jordan was a winner. Once again I'm a loser.

I inadvertently bumped into a young black man, shorter than I am, in a beige turtleneck and khakis. He raised his voice above the crowd and held out of hand. "Andre Marshall. Congratulations. Listen, I've got an All-American prospect for you. Point guard in the NATO Army. No one knows about him. And if he lives . . ."

"That's what it's all about," I said. "If he lives . . ."

Marshall gave me a questioning look. Then he said, "Hey, I'll stay in touch. And good luck tonight . . . High school coach to NCAA finalist . . . Every high school coach in America wishes they were in your shoes."

My eyes locked on his. "Don't bet on it."

I was continuing across the room past a coffee stand when someone tapped me on the shoulder and said, "Coach Byrnes—James Adams." He was Black, well-dressed, with movie star looks. Maybe fresh out of college. He pointed a finger at me. "You need an assistant. I'm yah man. I know New Yawk, AAU, street agents. And I'll get you Flex Anthony. Sixty big ones."

Flex Anthony—the pot head.

"Not interested."

I reached the escalator and was stepping up when a guy beside the lift spoke in a hushed tone. "Win tonight and Jordan's gone." I stopped on the first step, turned and watched a guy in a red baseball cap mill through the crowd. A dozen coaches in line for the escalator blocked me from going after him.

"Hey, stop!" I yelled. He kept going. My body ascending, The man disappeared in the crowd.

* * *

I entered a large ballroom upstairs, my stomach in knots, my hands wet and my head scrambled. The room was filled to capacity with coaches from all over the nation who were jabbering at tables for ten. I took an appointed seat with nine board members of the coaches' association at a dais near the door.

My mind still spinning with negative thoughts, I focused on the gold drapes across the room during the meal but saw nothing.

When I was called to the podium, I gathered myself and thanked the elegantly dressed M.C. who had just described DeCarlo as a fine man whose life was cut short just before he could reach his pinnacle of success.

I surveyed the audience of serious faces that I had seen only on *ESPN* and Network TV. Then, I cleared my throat, tried to smile in spite of my anguish, and said, "On behalf of Babe DeCarlo," but I thought: *On behalf of all the puppets, fuckin' bankrollers, and fixers at Sheldrake.* "I'm here to honor him . . . If Babe were here he'd say, '"You assholes finally made a good decision.'"

The coaches laughed out loud. Then someone blurted, "That was Babe!"

I continued, "Babe would also have said, 'Thank you very much from the bottom of my heart.'" I thought of something else. "Those of you who really knew Babe raise your hands."

Half the audience lifted their hands.

"Those of you he called 'asshole,' keep your hands up."

No hands came down.

"Thank you," I said. "That was Babe . . . And I'll tell you something else." I pointed up. "If Babe is up there, we all have a great chance."

I pace the empty locker room staring at the floor.

All my life I've wanted this moment . . . But now losing is everything.

I write a few strategic notes across the board. Not enough to bury us. I would have to do that own my own.

My FBI phone vibrates and I put it to my ear.

"I just landed," Kaycee says. "Agents found Jordan's room at the Masters Hotel, downtown. But he's not there. And Wills hasn't been located."

"He's got to be close."

"We'll find him. And Byrnes—that gun you wanted is in the vent on the wall in your meeting room. Anyone pulls a gun on you—defend yourself. But that didn't come from me or any of the agents who will be at your game—and there will be plenty. Be in touch." Click.

I hear the team coming up the hallway and take a hurried breath. I step up on a chair, reach up and remove the latticed vent plate. Then I pull out the gun, hitting the duct and making a dull metal sound. I replace the plate, jump down, and secure the gun under my belt in my lower back. *First time I've handled a gun.*

A minute later, I stare out at two rows of players who think they're going to win this game. The gun pinching my lower back, I give them thumbs up.

This is the moment they've dreamt about ... National champions. Something no one would take away from them—only me.

I say, "Very few ever get a chance to play in this game. Fewer win this game. But everyone remembers this game."

For a split second I'm confused and think about winning. I yell, "Go get 'em," then remember my brother Jordan. And my gut wrenches.

CHAPTER 64

My team fires out the door. I slowly trail them to the bright light at the end of the tunnel where seventy thousand cheering fans rise to their feet. The players run through two rows of gold-clad Mardi Gras waitresses in skimpy attire, who double as Sheldrake cheerleaders. They shake their green-and-gold pom-poms and everything else. In formalwear at the far end of the court, the Mardi Gra hotel's band plays my swan song—"The Saints Go Marching In." Hundreds of multi-colored balloons drift slowly from the top of the scoreboard towards the ceiling.

At the edge of the court, a short bald man in a suit and tie sticks a microphone in front of my face and says, "Coach Byrnes, it's been an exciting year for you."

I gaze at him for a long moment. "Sheldrake basketball and excitement are synonymous."

"So, Coach, what's going through your mind right now?"

Fear.

"There's no tomorrow."

I step away. He moves with me as if he's chained to me. "One more question, Coach Byrnes. Pico Rimpau is an emerging star. Can you comment on his adjustment to college basketball? Nine months ago, he was a street guy. Now he's starting in the NCAA Championship."

"It's been a whole new life for him, but he hasn't forgotten where he came from."

I walk apprehensively to our seating area as I watch last-second warm-ups. A minute later the horn sounds, and players hustle over to their seats to await introductions. I scan the lower level seats around the stadium. No Townsend, Tully, or Wills. My eyes shift to the boxes above the bleachers in the corner where the glare of stadium lights blinded me.

I'm an easy target from there.

My heartbeat picks up.

Sheldrake players in gold and NYU in dark blue receive enthusiastic applause as they're introduced at mid-court and the pom-pom girls shake and bake.

My Sheldrake cell vibrates and I quickly put it to my ear. A man growls, "Jordan wants to talk to you."

A blood-curdling scream, then the phone goes dead.

I yell, "Jordan!"

Suddenly, I can't think, breathe, or hear.

The phone still to my ear, a long moment goes by before I regain my senses.

"Hey, Byrnes," someone yells from the front row, "you coaching or ordering pizza?"

Then the reverberating announcement, "And the coach of Sheldrake College Conrad Byrnes," rocks my soul.

The team sprints to me to gather around. Thinking about Jordan, I squeeze out, "Let's be proud of ourselves at the end of this game." I automatically extend my palm in the center of the huddle. The players' place their hands on top of mine. Now, more than ever I'm ready to lose.

Thousand of flashbulbs brighten the court at the tip-off, and I stand on the sideline discovering new sweat glands, hoping that the ceiling falls in on me.

Minutes pass and neither team takes a bad shot or a bad pass. I pace the sideline in front of our bench waiting for my moment to destroy any chance of winning.

With the score tied at ten, Nitro motions for Pico to give him a high-post screen. Then Nitro drives to the basket and goes up for the lay-up, arm outstretched, ball about to roll off his fingertips. Simmons, his trailing defender goes up with him, grabs his shoulder, and slams him to the floor as the crowd roars. They skid into kneeling photographers behind the baseline. NYU players run towards them shaking their fists as if they mean to crush us every time we take a lay-up. Nitro springs from the floor and is shoved away by his defender. Whistles blare. Hard looks are exchanged. Players are separated from each other. Finally, Nitro hits two foul shots and one technical.

Seconds later, Pico receives the ball down low. He's double-teamed by six-eight Simmons and a slightly shorter Ellis. He goes up for the dunk with a hand, a limb, and a torso on him. Somehow he manages to score, then he's pushed out of bounds by Simmons. I spring from my chair, forget about losing, clench my hands, and yell to the closest official, "Protect Jordan . . . mean, protect Pico." *Man, is my brain screwed up.*

I call timeout, walk onto the court, stare at the official to make him feel guilty about making calls against me as the players pass me to our bench. When we huddle up, NYU's band plays so loudly I can't hear myself talk. A hand-held camera peeks over my shoulder. Not caring what forty million viewers are going to think of me, I lace my remarks with profanity and tell the players to take the next NYU driver into the post.

After Pico hits the backend of two free throws, we recover on defense and Nitro defends NYU's point guard, Howard, at the top of the key. Howard gets a screen and drives by Nitro, who jumps on his back and rides him for a few feet towards the hoop. They crumble to the floor. Whistles blow. Nitro struggles to his feet, points at Howard as if to say "an eye-for-an-eye."

I yell out to Pico, "Stay in the key. Defend the basket."

Time ticks down and we match NYU point for point.

On four straight possessions NYU drains four straight three-pointers on fast breaks and they lead 30-25 and I'm a successful failure.

4:20 LEFT IN THE GAME

I feel my FBI cell vibrate in my pocket. It's a text from Kaycee. My hand shakes as I read the message.

WILLS HAS A ROOM UPSTAIRS. WE'RE GOING IN.

I slip it in my pocket, seeing nothing but players sprinting back and forth, and hearing nothing but shoes squeaking on the highly varnished floor.

By the time I refocus, NYU has scored two consecutive, breakaway fast breaks and leads 34-25. We're a step behind and need to call time.

Breathing hard, Nitro dribbles up the court and glances at me.

He's thinking: We need a timeout. I'm thinking, Save Jordan. Don't call a timeout.

I walk down the sideline to mid-court. In front of the announcers' table I applaud, and yell, "Let's go." Behind me, one of announcers says, "Twelve months ago Byrnes was a high school coach. Now he's got to make big-time decisions. No place for a rookie."

00:05 SECONDS LEFT

I go to a knee in front of the announcer's table, and my cell goes off. A text from Kaycee reads:

JORDAN'S ALIVE. WILLS DEAD.

I take a deep breath. *Now only MY life is at stake.*

One of the announcers says, "Can you believe that . . . Byrnes is text messaging during the game." He laughs, "That's criminal."

The horn sounds ending the half. I look up at the clock. We're down ten, 42-32.

I brush the back of my hand over my gun in my lower back and trail the players to the locker room, knowing I'm too honest to be a Sheldrake coach and live.

CHAPTER 65

Inside the austere locker room there's an eerie silence. The kind of silence that comes with being down ten. Players sit with elbows on knees, heads down, towels around their necks, dotting the floor with sweat. The putrid sweat that comes from being way behind.

I pass through the locker room to a bathroom stall in the next room, take a deep breath and blow. The air stream ruffles the hanging toilet paper. I lock the door. My finger thumps my cell.

KAYCEE. GOING TO PROVE MYSELF. SEE YOU IN ANOTHER LIFE.

Back in the locker room, I listen to the silence for a moment, then erupt. "Wake up! Wake up! I take all the blame. It's not your fault. I got you into trouble and I'll get you out." I pace the floor, clutching my program containing my last will and testament. "You have to trust me one more time. I have the answer. We can't play their tempo. We have to play our tempo. That's the answer. The team that controls the tempo wins the game.

"Nitro, you pick up Howard when he gets the outlet pass and slow him down from running the fast break. Guide him slowly down the sideline where they don't run their break. Then at the half court, get through the Simmons' screen.

"Pico, you stay home in the key. Simmons will come back to you looking for the pass. Then you take care of him.

"And no fouls, Pico. You're the only center we've got."

"I know, Coach," he answers somberly.

I search for Willard Penn. Find him dripping sweat in front of me. I bark, "Willard, block out someone when the shot goes up or I'll kick your ass."

"Okay, Coach."

"Be patient. Good things will happen. We've come a long way."

On fixed games.

"And we have what it takes." *Believe that, you'll believe anything.*

"Do you believe that?"

"Yeah," the squad yells back.

"Are you ready?"

"Yeah," they yell in unison.

"Go get 'em!"

The players storm out of the locker room as I mumble, "And death to the winner."

CHAPTER 66

We charge from the tunnel onto the court. The blare of Mardi Gras bugles comes alive. The crowd wakes up with a deafening cheer, waving their pom-poms in sync with the band.

From the bench I spot Townsend in a corner seat at floor level, next to cheerleaders and photographers. Our eyes meet. My gut turns, my head swims.

He's thinking one billion. He doesn't know what I'm thinking. Twenty minutes and he'll know I choose winning and death. Twenty minutes and I'll prove myself, you son of a bitch.

For the next ten minutes the action is up and down. Fast and furious. We have absolutely no control.

Finally Howard receives an outlet pass and Nitro remembers to force his dribble to the sideline, below the mid-court line.

I glance down at the NYU coach. He holds up one finger—a play signal.

My head cloudy, I shout to Nitro, "High-post screen. Get through it."

Howard dribbles off a Simmons screen above the key. Simmons cuts to the hoop and receives a pass from Howard. He meets Pico, stops, goes up and shoots the jumper. Pico springs, stretches, snatches the ball in mid-air. In one motion, he flings it downcourt to Nitro for a break-away dunk. NYU players give Pico a double take as if to say "Who is this guy?" as the crowd goes wild. I applaud, but keep my head in the game.

It's not over yet.

Minutes tick by. We take our time on offense. Nitro gets hot—hits three treys in a row. Our Saran Wrap defense holds NYU scoreless for seven minutes.

Then Nitro effectively stops Howard, and Pico blocks a couple of Simmons' jumpers.

We score, they don't.

We pull up to 55 all.

TIME LEFT: 10:20

I glance at Townsend. Our eyes meet again. He slowly slides a finger across his throat.

I feel like I'm breathing through a straw.

Suddenly, I see myself as two beings—one in the here and now, a winner, the other in the air, gone. Then the thoughts, *I'll miss Kaycee and Pico . . . Will I feel the bullet? . . . How many people will die?*

Just like I left, I came back, and realize that the only way to get through this is to accept my fate.

I get into the game, pace in front of our bench.

Nitro breaks it and takes it.

"Way to go, Nitro!" I yell.

Nitro wants the rim. He penetrates to the hole . . . And a foul.

"That's it, Nitro. To the hole. They can't stop you."

Simmons too strong against the iron.

Nitro, a cross-over. To the hoop. Foul

"Hit the deuce, Nitro."

We just might win this.

Next time down the court, Nitro wedges between two players like a running back charging for a first down. Somehow he gets to the hoop. Simmons picks him up. Nitro flips the ball high to Pico who slams it home. And the crowd goes wild.

We sprint back on defense setting the tone for the next seven minutes of play.

TIME LEFT: 3:00

64-60, Sheldrake.

My breathing is labored. My mind rewinds.

Remember Jordan teaching you how to play ball. You barely got the ball to the rim. Remember the day Pico walked into your gym. And the first time you met Kaycee . . . Going to miss them.

I refocus.

Pico blocks another Simmons jumper. Pico is toying with Simmons. He fakes then goes up when Simmons goes up. Swats away another shot.

We score. Then NYU answers with a Howard jumper from the corner.

They score again. We're down one, 70-69.

The clock ticks down.

I clutch the will in my hand, pacing, applauding, coaching.

TIME LEFT: 00:10

Trying to keep things in focus, I stare up at the scoreboard again, mumble, "70-69. Down one."

Howard dribbles across mid-court, calls time.

The team huddles around me. I look into Pico's eyes. "When they take the ball out, step on Simmons' shoe and run him over. The officials will call the foul. It'll be a one-and-one. The clock won't start and there will still be ten seconds left. You hear, son?"

Pico nods.

The official hands the ball to the out-of-bounds man at mid-court. Simmons is a stationary screener near the mid-court stripe. Pico steps on his shoe and pushes him off balance. Simmons falls to the hardwood. Whistle blows. Foul on Pico. The clock is still.

Dead ball foul. Simmons to the line. Down one. Ten seconds left.

I call time, make Simmons think about his shot.

In the huddle, feeling like throwing up, I look in my players' eyes. "We have no more timeouts. Zero. When they rebound, we trap, steal, or foul. On offense, run play number one." I repeat the scenario twice. "We're in good shape. They have a non-shooter at the line."

Hundreds of fans edge out of their seats and drift down to the floor. A rope-line holds them back. Everyone is on their feet in hushed silence. Townsend stands just behind the rope in the corner, next to a cheerleader.

Simmons bends his knees. He straightens, rocks, and releases. The ball hits the heel of the rim and ricochets out. Willard Penn goes up. It hits off his fingertips. Simmons tips it back beyond the top of the key near the sideline. Howard sprints and recovers the ball in the corner near mid-court.

TIME LEFT: 00:08

"Trap, trap!" I yell.

TIME LEFT: 00:06

Nitro and Penn sprint to double-team Howard. Simmons is on the dead run to receive Howard's pass, top of the key. Pico sprints after Simmons. Howard snaps the ball toward Simmons. Pico in line with the pass, reaches out with his left hand and bats the ball forward.

TIME LEFT: 00:03

The ball bounds to our basket. Pico catches up with it in full stride across the mid-court line. My breathing stops. Two long dribbles and he's at the free-throw line. Out of the corner of my eye I see a blurry figure sprinting towards him.

Townsend! He's broken through the crowd.

As Pico springs for the jam, Townsend drives a shoulder into his legs tilting him toward the rim. The crowd gasps. Somehow Pico reaches out and wrists the ball through the cylinder with both hands. The crowd roars. Pico and Townsend go down like ten pins. The horn sounds. The scoreboard on the first level blinks, 71-70 Sheldrake. I rocket off my chair. Players freeze. Murmuring fans are held back. Two cops rush onto the court, pick up a struggling Townsend, and cuff him.

Townsend yells at me, "I'll get you, you son-of-a-bitch."

Pico struggles to his feet.

Townsend is muscled upstairs through the crush of fans.

My shirt wringing wet, I force a breath. Await a bullet, frozen in place.

Pico raises both fists flashes a winning smile. Our players jump like they are on pogo sticks. They surge to Pico, surround him, loft him onto their shoulders and march him around.

I scan, the boxes, the catwalk. No shots ring out. Then I realize that Wells and Townsend kept murder in-house, and there was no one left to shoot me. I take a deep breath that I thought I would never get.

Police begin to circle me like a blanket. One says, "We're gonna be around."

I watch Pico, then my eyes shift to the scoreboard.

I couldn't get over it. Pico did it. He really did it.

The players set Pico down in front of me. My sweaty hug with him follows. We'd been down a very dark tunnel.

Minutes later, I carefully climb the ladder to cut down the net, still dulled by dodging death, drained of emotion, stunned that we won. On the top step, I grab the bright orange rim and scan the crowd starting to empty out of the stadium. The guy who came out of the stands to tackle Pico would be a topic of their conversation. But no one will ever know why he did it unless I tell the truth.

"Hey, Coach," Pico yells from the floor.

I look down to find Pico at the base of the ladder, surrounded by cops, photographers, and eager players waiting to cut off their strand of netting.

"Stand still. You're going to want this picture for your living room wall," Pico says with enthusiasm.

I shake my head. "That's not me anymore." And with unsteady hands amidst a shower of light bulbs, I cut off a strand of netting that meant so much it sent four people to the morgue and was going to send a gambling ring to prison.

CHAPTER 67

Two weeks later, in a no-frills, Philadelphia FBI conference room, I conclude my deposition for the "United States versus Peter Townsend III."

After the court reporter and U.S. attorney leave the room, Kaycee and I study each other across the glass table.

Straight faced, she says, "Good thing Tully opened up so we could bury Townsend."

"Anything to save his own skin."

"So what are you going to do now?"

I push away from the table. "I'm going back to Atlantic City, pack and get out of town."

"Well, you got what you wanted," she says with resignation.

"Not the way I wanted it . . . It's ruined basketball for me. I don't want to wake up one morning and find I'm Babe DeCarlo, buying players, fixing transcripts, and doing deals with HotShoe. I would cross a line I didn't mean to cross. And if I crossed it enough times, that line would disappear forever. Then I'd be just another piranha in the dirty water."

* * *

One month later, I open the sports section of *USA Today* and read the following news briefs:

> *Based on earthshaking scandals at Sheldrake College of Atlantic City, the institution has decided to cancel its basketball program. Its star player, Pico Rimpau, the only remaining undergraduate, will transfer to another school.*

*   *   *

> *Peter Townsend III, a Sheldrake College booster and owner of the Mardi Gra Casino in Atlantic City, will stand trial for murder, money laundering, bribery, conspiracy, and fixing basketball games.*

*   *   *

> *Four basketball players have been arrested for taking bribes and throwing NCAA tournament games against Sheldrake College. They are Sky King of Colorado State, AC Johnson of Cal, Junior Mason of Missouri, and Notre Dame's Robert Charles.*

*   *   *

> *Hotshoe Incorporated announced that they have signed Marquee Smith of Philadelphia to a long-term shoe contract. Smith, a high school phenom, has decided to forgo college basketball, opting for the NBA draft. "He's a high first rounder," said, Jimmy Wheeler, Hotshoe vice-president of marketing.*

CHAPTER 68

Two months later on a sunny morning, I meet Pico at Shattuck Park, near MacArthur and Alvarado, where his training began. He's visiting Southern California universities and I'm searching for a job. There are familiar park sounds—the chirping of the birds in the trees and the whir of traffic on Wilshire Boulevard. The park hasn't changed, but we have.

I open the gate and step inside the fenced basketball court just as Pico releases a fifteen-foot jumper from the free-throw line.

"Follow through!" I yell.

In Sheldrake sweats, he rebounds the miss on a sideline, turns to me with a broad smile, and almost shouts, "Always the coach."

I approach him. Pico clutching his basketball to his hip, we shake hands, then go to the half-hug.

"Good to see you," I say. "Still thinking about playing in Europe? In our last phone call, you were into that."

"Good money and no books sounds good."

I glance at the blacktop. "You can always make money at this game. You can't always get an education."

"That's what the coaches I've been visiting have told me," Pico says with a shrug.

"Since Sheldrake cancelled its basketball program, you're immediately eligible at any school you transfer to. You don't have to go to Europe to play, and you'll be getting an education. You need that. Choose a school with the best low-post coach and where you can get the most help academically."

"I've thought about all that. Hey, want to see my free throw? I've got it down now." He dribbles to the free throw line, assumes his stance and snaps one off. It goes down.

"See," he says, shaking a fist in the air. "I can shoot a free throw on any court. Even your old condo."

"No, you can't."

"Yes, I can."

After we argue for about a minute, I acquiesce and drive him north of Franklin into the Hollywood Hills toward the hoop above the city.

On the way up he says out of nowhere, "You need a roommate?"

I give him a longer look than any driver of windy hills with short turns wants to give a passenger. "I'd like to have you as a roommate. But you need to live on campus with people your own age. We can hang on weekends if you like."

"I'd like that." With a smile, he turns back to the windshield and a view of the horizon.

I slow down on the last hairpin turn. "Are you sure you want to shoot the free throw?

I know how much the ball means to you."

"Keep going," he says firmly. "I've thought about it all year, and I've been shooting a hundred free throw every day. I even brought a camera."

Seconds later, we pull in front of my former residence and get out. Nothing has changed—not the beige condos, not the hoop, the wind, or the tall buildings below. Pico, gripping the ball in one hand, gives me a camera with the other.

As we walk to the free throw line, Pico asks, "You going to see Kaycee again? She's a nice lady."

"I've spoken to her. But we're on different coasts. Maybe I'll see her when she comes to L.A. But, hey, you need to concentrate on the shot, not my life."

At the free throw line, Pico bounces the ball once and looks up at the hoop, when a sudden cross-breeze blow from left to right.

Standing behind him, holding the camera high, I say, "The wind can change up here in an instant. Be careful. I know how much the ball means to you."

"I've been practicing with the wind."

"Wait until the wind stops."

"I can handle it."

"Hey," someone calls with a gravel voice from the direction of the nearest condo. "Mr. Byrnes, is that you?"

My head pivots to a woman about sixty, standing on the steps of my former residence. Tall, dark-haired, in a blue suit. I recognize her as the buyer of my unit.

I explain why I'm up here, and that Pico is trying to make this once-in-a-lifetime shot.

"Well, go ahead," she says, adding, "I've never seen anyone make it."

"I'm different," Pico says. He turns slowly toward the hoop that over-looks the city and sets the ball above his forehead.

I glance at his alignment. *Elbows in. Arm straight. Knees slightly bent. Elements of a fine shooter.* I reposition the camera to get this shot.

He extends his legs and snaps the ball forward just as the wind stops.

I click the camera.

The ball heads to the left of rim, misses the rim entirely, then disappears over the cliff.

"Damn!" blurts Pico as he rushes to the cliff's ledge. There, he follows his ball as it bounds down.

After a long moment, he points in the distance. "I see it! It's caught in the brush behind that white house, way below. We can drive down and get it."

"No, we can't."

Pico opens his hands. "Sure we can."

"No, we can't. That's poison ivy down there."

"Then you owe me a ball."

"You knew what the risks were." I hand him back his camera.

But seeing Pico lowering his head as if he's lost his best friend, I say, "I'll get you another ball."

"It won't be the same," he mumbles.

"Nothing is ever the same. For one thing, you're a man now—with a career ahead of you."

He lifts his head. "What about you?"

The events of last season race through my brain. "I'm alive. And tomorrow is a new day."

THE END